The Accidental Malay

Karina Robles Bahrin got her first break as a writer when she guest-edited a weekly teen column in the *New Straits Times* a very long time ago. Her short fiction has been published in *Urban Odysseys: KL Stories, KL Noir: Blue, A Subtle Degree of Restraint and Other Stories* and *Malaysian Tales: Retold & Remixed*. She is a former columnist with *The Heat*, a weekly by Focus Malaysia. She currently lives and works on the island of Langkawi, Malaysia. *The Accidental Malay* is her first novel.

Karina Robles Bahrin

The Accidental Malay

PICADOR

First published in Singapore 2022 by Epigram Books

First published in the UK 2024 by Picador
an imprint of Pan Macmillan
The Smithson, 6 Briset Street, London EC1M 5NR
EU representative: Macmillan Publishers Ireland Ltd, 1st Floor,
The Liffey Trust Centre, 117–126 Sheriff Street Upper,
Dublin 1, D01 YC43
Associated companies throughout the world
www.panmacmillan.com

ISBN 978-1-0350-3237-2

Published by arrangement with Astier-Pécher Literary Agency.

1 3 5 7 9 8 6 4 2

A CIP catalogue record for this book is available from the British Library.

Typeset in Electra LT Std by Palimpsest Book Production Limited, Falkirk, Stirlingshire
Printed and bound by CPI Group (UK) Ltd, Croydon, CR0 4YY

Visit **www.picador.com** to read more about all our books
and to buy them. You will also find features, author interviews and
news of any author events, and you can sign up for e-newsletters
so that you're always first to hear about our new releases.

For M.

Siapa yang makan cili, dia lah yang terasa pedasnya.
He who eats the chilli is the one who feels its heat.

–Malay proverb

1

So much for torrid sex tonight.

Tomorrow, Jasmine Leong Lin Li might make an obscene amount of money. But right now, she slams back five shots of tequila alone in her favourite bar on Changkat. Iskandar, her lover, is not coming after all. His wife has taken ill with a cold.

At forty-one, she is the ideal mistress – not a wife, never a mother, and gainfully employed, with little need for matrimony to complicate matters.

There goes their little celebration. And after months of her haggling with leery merchant bankers, way past the hour the men should have gone home to their spouses. At least the bartender is used to her waiting, sometimes for a little while, but other times till closing.

At some point, in snatched phone conversations, there was talk of a vacation, just her and Iskandar, to a jazz festival or on a safari. He was meant to conjure up some business deal so they could get away for three weeks. Except now he isn't here for even one miserable drink.

It is 1 a.m. on a Wednesday. There are only a few stragglers left by the time she exits Luccio's. The concrete pavement is slick with leftover rain, steam rising from the asphalt on the road. Her thick, wavy locks instantly go frizzy in the humidity.

She pulls an elastic band off her wrist and gathers her hair into a messy topknot. It is late; no need to fuss with the hairdo.

She is attractive but not beautiful. Men have described her as 'interesting', their blooming desire quelled by a hint of fear. A warning sign that if they get too close, she might possibly render them stupid, all their weaknesses revealed.

The bartender hails a taxi for her and Jasmine climbs in, waving a tipsy goodbye. The driver noses the vehicle through the detritus of Ladies' Night Wednesday. They slip down narrow Jalan Alor with its fierce flaming woks and flimsy plastic stools, through the expanse of shiny Sultan Ismail's skyscrapers and out onto the expressway.

Here, and sometimes even overseas, people call Jasmine 'The Bak Kwa Princess'. To the city's other socialites, it is cause for some derision. Being named after sticky pork jerky is hardly the height of glamour, unlike those whose fathers run fleets of private jets or hock jewels to their rich friends' wives and mistresses. But to Jasmine, it is only a name.

After all, the country's capital in 2010 isn't any worse for wear despite its swampy origins. KL, Kay-Yell, Kolumpo, Koala Lumpa – nothing people call it reminds them of the mud. Yet it is there, crippling its inhabitants' legs, willing them to stand still if they get too ambitious, its cold, squelching grip a reminder not to stir up the water too much. By now, people's noses no longer wrinkle from the stagnant stink. It has seeped into their bodies through the shuffle of their footsteps, muddling their moral compasses, blurring the bright black lines between gods.

2

It has taken several lifetimes to get here.

Thirty seconds to 9 a.m.

On stage, Jasmine gives her sombre charcoal jacket a cautious tug, hoping its drooping top button will not fall off. Its thread is anchored on the jacket's inside with a scrap of Sellotape scrounged from her car's glove compartment. She didn't double-check today's outfit last night, too drunk by the time she got home.

Only one other woman stands on the small podium, flanked by a retinue of men. Jasmine's grandmother, Madam Leong, is the company's CEO. Her son, Jasmine's father, was murdered in the racial riots of 1969. Her husband died the year before that from cancer. Decades of cutting through the coarse male fabric of business dealings have left her insides scarred and hardened. She has seldom, if ever, shed a tear since her husband's passing.

In seconds, Phoenix Berhad will debut on Bursa Malaysia. The Leong family company, more than a hundred years old, is becoming a twenty-first-century entity.

Though they stand in KL's stock exchange, Phoenix got its start in Ipoh, the northern town once famous for its tin ore. The company now owns one-third of Ipoh's property developments. Yet, despite its name being plastered on billboards heralding new townships and commercial districts, everyone still knows it for its bak kwa. Malaysian Chinese living abroad acquire cartons of it on their homecoming sojourns. Phoenix bak kwa is the staple of Lunar New Year reunions, boxes of it stacked for sale in front of shops next to crates of mandatory mandarin oranges. People flock to Ipoh on weekends to take photos inside the flagship colonial shophouse, a national heritage property.

There are rumours that Phoenix intends to distribute its bak kwa abroad. A sure bet, some say, thanks to the Chinese diaspora spread across all corners of the globe. A Michelin-starred chef once pronounced Phoenix's pork jerky the most heavenly mouthful he had ever savoured. Jasmine can almost taste the sharp tinge of victory in the back of her throat. She leans towards her grandmother, her Jimmy Choos shooting vertiginous pain up her calves. 'Poh Poh, I think we might be worth a billion ringgit in a moment.'

One moment could balance out the ledger of debt a granddaughter has accrued since being orphaned at birth. One moment could make eighteen long months of boxed lunches and late-night pizzas in the office all worth it. One moment could shift the compass of her fate, edging it truer north, where she might at last feel she belongs.

For an instant, Jasmine is five again, holding up a piece of clean white paper by its corners, afraid to smudge it with her fingers. On the last day of her first year in kindergarten, Jasmine knocked on her grandmother's bedroom door. She had something to show her. The result of endless attempts at learning to write her own name, which was very long, far longer than 'cat' or even 'ambulance', or whole sentences copied from her Dick and Jane books.

Poh Poh loomed – slim, severe and complete – in a black, knee-length samfoo with tiny pink flowers.

Jasmine held up the piece of paper, her damp fingers careful to pinch only its upper corners. All the way home from school, on the twenty-step walk to the gates from class, in the back seat of the car, up, up to her grandmother's doorway, she had held it, arms now aching a little.

'Poh Poh, I can write my whole name. I don't need to go to school any more!' An offering held up for scrutiny, obscuring Jasmine's view of Madam Leong.

Poh Poh laughed, a tiny snigger, fingering the words on the paper, before snatching the gift from Jasmine's grasp. She reached down and pinched Jasmine's chin between bony thumb and forefinger, holding the child's gaze.

'You think this is all it takes? Well, at least you're better off than your cousin Kevin. I am told he cannot even read yet. But then again, boys are always slower. At least at first. Because the world waits for them, they are in no hurry. But you, you are a girl.' Poh Poh tapped the tip of Jasmine's nose. 'You can never do enough. You will always need to do better. Nothing is ever promised to girls.'

As the crowd counts down, Jasmine realizes no one really sees her.

It is difficult to be noticed next to Madam Leong, who stands straight despite her eighty years, her almond eyes elongated by her taut silver chignon. Poh Poh never wears heels; she does not need them. Her presence diminishes the tallest of men, their eyes widening in fear of her shadow.

At zero, the audience roars in unison.

Madam Leong strikes the gong with a resolute blow. Its

sonorous timbre echoes round the listing hall. For a moment, it is the only sound, until the giant screens in the gallery flicker to life, signalling the market's opening. Rows of letters and numbers fill the screens, representing companies listed on the stock exchange. Somewhere down the middle is Phoenix, denoted by its code: PHX. Next to it, figures glow green. Jasmine watches as the digits tick upwards, her hands clasped beneath her breastbone like a choir girl. The nails from her right hand form small indentations in her left palm.

The company debuts at almost twice its initial asking price. Phoenix Berhad is now worth 950 million ringgit and rising. Not quite a billion. Not yet.

'Perhaps tomorrow,' Poh Poh mutters, staring into the crowd, lips stretched in a practised smile.

Still, raucous applause rises from the din. Cameras flash in a frenzy. The stock exchange's chairman offers Madam Leong a timorous handshake in congratulations. The merchant bankers' nervous frowns stretch into open-mouthed schoolboy grins. The men pat one another's backs, pumping their fists, giving high-fives.

The media photographers and cameramen edge closer to the stage. Jasmine and her grandmother join hands and raise their arms in victory.

Yet Jasmine feels unmoored. The tips of her fingers tingle with doubt. The iron grip of her grandmother's hand while the shutters click leaves her bones throbbing with a dull, empty ache.

If asked, most in the room, except maybe the catering crew, can name her. And perhaps tag on 'multimillionaire' as a descriptor. Beyond that, she is unknown to this sea of people. Not someone whose presence creeps into their dream-filled sleep or invades their idle thoughts with worry over her well-being. And certainly not one whose empty seat would be noticed at family gatherings.

The only chair waiting for her is on the eighteenth floor of an office tower in Damansara Heights. In a city ignorant of her exile, her only custodian is work.

Except, perhaps, for Iskandar.

Scanning the room, she spots him, a lanky apparition that catches her by surprise, leaning against the large glass windows, at a distance from the crowd. He winks with a slight incline of his head, a lazy smile crossing his face. He gazes at her for a brief moment before walking away to the coffee station.

Jasmine lets out a small sigh, rubbing one ankle with the pointed tip of the other foot's shoe, feeling the tug of desire rise in her throat. At least he made it this time. But before she can reach the buffet line, a parade of waiters emerges, bearing trays of food. Weaving between them, she almost collides with the last one.

'Oh, ma'af, Puan,' he addresses her in Malay.

She glances at his fair-skinned face, his narrow eyes and thin lips. The slant of his cheeks, the tonal seesaw of his voice. Chinese.

She thinks to correct him, but doesn't. They all get it wrong, anyway. Chinese men think she's Malay. And Malays assume she's Chinese. Always addressing her in the other's language, so sure they are that she isn't one of their own. Indians stick to English, probably on account of her expensive handbags.

There were times in the past that she wondered about this confusion. She used to spend hours late at night in her youth, gazing at her reflection in her cotton nightie, trying to pinpoint what made everyone unsure of who she was. Perhaps it was her oval eyes that end in an upward tilt, the hair that tumbles down her back in waves, her breasts that are just a little too generous, her brisk stride. The full mouth anchored by a dimple on each side. The careless toss of her handbag on car seats. The lack of a cooing, flirtatious lilt in her voice, even when she wants a favour.

These days, she merely lets their perplexity slide, using it to her advantage when possible. Strangers are still uncertain when they encounter her, until she tells them. At times, she is tempted to lie, but she hasn't, although there are moments when it is hard to resist. Like when she is buying batiks on Jalan Masjid. Except her accent would give her away – Malays sussing out her Chineseness from her stilted, sing-song pronunciation. But always, once she reveals the truth, there is a spark that flits across those previously puzzled gazes, and a small grain of relief settles in the questioning faces. People are always more amiable then, dispensing a small favour here, an extra handful of crispy pork lard in the char kway teow there, or even a seat in their already packed coffee shop during lunch hour.

By the time she manoeuvres her way to the coffee station, Iskandar is nowhere in sight. Rake-thin Mr Chew, her grand-mother's assistant, is waving from the edge of the room, his finger jabbing the face of his watch.

*

It is a rare ability to pull off mustard yellow with panache, but the pert reporter wears her pencil-line dress with the air of a haughty swan. As the woman settles into her seat, fiddling with her tape recorder and flipping the pages of her spiral-bound notepad, Jasmine eyes her in silence from across the conference table.

Outside, refreshments are being served, with the fragrant aroma of nasi lemak seeping under the meeting room's doors. Jasmine remembers that she skipped breakfast, and hopes there will be some food left once the interview is over. The creamy coconut rice and sambal served at company listings is reputed to be the tastiest in town. She jiggles her leg beneath the table, impatient for a plate because, by God, she's earned it.

The reporter is from the *Market Watch*, the nation's leading business paper. Its Sunday edition is scrutinized at length by financial executives over cups of viscous Hainanese coffee or bitter weekend espressos. Phoenix has been the talk of the town, making headlines each week with analysts weighing in on its forecasted listing price.

Today they beat all the pundits' expectations.

The reporter appears ready now, her spine straight, pen poised in her left hand. 'Right, shall we start?'

At first, the questions are standard-issue. Jasmine answers them in her usual perfunctory manner, reeling off sales projections and market share numbers. In truth, she finds most local journalists boring, with their vapid questions that she can easily tick off on her mental checklist.

'Miss Leong, are there plans for you to take over leadership of Phoenix?'

This catches Jasmine off guard. Most local journalists are not normally this forward.

The reporter notices. 'Madam Leong is getting on in years, and I thought with the listing . . .'

Jasmine stiffens. The issue of her grandmother's retirement

has only been raised by her two aunts, the other major share-holders of Phoenix. But never discussed directly with Madam Leong, and certainly not with outsiders.

*

Last Lunar New Year, Treasure Leong, Jasmine's second auntie, mounted a small inquisition during her annual visit home from Vancouver, where she had lived for years with her own family. Over the mahjong table, after Poh Poh had retired for the evening, Seh Gu Treasure made the first overture.

'Ma Ma needs to let go. She's already eighty. It is time.'

Seh Gu's older sister, the formidable Tai Gu Ruth, sniffed. 'Seventy-nine. She's seventy-nine. We're all getting old.'

This was where all big conversations began in their family, or perhaps most Chinese families now, for hundreds of years. Fingers picking up and sliding smooth mahjong tiles on the felt-covered table while marriages were dissected, children waved like trump cards, and husbands, oh those husbands, bemoaned as the acquired handicaps that are the necessary burden of a responsible Chinese wife. For decades, it was Poh Poh and her two daughters at the table. But five years ago, the matriarch announced her withdrawal from the post-reunion dinner custom, choosing instead to retire to her room after the last dish had been cleared. Since then, her seat has been occupied by Jasmine or one of her cousins, whose presence has done little to curb the Leong sisters' frank debates. Sometimes the pair, addled by a touch too much wine, break out into songs from their giddy youth, their drunken wails of laughter keeping Seh Gu's husband and children well away. Everyone knows not to interrupt the Leong sisters and their rare merry-making.

But most of the time, it has been like this. Small vipers of shared but unspoken thoughts tossed out, writhing into the open without warning, uninvited.

That night, it was Jasmine's turn to take the third seat at the table.

'It's easy for you to say, you don't even live here. Your life is good.' Tai Gu Ruth straightened the row of tiles she had stacked.

'What do you mean? As if yours is any worse,' Seh Gu Treasure shot back. The deck now complete, each of them drew their own thirteen tiles to start the round.

Jasmine examined her own tiles, arranging them to form clusters. The hand was a good one. She might win.

It was Tai Gu's turn to start. She tossed out a tile and exchanged it for another from the deck, her poker face giving nothing away. 'At least you still have a husband.' Her tiles click-clacked in between her words as she rearranged them in a new order. 'And your children don't want to come back here anyway. Why should you care who runs the company? As long as the cheques keep arriving.'

Seh Gu looked up from her hand. 'Who says? Eh, this is Ba Ba's company we're talking about, our heritage. As for husbands, have you seen mine ah? He's not exactly Rock Hudson, you know.' She picked up a new tile with a grimace, gesturing to the snoring lump on the sofa.

Tai Gu cackled. 'Rock Hudson? Rock Hudson's gay lah! What for you want a husband like that?'

Her sister sniggered. 'Who knows? Maybe if you had a husband like that you would still be married.'

'Iieeeyeeerr! Talking nonsense lah you!' Tai Gu Ruth's screech-ing laugh rang through the living room. 'Nah, Jasmine, your turn!'

Jasmine drew a tile from the deck. It formed a meld with two others in her hand. 'Pung!' She set the three tiles down in front of her, discarding another.

'Wah! So fast! See, Che,' Seh Gu said, addressing her older sister. 'This is what we need, someone who moves quickly. Jasmine should just take over Phoenix.'

Jasmine resisted the urge to reach out and squeeze Seh Gu's hand in gratitude. Instead, she pushed her mahjong tiles into the centre pile, swirling them to commence the next round.

Tai Gu Ruth stayed silent, her mouth set in a firm, straight line. But her vipers remained in their nest that night. The fluorescent glare of her baby sister's words left no hidden space for negotiation.

The rest of the game progressed without a word uttered at the table except to declare a meld. In the distance, a lone dog barked in the muted, lukewarm evening. A string of firecrackers went off in successive bangs two houses away. A motorcycle squealed down the road. The grandfather clock in the living room struck eleven. And the conversation hung unfinished in the smothering night.

*

The haughty swan reporter reaches a slim arm across the table to grab Jasmine's hand. Looking her subject in the eye, she lowers her voice. 'If I were you, I'd want to be CEO. You've certainly earned your seat at the table. After all, there aren't any men you have to climb over. Not like the rest of us.'

Jasmine withdraws from the woman's grasp. A knock at the door reveals Mr Chew. 'Madam is leaving,' he says.

'I'm sorry, I have to go.' Jasmine promises to answer further questions via email. 'Maybe you could come to our party this evening. At the Hilton. Everyone will be there. Mr Chew will get you an invitation.'

As she strides across the listing hall, Jasmine stops several times to shake hands with well-wishers. She reaches the foyer to find her grandmother already standing on the top step, waiting for her car.

'Your jacket is missing a button,' Poh Poh says. 'I presume the interview went all right?'

Jasmine takes in a sharp breath. Poh Poh always knows when she is off-kilter.

'Oh, it went fine. The usual.' Jasmine shrugs her shoulders.

'I don't suppose she asked when you were going to become CEO?'

'Wh-what?' Jasmine's eyes widen a little, her breath stuck in her throat.

A soft laugh escapes Poh Poh's lips. 'And you didn't give her an answer.'

Jasmine presses her lips together, tilting her chin forward. Drawing herself up taller, she says, 'It's not my place, Poh Poh. I have no doubt you'll tell us when you're ready.' It never pays to confront the matriarch. Things must be allowed to take their course. Still, Jasmine cannot help but fear that her grandmother may have other plans, despite all the years Jasmine has spent at the old lady's side.

The car arrives. Poh Poh steps into the back seat, the driver closing the door. The window slides halfway down, and her grandmother beckons Jasmine closer.

'Tonight's party. Make sure you keep the merchant bankers happy. Who knows? Maybe you might meet one that you like.

I am heading back to Ipoh. This city is too noisy. Or perhaps I'm just tired.'

'Yes, Poh Poh. We'll manage.'

'Of course. But you are the host, Lin Li. Stop letting your Tai Gu bully you. And make sure the drinks are flowing.' The window rolls up, leaving Jasmine staring at her own tilted reflection in its tinted surface.

She watches the car glide down the slope of the stock exchange's driveway, towards the oncoming crush of lunchtime traffic.

Nothing escapes the old lady. She must sleep with one ear awake.

3

Even without Madam Leong present, the Hilton ballroom teems with KL's rich and infamous. Pastel lights cast blue and mauve shadows over the cavernous hall. This is not the usual Phoenix dinner with its old web of Chinese tradespeople. Those are in brightly lit Chinese restaurants, the loud clanking of chopsticks against bowls and frequent cheers of 'Yam Seng!' forming a cumulus of chaos over the room.

This is a lot more civilized. A string quartet accompanies the soft chatter. Walking through the crowd, Jasmine catches snatches of Hakka and Cantonese amid the English conversations. Some of the old tradesmen look like uncomfortable schoolboys, pulling at ties and shoving hands down their trousers to tuck and re-tuck shirts that keep bunching at their waists. Their wives have predictably almost risen to the occasion: the off-the-rack sequinned gowns and tulle skirts only give away their less-than-couture origins upon close inspection. It is not often their kind gets a chance to dress up to the nines and rub shoulders with the who's who of KL. The haughty swan is present, scribbling in her reporter's notepad, sheathed in a high-necked, turquoise cheongsam.

Jasmine wades through the crowd, shaking hands and trading small talk with the men and their wives. They congratulate her on the successful listing. The merchant bank's CEO is also present. He claps her on the back in approval. 'This girl ah, always pushing me to increase the IPO price. I said cannot lah, but she kept insisting!'

The initial public offering price for Phoenix's listing had been a point of contention between Jasmine and the bankers for months. In the end, she wore them down, and today's success was proof she had been right all along. Phoenix's initial offer price had been thirty per cent higher than the bankers' initial valuations. And its debut at the listing had bested even that several times over.

The CEO casually slides his arm around Jasmine's shoulders. A gesture of comradeship, perhaps, except his oily smirk suggests something a little more. She smiles, casting him a sideways glance, gently unwrapping his arm from her shoulders. His sort is a familiar presence in her years of boardroom dealings. Turning to him, she says, 'You lot should know better by now. We women have instincts that can sometimes be more reliable than those spreadsheets of yours.'

Tired of small talk, Jasmine finds her cousin Kevin at the champagne table. She snags a bottle from the bartender. 'Grab the glasses,' she says, gesturing.

From their vantage point in the rooftop garden, city lights wink in the distance. KL looks all grown-up, a far cry from its mosquito-infested beginnings. A rare breeze blows, cooling Jasmine's bare shoulders. A couple of wrought-iron chairs and a table sit in the middle of the astroturf.

Jasmine plonks herself onto a chair, cross-legged, her evening gown hiked up to reveal thighs starting to show hints of cellulite. Already there is a tiny tear in the hem of her dress delivered by the heel of her Louboutin. She should have had the darned gown shortened before tonight, but really, she has little time for such trivia. 'Gimme,' she says, holding up the bottle.

Kevin hands her a champagne flute with a flourish. 'And there it is. The Ipoh in you comes out after all.'

She pours herself too much champagne, lights a cigarette. 'Does it ever leave?'

Kevin takes a swig straight from the bottle. 'Not when half the town is in there.' He waves towards the ballroom. 'Speaking of which, can you believe Lau Kuan Yew is now calling himself Olivier?'

Jasmine's brow wrinkles for a second as she tries to recall the person. Then, the realization strikes her: the boy whose naming caused a stir among the Chinese community in Ipoh, the one whose parents saw fit to christen him after the prime minister of their southern neighbour Singapore, instead of a famous Malaysian Chinese. To the Laus, it was merely a dream expressed – that one of their children would become a towering man, like the one they so admired. The rest of Ipoh, especially the monied crowd, put it down to bourgeois aspirations. After all, the Laus were only goldsmiths, not descended from the owners of actual mines.

'Kuan Yew, the jock from Ipoh? The goldsmiths' son? He's the Olivier who is the new managing director of RSE?' Royal Swiss Equities is an important potential investor in Phoenix.

'Yep,' Kevin says with a grin. 'One and the same. He just moved back here from Australia.'

'Holy shit, he just introduced himself to me. I thought he looked familiar. Why didn't he say anything?'

Kevin shrugs. 'I hear he's in the market for a wife. His father is on his case for a grandchild.'

'He can't need his father's help in that department.' Kuan Yew's broad shoulders have stood him in good stead. Jasmine imagines that many women wouldn't mind being swept up by someone of his stature. 'I should have known it was him with that deep voice.'

*

After finishing her A levels at an English boarding school, Jasmine went home to Ipoh for the summer before beginning university. Poh Poh surprised her with a graduation gift – a slim gold bracelet in a modern design that encircled Jasmine's wrist, catching the sunlight.

The small act of generosity was unexpected. Her grandmother's gestures were usually more austere. Jasmine wore the bracelet every day with pride, never taking it off. But it was a tad loose, too large for her bones. One day, out of boredom, she offered to help Ah Tin, the cook's daughter, in the kitchen. The maid dispatched Jasmine to do the dishes; there had been a gaggle of Phoenix's most important distributors at lunch. A stubborn wedge of chicken curry, slightly burnt, proved too much for the dish sponge, despite Jasmine's vigorous scrubbing against the wok. She picked up a piece of steel wool and attacked the wok with more vigour, her hand moving roughly back and forth over the blackened crust.

By the time she noticed, it was too late. Her wrist was bare. The bracelet had slipped into the sink's yawning drain hole.

'Shit!' Her heart pounded with alarm. 'Shit, shit, shit, shit, I've lost it! Ah Tin!'

At the sound of Jasmine's voice, Ah Tin stopped chopping onions, rubbing her hands dry on her sarong. Peering down the sink hole, she stabbed with a chopstick in a desperate attempt to fish out the bracelet. They shone a torch light down the hole, but nothing gleamed back. The bracelet was gone, washed down the old pipes, sentenced to a death among Ipoh's sewage.

Distraught, Jasmine sat on a wooden stool, trying to slow her laboured breathing. 'Ah Tin, quick, where did Poh Poh buy it? I have to get a replacement before she finds out I've lost it.'

The maid told her the bracelet was procured from the town's goldsmith. But she didn't know how much it had cost.

Jasmine still had some British pounds in her wallet, left over from her travels and savings from school. She counted the money with care, shoving it deep into her jeans pocket. Grabbing her bicycle, she checked her watch; her grandmother was taking an afternoon nap, giving Jasmine two hours to cycle to town and back. She slapped on extra sunscreen, Poh Poh's warnings about the damages of UV rays echoing in her ears. Checking her reflection in the mirror, she patted down the frizzy strands of stray hair and slicked on some lip gloss for good measure. It wouldn't help if the townspeople saw Jasmine Leong looking too frazzled.

The shop had not changed much over the years. A row of glass cases flanked each mirrored wall. They were filled with gold trinkets on beds of red velvet. Bracelets, necklaces, rings, earrings, and the obligatory section of jade pendants. Standard for a Chinese gold jewellery concern.

There was not a person in sight when she entered the shop.

It was Ipoh; no one robbed stores in broad daylight. Walking towards the rear of the shop, she poked her head through a curtained doorway into a dark corridor. A wall divided it from the rear of the establishment. She could hear Depeche Mode blasting through the thick air.

'Mr Lau? Mrs Lau?' Jasmine shouted above the din.

There was a stirring, then the music turned down. Kuan Yew emerged, his hair in a short, spiky fauxhawk. He was wearing an old singlet and a pair of sports shorts with twin blue stripes running down the sides. Sweat slicked his broad, square shoulders.

'Oh hey, when did you get back?' Kuan Yew said with a surprised smile. The last time Jasmine had seen him, they were twelve. He led them both back to the front of the shop.

'Just last week.'

Taking his place behind one of the glass cases, Kuan Yew propped his elbow onto its surface, resting his chin in his cupped hand. He gestured for Jasmine to sit on one of the swivel stools across from him.

'Man, you've changed,' he said, his grin mischievous. Jasmine looked down at her jeans and T-shirt, puzzled.

'The make-up, the hair . . . You sure you're Jasmine Leong ah?'

She swiped off her lip gloss with the back of her hand.

'Oh, wait, you've . . . You got a little of that stuff on your face.' Kuan Yew reached out for a tissue from the box on the counter, then blotted her left cheek. 'There, all better,' he said, still grinning.

Jasmine felt her cheeks burn. If not for the fact that she was in a jam, she would have fled the shop already.

'Can you keep a secret, Kuan Yew?'

He sat up, alert. 'Hey, buy me lunch? I need someone to tell me what it's like, living abroad. I'm leaving for Australia soon. You're the only person I know who has done it. Left here, I mean.'

Jasmine heaved a sigh of relief. This she could do, no problem. It was a small price to pay for his confidence. She told him about her predicament, how the bracelet her grandmother bought her had been lost. And she needed to purchase a new one, so Poh Poh didn't notice.

'Ah, my father told me about that bracelet. Your Poh Poh came in to buy it last month. Spent a long time in the shop too. I think it's over here.' He moved to another glass case, retrieving an identical bracelet to the one she lost. 'Except I should adjust it, so it doesn't slip off your wrist again. It'll take a week. Think you can delay your grandma till then?'

'But what about your father? He'll tell her.'

Kuan Yew smiled with a small shake of his head. 'Don't worry about it. I'll just write up a bill for some fake person. Tell him it's some girl I know, and I'll deliver it once it's done.'

Jasmine narrowed her eyes, lips pursed. 'Some girl in some nearby town, I'm guessing?'

He threw his head back, his thundering laugh a familiar comfort.

Jasmine giggled in return.

They went to a char kway teow stall in a quiet side lane. He ordered for them, pulling out a plastic stool for Jasmine so they could take their seats at a rickety fold-out table. Jasmine inhaled the steaming black noodles, polishing off her plate before he was even halfway through his meal. She told him stories, of how alien she'd felt when she first got to England, and how white people ate rice with forks instead of spoons. Of the cold and the wet, the unending dreariness of it.

'But at least you're going to Perth. It's not that bad there, I imagine.' Jasmine wiped her lips with the back of her hand.

Kuan Yew nodded. 'I hope so. My mum's packing me sweaters and a jacket. I managed to get one on our last trip to KL. Is winter colder than air con ah? We don't even have air con in our car.'

'You'll be fine, Kuan Yew. I can't imagine you won't.' Unlike her, Kuan Yew had always seemed comfortable in his own skin.

Except this time, there was a glimmer of fear in his eyes. 'I – I've never been anywhere else, Jasmine. Never even been on an aeroplane.' He looked down at his hands with their clipped, broad fingernails.

He didn't say it but Jasmine caught the hesitance in his voice. Kuan Yew was not exactly the model student. Despite his stellar grades, teachers used to label him a trouble-maker for riling up the other jocks and heckling the headmaster during the latter's rambling school assembly sermons. Occasionally, Kuan Yew skipped school altogether, resulting in him being put on detention. But Jasmine knew he wasn't merely playing truant. His absences were often a result of him having to babysit his youngest sibling while his parents went off on trips to Kuala Lumpur to procure new stock for their store. He had been too embarrassed to tell the teachers the truth. It was Ah Tin who had told her this once. The maid had a soft spot for Kuan Yew's family. They were at times the object of mild ridicule among Ipoh's well-heeled for their less than privileged ways. But now their son was going overseas to study, just like the kids from well-to-do families. Like Jasmine.

She took a deep breath, then exhaled. 'Look, if I can do it, you certainly can do it better. No one's gonna mess with you. Not you. Just, you know, put on your best Travolta face. Over there, no one will know you. So you can be whoever you want.'

When she tried to pay for their meal, she realized she'd only brought British pounds. Seeing her crumpled fistful of notes, Kuan Yew broke into one of his huge laughs. 'I don't think Uncle Kee accepts gwai loh money. My treat this time, Jasmine Leong Lin Li.'

A week later, he met her outside the town's cinema. 'Your new-old gift from your Poh Poh, all done.' He handed her a pink plastic jewellery box. She opened it and he took the bracelet out, then fastened it round her wrist. The British pounds she had saved up more than covered the bracelet's cost once she had exchanged them for ringgits. She gave Kuan Yew the money in a red ang pow packet.

He grinned, slipping the small envelope into the back pocket of his jeans. 'Pleasure doing business with you, Miss Leong.'

The bracelet looked just like the one she'd lost, except there was now much less risk of this one slipping off.

*

A cloud promenades across the inky sky, revealing a full moon.

Kevin takes another swig of champagne from the bottle. 'His younger brother is taking over the family business, you know. Kuan Yew isn't interested.'

'And you?' Jasmine's eyes narrow, fixing her gaze on her cousin's face. 'Do you ever think of coming back? Running Phoenix?'

Kevin rolls his eyes. 'You know my mother would love it.'

At dinner earlier, there was a mild skirmish when Kevin's mother, Tai Gu Ruth, took Madam Leong's empty seat at the head of the main table. But Seh Gu Treasure intervened, informing her older sister that the seat was Jasmine's. Poh Poh's instructions. Jasmine knew Tai Gu was seething with discontent.

'Would you?' She takes a drag of her cigarette, exhaling a thin stream of smoke.

'I don't know. Never really considered it. I mean, how can I possibly come back? At least in Singapore, I have some measure of freedom. Here, if I even look at another man, Ma Ma would hear about it in two seconds.'

'This town is too damn small.' Jasmine grits her teeth. 'We're both over forty now, Kev. Fucking forty. We can't let these old ladies rule us for the rest of their lives.'

'Well, at least your paramour isn't interested in going public. Where is he, by the way?'

Jasmine doesn't know. Iskandar has not answered her calls. Texts to him appear still unread.

'Probably at some boring wedding.' She flicks a column of cigarette ash onto the astroturf. 'I think you should tell your mum at some point, though, that you don't want to come back. Or not, and just come back here to live. I could use the company. It'd be like old times.'

Kevin guffaws. 'You and me? Superman and Wonder Woman? Racing round KL, saving the city with bak kwa ah?'

'Hey, watch it. I'm telling you, this rebranding could be just the thing.'

Jasmine has arranged for swag bags with surreptitious samples of Phoenix bak kwa for the non-Muslim guests to take home.

24

Except not in their traditional boxes. She has spent the last few months developing a new look for potential international markets. The guests tonight are her first test cases, and so far, word has been positive.

Even though Phoenix has become a diversified conglomerate, Jasmine still holds a sentimental attachment to their pork jerky business. As Poh Poh has told her many times over, it is, after all, what saved their family from the brink of bankruptcy. The bak kwa business started years ago, after the Japanese Occupation. Traders were struggling to get back on their feet then, toes curled from poor diets of tapioca and rice, with a rare chip of salted fish thrown in on good days. People found it hard to stand straight, joints wracked with malnutrition and leftover fear.

It was Jasmine's great-grandmother who struck upon the idea of selling bak kwa to raise cash and restart the family's enterprise. Any gold and silver they previously possessed had been pawned during the Occupation for food, clothing and favours to keep the barbaric soldiers away. Grown weary of her household's hungry faces and her husband's constant presence in their home, she dug up an old family recipe and commandeered the house help into action. All day they boiled and pounded raw pork into paste, mixing it with a blend of spices and sugar before rolling it out on bamboo screens to dry in the constant afternoon sun. At night, the servants tended small fires in the back kitchen, swatting mosquitoes while they barbecued the meat until it caramelized into pliable sheets of chewy, salty-sweet goodness. The smoke sailed through the black of night, passing through dreams before settling in the dense kapok pillows among spiders and little insects.

Without it, Towkay Leong might have succumbed whole to his drinking habit. Without it, his wife would have perhaps gone mad and taken a parang to her sleeping husband's neck.

But news of the Phoenix bak kwa travelled fast. Before long, people arrived from neighbouring towns, on rickety bicycles carrying whole families and in fat, curvy cars bearing rich heiresses, maids in tow, in search of the family's famed pork jerky. Towkay Leong was able to restart his business and reclaim his place in the Tin Mining Club at night, leaving the matriarch in peace for days.

If the older Madam Leong saw Phoenix today, she would probably light a thousand joss sticks at the temple and remind all her sons' wives to thank her for the tranquil absence of their spouses. But she might also be surprised.

Jasmine knows her attempt to modernize their traditional bak kwa business isn't just a necessary step. It is her homage to the women in her family. And a way for her to leave her own mark on their legacy.

The bottle now empty, Jasmine and Kevin walk back to the ballroom. There, the wine and whisky still flow, but not a trace of the prized Phoenix pork jerky is in sight.

Somehow the Malays she deals with, even the ones who abstain from liquor, don't mind the presence of alcohol in their midst. Especially when it comes to occasions like this, where drinking is de rigueur unless one wants to appear gauche. But the mere whiff of pork sends them retching, running helter-skelter in disgust. Their selective blindness never ceases to amaze Jasmine. Their terror of accidental sinning is so great, not even the Pope could outdo them in the fear-of-God department.

Yet there is always the odd one out. Tunku Mahmud, an

elderly vestige of an old royal family, sidles up to Jasmine, whisky in hand.

'Grand party, young lady.' He strokes his carefully groomed white beard. 'I say, I hear you're giving out special treats to some VIPs.' His clipped accent betrays his English public school upbringing. His relative was once the prime minister.

Jasmine hugs the old man, inhaling the lingering aroma of cigars on his jacket. He was a friend of her grandfather, the other unknowable man in her life. Death has tossed her no favours. Since making Tunku Mahmud's acquaintance at the Ipoh Country Club one summer, Jasmine always seeks him out when she is back in her home town. Over the years, they have forged a covert friendship, sharing whiskies in the gloom of the club's worn-down bar. Her grandmother probably knows of their meetings. After all, Tunku Mahmud occasionally dines at their Ipoh home, of late without his wife, who has become more devout, haunted by the advancing spectre of dying outside God's favour; she would rather not risk eating off plates that may have known the smear of lard.

'I've already given a box to your driver, Tunku,' Jasmine whispers, a gleam in her eye. 'And I told him to put it in your study when you get home.'

'That's my girl. Can't be too careful these days. Even the servants are becoming all holy-moly. Although what are they going to do? Report me to the religious police? Still, I suppose one should be careful. Not worth the trouble if word gets out.'

Things have changed. Phoenix's Lunar New Year celebrations are now held in halal restaurants, to the chagrin of their Chinese distributors. No more whole roasted pig on the table; otherwise they lose necessary allies for the company's diversifying interests.

Without the Malay town council heads, district officers and chief minister, no property developer could hope to build even a dog kennel.

'Make sure you let me know when you next come to Ipoh. This old man is running out of company at the bar.' Tunku Mahmud squeezes Jasmine's hand and plants a kiss on her cheek.

At the dessert station, she bumps into Kuan Yew. 'I believe I still owe you lunch,' she teases, reaching for a strawberry tart. Her debt from their char kway teow encounter years ago remains unpaid.

He is even more handsome now, his eyes softened with faint wrinkles at their corners. It has been decades since they last met, and time has been more than kind to him. There is no longer a hint of his small-town cockiness. He is polished and assured.

He suppresses a smile. 'I was wondering how long it would take before you realized who I was.' His voice, still deep, now carries a slight Australian drawl.

His eyes sweep over her and she recognizes that he likes what he sees. Unlike their last teenage encounter, her instincts this time don't urge her to flee.

'Jasmine Leong. I always figured you'd end up doing something big.' He shifts his gaze around the room, a slow grin spreading across his face. He offers his business card. 'We should catch up. Maybe drinks, soon?'

'Yes, I'd like that.' She means it and smiles back.

Walking away, he turns back to look at her. 'It's nice to know I was right all along. And I see you've managed to hang on to the bracelet.'

Jasmine glances down at her wrist. If Poh Poh ever suspected, she never let on, even after all these years.

Kevin waves at Jasmine to come forward, just to the front of the stage. It is time for the obligatory group photographs. The two aunts take their places in the centre, flanked by the rest of their small clan. Mr Chew, whose bow tie is already crooked, directs the motley crew, his skinny frame drowning in a dark-blue polyester suit.

As Jasmine approaches, Mr Chew makes a sweeping gesture with his hands, parting the Leong sea down the middle and inviting Jasmine to fill the vacuum. The family closes ranks and smiles.

After the last guest leaves, Seh Gu Treasure corners Jasmine in the washroom.

'I thought I saw you talking to Kuan Yew.' She powders her nose, even though she is only going upstairs to her hotel room.

'It's Olivier now. Or didn't Tai Gu tell you?'

Seh Gu Treasure picks at a stray strand of grey poking out from her coif and pats it in place. 'I think you and him would make beautiful babies. He's turned out such a good-looking fellow too. And smart. Like you.' She shoots a glance at her niece's reflection.

Jasmine dries her hands on a towel and drops it into a basket below the countertop, avoiding her aunt's eyes. Seh Gu Treasure, the benevolent fairy godmother. Unlike huntress Tai Gu, who pounces unannounced.

'All I'm saying is, you shouldn't be alone lah, girl.' Seh Gu places a warm, soft palm on Jasmine's cheek, her eyes kind and tender. 'Once your Poh Poh goes, you won't have anyone. I mean, there's still us, but it's not the same, and I'm all the way in Canada. Kevin will one day have his own family. Find someone to be with. It's not good to grow old alone.' She clasps Jasmine's hands.

But what about love? Jasmine wonders.

Later, she watches her aunt walk towards the lift, arm wrapped round her husband's, their three twenty-something children tailing them. They don't notice her, cocooned in their own shared banter, the threads that bind their immediate family so palpable that Jasmine can almost reach out and pull them close.

She checks her phone for the thousandth time. No sign of Iskandar.

Not even a text.

4

The first time Jasmine and Iskandar met, she was wrestling with a platter of ketupats on a buffet table in London's Malaysia Hall. She was nearing the end of her second year at the London School of Economics and Political Science. The rice dumplings packed into woven palm leaf pouches had become tangled, their thin, leafy cords intertwined. As she tried to extricate one from the bunch with her fork, several others trailed onto her plate.

'You should just use your fingers.' A slim, attractive young man in a blazer and T-shirt stood next to her, bemused. He looked like a Malay version of John Taylor from Duran Duran, Jasmine's favourite band.

'May I?' He pulled a string, shaking its attached dumpling free. He passed it to her on a clean plate, switching it with the one she was holding.

'I'm Iskandar, but they call me Alex here. Short for Alexander. I guess the Arabic version is too difficult for white tongues. Let's get you some rendang.' He took her hand, clasping it tight, as if that was the way things had always been between them.

It was the end of term, the weather turned cold, and her stash of instant Brahim's rendang hauled from home had only lasted till the final exams. She was tired of the fish and chips from the place near her flat, and cooking was out of the question. The last time she'd tried, she set off the fire alarm in her kitchen. She yielded to his invitation, anticipating the taste of the rich, spicy beef stew on her tongue.

It was the Malaysian High Commissioner's annual student meet-and-greet. Jasmine had only come for the food, otherwise wanting to avoid contact altogether with other Malaysian students living in London. Her friends were mostly British, with a sprinkle of other foreign students from exotic places like Brazil, Kenya, Costa Rica, Japan. There was never a risk of them knowing anyone from home.

But that evening her weariness from gruelling exams had worn down her guard. She yearned for the familiar, and Malaysia Hall seemed like the only place that would fit the bill. Built as a centre for Malaysian students, the place had a long history that stretched beyond its base mission of providing food and shelter. And that night it smelled like home. The aroma of the generous buffet spread, with its heady spices and rich coconut stews, the sambals and the colourful riot of kuehs for those with a sweet tooth all felt familiar and comforting in a way no shepherd's pie or mushy peas could match.

Iskandar heaped spoonfuls of rendang onto her plate, leading her to a table already occupied by some other students. They were all Malay from what she could tell. A clutch of bored, attractive girls and their designer handbags ringed the table. The boys dotted between them looked like more Duran Duran knock-offs.

Iskandar was still holding her hand. 'Guys, this is . . .'

'Jasmine,' she added in haste, forcing a smile. She had not

planned on making small talk. Next to them, she was under-dressed in her hoodie and jeans. She and Iskandar sat and tucked into the rendang.

The other Malaysians assumed she was from KL. Jasmine didn't correct them. It turned out one also attended her university, but they had never met before. The group was going to a club after dinner. Jasmine faked a yawn.

'I'll drive you home,' Iskandar said as they all got up. It wasn't an offer. The night wind blew its sharp winter chill, making her shiver. Perhaps it wasn't such a bad idea.

The car was warm and new. She sat with her coat on as Iskandar fiddled with the dials on the radio. 'You actually went to Malaysia Hall all alone,' he said, as if it was such an incredible thing. 'Lucky me, then.'

*

Like a slow mulled wine simmering on the stove, their relationship took root over Christmas, then New Year's, settling into the months that followed, without him asking for permission, and with her not saying no. They fell into an easy rhythm, curling around one another, each reading their own assignments in libraries, on couches and park benches.

She found herself eating less bacon and ham, seeking out halal grocers to stock up the fridge. It felt like a secret rebellion, one her grandmother would not condone. He made an exception for her favourite Chinese roast duck in Bayswater, picking the leavings from her share every time they had a meal there. He mastered the art of eating rice out of a bowl with chopsticks. She learned how to use her hand, cupping the white grains at the tips of gathered fingers, her thumb sliding food into her mouth. As spring approached and the days lengthened, she retrieved his lost sock from under her sofa one morning and realized they were living together. It was easy in London. His friends, despite their intermittent curiosity about the two of them, didn't ask pressing questions. They mingled like a herd, jumping in and out of each other's cars, flats and beds. But the boys never tried to flirt with Jasmine, and the girls circled her with a resigned weariness.

Her friends – the assortment of people she had round to her flat some evenings – were more inquisitive. At first, they were excited by the prospect of fate in bringing the pair together, two people from a 'small' country – at least in their minds, though Malaysia was two and half times bigger than England – meeting in a city as large as London. Iskandar was the only Malaysian most of them had met apart from Jasmine, and he was nothing like her. They struggled to understand how, the whys not even arising in their consciousness.

She and Iskandar didn't offer explanations, the pocked terrain of their coupling a subject too scabrous to broach. Because it only mattered back home, where their differences were apparent in their mere names.

By summer, it was time for graduation. Neither attended the other's, not wanting to enter into difficult conversations with their respective families. Instead, they met afterwards, his posse and her rag-tag bunch at Turnmills, for one last, epic blow-out.

They packed up her flat that weekend, and spent their last night in London at his – a one-bedroom in Bayswater where many Malaysians seemed to end up, like ants marching a trail of crumbs to the nest.

In two days, they would arrive home, back to the sweltering, thick dampness of their birth country, their boxes of sweaters and coats to be stored in closets, unopened. In two days, they would return to the layered folds of their respective families, ignorant of their combined existence. The tangle and twist of things that had been absent from their affair in London would reach out and ensnare them, throwing doubt on their audacity and light on the impossibility of their secret togetherness. She knew she could not face it.

Jasmine was to join one of the big accounting firms. Poh Poh had arranged it. Iskandar had a job waiting for him at the national oil conglomerate. Like many other Malays (even those from well-off families), he had to serve out his scholarship bond. His parents never had to worry about putting their children through university: the government took care of that. Unlike the Chinese, who had no safety nets waiting to catch their fall.

Jasmine watched the street traffic outside his bedroom window. She had never spent the night there before this. Too risky, with his block of flats occupied by Malays of all kinds: PhD students with their wives and three children in tow, embassy personnel who observed both Malaysian and English bank holidays, other government types from dubious depart-ments one barely knew existed back home, even a sprinkling of corporate sorts who could never bring themselves to stray too far from the familiar. In Bayswater, rendang was easily found; all you had to do was knock on some doors.

His flat was now stripped of his presence, leaving only the standard-issue furniture and crockery. She traced a finger down the windowpane, chasing a trickle of rain.

He came up behind her, resting his chin on her head. 'Duck rice?' She declined to dine out, so he volunteered to get takeaway.

They sat in separate armchairs in the living room, eating their dinner. Already she could feel them pulling apart, like two halves of a cell dividing, their easy rhythm stuttering to a halt. A half-empty bottle of whisky stood on the coffee table.

'What's going to happen back home, do you think?' She chewed on a duck wing, watching him in the waning light. They had never talked about this before.

He pushed a shock of wavy hair off his face. 'We're not in the nineteenth century, sayang.' He only used the term of endearment when he knew he was on rocky ground, needing some added traction. 'Although I didn't think you'd want to get married so soon.'

She hadn't even considered the possibility. Conversion to Islam was not an option for her. Poh Poh would never allow it. And he could only marry a Muslim; the law said so. Either of them breaking tradition would cause a seismic crack in their families.

'Maybe this is where things end.' Her eyes welled with tears. 'So we don't have to say goodbye later. Because . . . we will.' She lifted her gaze towards him, reaching for his hand.

He looked as if she had just slapped his face. 'What the fuck, sayang? You're leaving me?'

She buried her face in her hands, rocking herself back and forth, crying without sound.

He kneeled in front of her, wrapping her in his arms. 'We'll make it work. I'll find a way for your grandmother to love me. And my parents, they'll adore you. We'll get married, and . . . and maybe have babies.' He was pleading now, his weight sinking, her body his ballast.

She straightened herself, gripping his shoulders. 'We won't.

It's not going to happen. I won't become a Muslim. I don't want to. And you cannot change who you are.' The truth, the real of it, the heart of them, had finally entered the room. And she had let it in.

Later, as the plane taxied on the runway and turned into its bay at Subang Airport, she planted a surreptitious kiss on his cheek. Already there were a few too many inquisitive eyes watching.

Retrieving their bags, they hugged like two firm friends, and walked towards the glass doors. His family engulfed him the minute he appeared, while she stood alone waiting for Uncle Boon, Poh Poh's chauffeur. Iskandar looked back once, a hint of sadness tinged with hope in his eyes.

*

In the end, it was he who left her, two years after they returned from university, in a restaurant, halfway through dinner, in a room full of people. They rose from their seats right after he said it, her face concealed by her handbag.

He waved for the car jockey when they reached the street, one hand still holding hers firm in his grasp. He hugged her to his chest while they waited for the car, trying to bury the sorrow that carved black trails of mascara down her cheeks.

His father had just had a bypass. Things were brittle and uncertain. His mother wanted him to marry the daughter of family friends: a Malay girl she approved of.

None of it surprised Jasmine, really. She had been right after all. The reality of their lives had finally cleaved her and Iskandar apart.

In the first few months after the break-up, she sometimes

awakened in the dead of night, a strange fear caught in her shallow breath. As if she had been on the verge of discovering some secret loophole that could have allowed Iskandar and her to remain together. A universe where she didn't have to change God allegiances. And one where his wouldn't mind.

If Poh Poh noticed the dark circles under Jasmine's eyes, she never mentioned them. Instead, fortifying supplements appeared on Jasmine's office desk some mornings. Brand's Essence of Chicken. Ginseng tea. Herbal concoctions meant to cool troubled digestions.

And Poh Poh herself darkening Jasmine's doorway before day's end, insisting on witnessing her sleep-deprived grand-daughter's consumption of said remedies. If anything could scare away heartbreak, Poh Poh's often bitter panaceas did. Or at least hastened Jasmine's determination to plunge herself deeper into work in an attempt to exhaust herself into uninter-rupted sleep.

Until at last, some years had passed, and Iskandar became a mere thought that sometimes flitted across Jasmine's mind when she was not paying attention. Then a small flutter of wistfulness would wash through her before disappearing into the ether. But the hurt of the heartbreak was gone. Or so she thought, until one night in 1997.

That evening, rain fell in torrential gashes, slashing its wet through the black Hong Kong sky. The Chinese were reclaiming the city after a hundred and fifty years, and she was twenty-eight years old. She was there for a good time with an English lawyer she had met in KL. Since Iskandar, she had stayed away from attachments, and besides, work kept her more than busy.

The party on the fifty-foot yacht was heating up, despite the chill of the churning rain. Revellers huddled under a canopy on the boat's deck, trying not to spill their drinks every time the vessel swayed. Causeway Bay was filled with others like them, all jockeying for the best position to watch the fireworks.

The boat captain secured a spot at the front of the cordon. Before them, Hong Kong loomed, the tall columns of its buildings illuminating the shore. Puddles of light bounced on the waves in the bay.

Her phone buzzed. She retrieved it from her handbag and flipped it open. An SMS from Iskandar:

I need to tell you something.

Her heart lurched.

She descended into the belly of the boat, legs shaking, found an empty cabin and shut the door behind her. He picked up on the first ring.

'Hi.' His voice sounded weary. 'I'm sorry.'

After years, suddenly an apology. 'Iskandar, are you okay?'

'No.' Pause. 'I don't know. I need to see you.'

'I'm in Hong Kong.'

Silence. A stifled sob. Or perhaps it was just static.

'I can't, Jasmine.' His words came in staccato. 'I keep trying, but you're still there. Even if I . . . haven't seen you. Even if . . . we haven't spoken. You're here, in my head. I—'

'Iska, stop.' Her chest tightened. She couldn't breathe.

'I messed up, Jaz. It was my fault. I should never have left you.'

'Iska, why are you calling me now?' She didn't know what she wanted him to say.

39

'I . . . I'm getting married.'

Anything but that.

She had thought, all this while, that he had already been married to the woman chosen by his family. By now, there would have been babies.

But she should have known after all. Iskandar had a way of stretching things out longer than they needed to be. Tasks, books to be read, university assignments, house chores, affairs. His preference was always the more circuitous route, unlike Jasmine's cursory way of dealing with life.

She could hear the muffled cracks of celebratory fireworks as they exploded in the sky, defying the rain. In the corner of the cabin, she curled into a foetal position, dry heaving, her body wracked with tears that did not come.

Later, she emerged to the rain thumping on the canopied deck. She made her way to the stern of the boat, staring into the black, choppy water. A part of her wondered what it would feel like to jump into its depths, the cold enveloping her, shutting out the pain.

'Hello, miss! Are you okay?' A coastguard in the boat next to theirs was waving. She nodded in response, not wanting to alarm him. He smiled and looked down at his shirt. He removed his metal badge and gazed at it for a moment before tucking it into his top pocket. Reaching into his trousers, he pulled out a different one bearing the new Hong Kong flag. He caught her looking and shouted across the pelting rain: 'Things change, but we mustn't forget,' and then shrugged, a sad smile on his face.

The day of Iskandar's wedding, Jasmine drank herself silly alone in her condominium. It was Lunar New Year, but she didn't go back to Ipoh, unable to brave her relatives, especially Poh Poh, afraid she would break down over the reunion dinner.

Phone calls went unanswered. Messages unread. She played Billie Holiday on the stereo continuously, turning it up to drown out her confusion. After all, she and Iskandar had not been together for years. She couldn't understand her despair.

It was Kevin who finally dragged her out of her stupor. On the third day of Lunar New Year, he turned up at her doorstep bearing bak kwa.

'Everyone's wondering where you are. I told them you have a suspected case of mumps.'

She opened the door and let him in.

'Don't even ask me to explain it.' She chewed on a piece of pork jerky, its familiar taste comforting, especially when chased with a swig of whisky. 'This shit actually goes together quite well.'

They both got drunk that night and fell asleep in the living room, her on the couch and him on the floor.

But she was never one to wallow for long. By the time businesses reopened after the holidays, she was back in the swing of things, the memory of Iskandar shoved in the dark, narrow crevice of losses she carried along with the fantasies she had of her father, the mother who was missing or dead, and all the love she would never know.

*

If not for the wedding of the KL mayor's son nine years later, Iskandar might not have figured in her life again. Except KL is a town, not a city, not really, given the three degrees of separation for just about anybody, so fate might likely have found a different way to intervene. They were unfinished business meant to collide.

After the dinner reception, she stood in the foyer of the Mandarin Oriental, waiting for her car.

'Jasmine?' The familiar, soft lilt made her catch her breath.

She turned and saw his guarded smile, the ghosts of their past selves lingering in the corners of his eyes. He looked like he might shed a tear and laugh at the same time.

She kissed him lightly on each cheek, clasping his hands as if they were mere acquaintances. It was probably the closest thing to the truth. Her travel schedule kept her out of the country at least a couple of weeks a month. He revolved in Malay circles, circumnavigating the periphery of powerful politicians on account of his father's association with them. His family had done well in recent years, scoring big construction projects across the country, thanks to his father's ties to a cabinet minister.

'Do you have time for a quick drink?'

So he still drank, of course. 'Maybe just one.' She rang her chauffeur and told him to wait. Iskandar's wife was at home, unwell.

They sat in a far corner of the hotel's lobby lounge, settling into separate club chairs. Talk was of things that were of little real consequence – work, his parents, her grandmother, the latest jazz album, that giraffe hotel in Kenya, how he had bought a guitar and taught himself to play.

'I bet you're quite good at it,' she said.

'I played a gig the other month!' A light, real joy, reflected in his eyes.

'I should come and listen, maybe one day.'

'I wrote a song, I played it that night.'

About us? she wanted to ask, but stayed silent. Because in truth, there had been no one in her life after him. At least, no one of consequence. Besides, Poh Poh kept her so busy she didn't even have any friends, really. Just people who invited her to places and parties, mostly work-related. Even baby showers and hen nights were obligatory drop-ins – things that kept her on the radar of the daughters of very important people.

They didn't make love, not then. Nor the next week when she saw him in a bar, where he played the song he had written. He strummed the guitar on stage and stared right at her, making her cheeks burn until she had to leave.

It happened a month later. He rang her one night, his voice jagged and torn.

'I just punched a hole in my bedroom door. I need to get out of here for a while before I do something I might regret.'

Jasmine was alarmed at the simmering anger in his tone. Without thinking, she invited him to her condo, imagining his slender frame broken.

He arrived sporting a swelling right hand, its knuckles beginning to show signs of bruising. She sat him down at her dining table, examining the damage. It looked superficial. 'Was it a teak door, at least?' She couldn't help the small giggle. 'Or one of those plywood things? Because if it was just one of those . . .'

He leaned forward and kissed her before she could finish. The sex afterwards was familiar, yet oddly new, a questioning urgency burning in her thoughts. All through it she wondered about the wife, but didn't ask, afraid he might stop.

After, he told her about his marriage. How he and his wife had been trying to conceive, except she kept miscarrying and was becoming increasingly distraught. A part of him felt relieved every time, but he couldn't tell his wife, of course. Guilt hung in the sag of his shoulders, hunched from the weight.

'I should never have married her,' he said. 'I'm just not brave enough, after all. Luckily, you knew better. Because God knows, the last person I ever want to hurt is you.'

She gathered him in her arms then, rocking his body like a small, forlorn child. Should she wish him a baby? She wasn't sure. All she knew was that his presence felt right, as if he had come home from a long sojourn, placing his battered, sorry burdens at her feet. The things that were missing from her life since they had separated were back, to be laundered and stored in some secret closet.

*

These days, home is a penthouse on Federal Hill, the kind where macaques sometimes still appear on the tennis courts, its grounds ringed by a thicket of trees. It has a SwimJet lap pool on its veranda, the kind that emits currents, allowing Jasmine to clock distances in never-ending strokes, the city a distant backdrop. Far enough from the thick of it not to taste the choking, daytime rush-hour smog. High enough not to hear the scream of racing motorbikes in the dead of night. Buildings and people are now merely faraway pinpricks of light, punctuating pockets of darkness where humans lie sleeping, or empty offices wait for morning. Jasmine is sipping a perfect martini (dirty and stirred) in her swimsuit when the front door beeps at 2 a.m. She is still buzzing from the excitement of the public listing and the gala.

'Oh, you're wet,' he says with a grin. 'Entertaining your Bond girl fantasies again, I see.' He walks over to the stereo, lowering the volume. 'Babe, pity the neighbours.' The unit below is empty; it belongs to Seh Gu, who is never there. But she has never told him that.

Jasmine slips back into the pool, her finger crooked, beckoning him in. He undresses.

'Well, this all seems a bit unfair,' he says as he nuzzles her neck, fingering the shoulder strap of her one-piece.

'Winner's pick.' She moves his hand down to her waist.

'You're KL's golden girl now. I need to up my game.' He is proud of her, she can tell from the way he holds her at arm's length, as if reappraising her value. He just made a few million ringgit himself from her company's listing this morning, despite Phoenix's bak kwa reputation.

Jasmine wonders how he reconciles it. 'You Malays are something else. You don't just have one set of rules, especially when money is involved. Sometimes I think you're more Chinese than I am. I never know where the lines are with you Malays . . .'

'I told you. We may not be your customers, but we certainly don't mind your money.'

Jasmine gives him a playful shove. 'That's not all you don't mind.' She climbs out of the pool and offers him a whisky.

He waves her outstretched hand away. 'Not tonight. It's almost Ramadan. Gotta face the music soon.' The annual cleansing of sins. Thank goodness she's not Catholic, merely Christian. She dangles her legs in the water, one hand stroking his now-wet hair.

'I really need to start working out.' She pinches her midriff, poking the modest roll of fat. All those nights working late and eating junk food have started to show.

'Maybe you could try fasting, since it's Ramadan.' He looks up at her, caressing her thigh.

'Stop it,' she sighs, pulling her legs out of the pool. 'Stop trying. I'm not going to be a Muslim. You know this.'

She doesn't see the point of it. After all, he is married to a bright-faced hijabi he still has sex with, judging from the miscarriages. She is more than a little tipsy when the words slip out. 'How did you manage to leave the house at this hour? Didn't your wife wonder where you were off to?'

He climbs out of the pool, wrapping a towel around his torso, shaking his head like a lean, wet dog. 'I just . . . left. She was sleeping.' As if this is an explanation.

Over the last four years, they have kept things going by gliding over the little details. Telling each other just enough, without letting on too much. It is their unspoken shield from wasteful hurt. Whatever time they spend together is confined to a small, narrow space, muffled by hours of missing the other, concealed beneath their external, everyday lives. Time is always in short supply, so it is used judiciously – for lovemaking and laughing, holding their secret dreams up to the light. He still wants to be a musician; she still fantasizes about going on safari. They don't have the luxury of a real good fight – skirting each other in a shared home, seething with anger and desire at the same time. Their arguments always have abrupt endings, with him walking out and them not speaking for days until one or the other gives in. Then they reconcile, the lost hours in between unmentioned, so there are gaps in their knowledge of each other, of things that perhaps don't matter, but in the end are of real consequence.

He motions for her to sit next to him on the lounger, and she acquiesces. He pulls her close.

'I can stay,' he offers. This time he knows he has missed

too much. She almost refuses, not wanting to make trouble. But she doesn't want to be alone tonight. She won today and wants all the spoils of victory, even if its shiniest baubles are make-believe.

So she leads him to the bedroom, activating the front-door alarm before switching off the light.

Their lovemaking is hungry, the kind of sex tinged with angry yearning that only the knowledge of parting precipitates. It is truth and lies sliding on sheets, the ones too painful swept to the ground like unnecessary pillows that only get in the way.

In the morning, his fingers are entwined in her hair. She lies there, not releasing herself from his sleeping grasp. She doesn't want to go to the office. She doesn't want him to go home – that blank vacuum they never speak of.

But life has a way of finding its path, its heft pressing in, demanding to be examined, laughed at and cried over in the spaces between the loving. The ridiculous wants to be made sublime. The dreary made special. And the minutiae of things magnified, shaping a fine mesh of nerves that fuse two people together.

5

By the time she gets to the office the next morning, Phoenix is worth a billion ringgit.

Jasmine finds Mr Chew waiting in the lobby. Seeing her, he stands, folding the newspaper in haste. They walk past the pool of a hundred or so employees, down a corridor that ends at a large red door carved with gold phoenixes. She stops just to the left of it and enters her office. Sunlight streams in through the half-drawn blinds.

This is what winning feels like. No different from before except for the little things – the extra-wide smile of the receptionist, the quiet nods from the workers in their cubicles. Before, they would bury their heads in their laptops, looking up only to acknowledge her grandmother.

Mr Chew has had too much coffee, a thin film of sweat shining on his brow. 'The merchant bankers want a meeting. And the reporter from *Market Watch* called. She needs you to answer her email. For the interview.'

'Tomorrow. I can meet them tomorrow.'

'Olivier Lau's secretary wants to know if you're free this evening. And your aunts are on the way.'

Jasmine's head jerks up. 'My aunts? Why are they coming here?'

'I don't know, Miss. I thought you had scheduled it. I'll set up the conference room.'

'No. I'll see them here, in my office.' The last thing she wants is to encourage the two older women to stay.

At eleven, her aunts arrive.

'This is a pleasant surprise!' Jasmine shows them to the sofa. 'Yum cha, Tai Gu, Seh Gu.' She offers them each a cup of tea. 'I didn't know if you had breakfast yet, so I only managed to get some pastries. If I had known you were coming . . .'

'Oh no, no, it's okay. I just thought we'd drop in on our way back to Ipoh.' Seh Gu Treasure is all smiles, but her voice is brittle around the edges.

They expect her to ask how they are going to get there, just as a matter of pleasantry, but she doesn't. She smiles back, her glance flitting from one aunt to the other, waiting for them to continue. She doesn't have time for small talk this morning. And they really should have called first.

Seh Gu clears her throat. 'Lin Li, your tai gu has something to ask you.'

Tai Gu Ruth takes a deep breath, her eyes shooting darts at her younger sister. Turning to Jasmine, she says, 'I want you to ask your grandmother to give Kevin a position at Phoenix.'

That viper, revealed at last.

'I know you've worked very hard these few years, girl,' Seh Gu coos, her head cocked to one side. 'And you must be tired, so tired. So maybe Kevin can help take some of the load off you. We just want what's best for you both. Think about it. You'll have more time. Maybe find a husband. Have children of your own.'

'We want him to be the new CEO,' Tai Gu interjects, her voice firm, unyielding. 'He is, after all, a man.'

And Jasmine is not. At forty-one, she is still just a girl who takes care of things, dusting the throne and tidying the palace until a male is ready to become emperor.

'Fuck you,' Jasmine mutters under her breath. Then louder. 'Fuck you! This is bullshit.'

She has never told them off before, let alone hurled expletives in their faces. It isn't the thing to do. It wasn't how she was brought up.

Tai Gu stands, bumping the coffee table's edge. The teacups tremble. 'Ni hi chung fan shu,' she hisses. 'Your mother abandoned you after your father died. If Ma Ma hadn't taken you in, you wouldn't even be here. Who knows where you came from? Your mother could be some nightclub bar girl for all we know.'

'But my father was a Leong, and so am I.' Jasmine is standing now too, her calves flexed for a fight. 'Kevin is a Chen. He is still his father's son. Not a Leong. Not like me.'

A small cry escapes Seh Gu's lips, her hands pressing her mouth. 'Oh Jasmine, I didn't want to do this. Of course you have every right to be angry, but I just thought . . .'

'Leave,' Jasmine retorts, holding the door open. 'Leave before I never speak to you both again.'

At the doorway, Tai Gu pauses, her eyes blazing with anger. 'You and me,' she says, pointing her finger at Jasmine, 'all three of us, are the same. Your seh gu and I made sacrifices for this family, all the while knowing it was only to make way for your father. A man. It's time you knew your place in this family.'

Poh Poh once told Jasmine that victory is a fragile thing. It can never long withstand the twin sledgehammers of ambition and envy, its armour crumbling at the first heavy thump of danger at the door. When the enemy is within, Jasmine's instinct is to flee. And perhaps seek solace close to home – a spot down the road where she can hide for a moment, one eye on the little fires blazing in her own windows.

She tries ringing Iskandar in the hope of some respite. A stolen lunch in some obscure restaurant perhaps, where her rage can be tempered by his soothing words, and maybe a bottle of wine or two. Or just some hot, angry afternoon sex.

But he doesn't pick up. And she doesn't bother leaving him a message. It was a long shot anyway. And she is used to solving problems on her own.

*

Two and a half hours later, Jasmine is at Ryokan, a Japanese restaurant housed in a bungalow on Embassy Row. The waitress leads her upstairs to a private dining room with a view of the garden below. She thinks she is early, but Kuan Yew is already there, waiting with a bottle of cold saké.

'Sorry, I know you said "drinks later" . . .'

She greets him as he stands, air-kissing his cheeks on both sides.

He laughs.

She throws him a puzzled look.

'It's just . . .' He waves his hand left and right of his face, then back and forth between them.

They both burst into laughter, realizing the strangeness of her earlier gesture. Their kindergarten selves would have been appalled.

They skim through the years, catching one another up. His mother's death two years ago. His father's gradual retreat from

51

the world since then. Her work at Phoenix, his in Australia after graduating with a degree in finance. Jasmine's college days, filled with bad food and the rations of Brahim's and Maggi cup noodles to stave off her longing for home. To him, they were staples that kept him alive. His meagre pay from working a pizza delivery job barely covered rent. His father only sent enough money for tuition and books; they couldn't afford more back then. But they don't talk about lovers.

Lunch eaten, she grows quiet, unwilling to leave. It feels safe here with him. No danger.

'Coffee?' he suggests, pouring the last of the saké into her cup. 'Unless you have someone waiting.'

She summons the waitress and orders an espresso. Double shots.

He leans back in his chair, a quizzical expression in his eyes. 'I've never seen someone win the stock market lottery and look like they wanted to give it all back.'

'You'd be amazed what crawls out of the woodwork,' she says. Because the world comes knocking when you have a windfall, with its long list of debts you never knew you accrued.

She didn't mean to, but she tells him about the visit from her aunts. Because he is an old friend, long-lost yet still familiar, a witness to a small part of her past, to whom her history doesn't need explanation.

When she finishes, he asks, 'And what about Kevin?'

She wants to say: *He's gay. Coming home would smother him. His mother doesn't know.* But that isn't her secret to share, so she keeps it. 'I haven't had a chance to speak to him today.'

'I doubt Madam Leong will let her daughters dictate things. Not while she's still alive.'

Maybe he's right. She should know, but she doesn't, her Poh Poh still an opaque entity. And this isn't the sort of conversation Jasmine can have with her grandmother over the phone.

Besides, her aunts have beaten her to it. By now, they will have arrived in Ipoh. Jasmine pictures them having tea with Poh Poh. Seh Gu twisting her fingers, wishing she were behind a stray garden bush. Tai Gu, the tiger, chin high, her long-stored tears locked away, bracing for the hurt, but prowling forward despite it.

*

By evening, Jasmine is exhausted. She unlocks her condo door and kicks off her shoes at its entrance.

There is music playing, a saxophone solo, its twirling notes lingering in the air. She sees a suitcase, enough for a week's stay, next to the shoe cupboard.

Iskandar is sprawled on the couch, smoking.

'I thought you quit.' She straddles his torso and plants a brief kiss on his cheek. 'I rang you this afternoon, but you didn't answer. Busy day?'

'Hey there, golden girl. Sorry, I let myself in. Surprise.' He sits up and stubs out his cigarette, arms circling her waist.

'Going somewhere?' Jasmine motions to the suitcase.

'That depends.' He averts his head and then mumbles, 'I left. Well, she threw me out. So, I left.' He lifts his gaze up towards her, questioning.

No wonder he didn't take her call. His real life trumped their secret one again.

'You walked out? Again?' Two years ago, he spent a month in her condo, back when his wife found out about them. But she thought Iskandar and his other half had reached a detente since then. Just like she has. Two women with separate lives, resigned to a common fate entwined in one man. Jasmine wonders if, this time, his wife has had enough.

He shrugs, shaking his head.

'Well, fuck.' She rolls her eyes. 'I guess I wasn't the only one who got blindsided today. Move over.' She pushes his legs away, making room for herself. A sheaf of magazines slips off the couch to the floor.

'Whisky?' He lifts his glass from the coffee table, takes a sip.

'No, I've had too much to drink.' She massages her temples, a headache forming at the roots of her hair.

He raises an eyebrow but doesn't say anything.

She tells him about her aunts' visit. He tries to soothe her, one hand caressing her back in long, slow strokes.

When she gets to the part where she cusses her aunts out, he stops her. 'You told your tai gu to fuck off? What the hell did she say?'

'She told me to dig a hole and plant potatoes. It's a Chinese thing. Essentially: go kill yourself.'

'Holy shit! Harsh!' he barks out, laughing.

She gives him a playful shove, pouting. 'I thought you were on my side.'

He reaches out, hugging her close, planting small kisses in her hair. 'Sayang, you know I am. Do you want me to stay?'

A small laugh escapes her lips. She feels like crying a little, but she mustn't. 'Or what? Let you run loose round KL so you can pick up some other woman? And piss off your wife and me even more?'

A hurt look crosses his eyes. 'All I've ever wanted is you.'

Except she cannot afford him. 'I can never compete with your family, Iska. The wife, your parents. God. The odds will never be on my side.'

She leans on his arm. He slouches down further on the sofa, her head slipping into the curve of his neck. The evening azan floats in the distance, calling Muslims to prayer. She frowns. 'Is that a new guy? The tune is a little different.'

'Sounds like it.' He pauses, eyes narrowed. 'I liked the old one better.'

'Me too. He had more style.'

'Yeah.' He nods. 'That guy was like a Thelonious Monk. This one's more like a . . . Kenny G.'

They laugh and snuggle closer. He traces a circle on the palm of her hand. The sky darkens. Sunsets in KL are sudden, a mere fifteen minutes. Unlike its languid descent from the English skies, the sun here departs in a hurry.

He straightens himself, facing her, both hands now on her shoulders. 'Let's get married. You can come work for my family's company instead. Fuck it. I'm done living life the way everyone thinks I should.'

For a moment, she is happy. Then: 'I'm not becoming anyone's second wife, Iska. And you know I don't want to be Muslim.'

'I'm divorcing her.' There is weariness in his voice. 'We don't love each other anyway. Maybe she loved me at one point, or thought she did, and I just did what I thought my parents wanted. But I am done, whether you marry me or you don't.'

She stares at him, open-mouthed, blinking.

Iskandar strokes her cheek. 'I think it's time I stopped being unfair to both of you. To all of us.'

She draws a long breath, not daring to hope. Her stomach grumbles. 'Let's eat,' she says, reaching for a stack of delivery menus.

After dinner, they watch TV on the sofa, one of those travel shows featuring eateries that only locals would know. They spoon like teenagers, his arm wrapped around her torso. He slips a hand under her blouse, seeking the familiar, soft curve of her middle.

'London,' she says.

'Mmm . . .' he murmurs. 'We used to do this a lot then, didn't we?'

'No, look! There's the street where we used to live!' She turns to glance at him, but his eyes are closed.

'Iska, that's where the fish and chip shop was.' She points to the TV screen. 'It's now an Italian bistro.'

He is paying attention now. 'Maybe that's what we should do. Just chuck this all in. Get the hell out. Leave. Things were good in London, when it was just you and me.'

Of course they were, away from Poh Poh's acid gaze and the realities of his tangled dependence on his family. When they were merely students playing house in a place that was not their home and few grasped the actual cost of their togetherness.

She twists round to face him, almost rolling off the couch. He catches her.

'What's really going on with you, Iska?'

He lets out a long sigh. 'My father wants me to run for office. He thinks it will help us get bigger projects.'

She sits up, turning to face him. 'What, politics? Stand for election? Do you want this?'

'Of course not!' He sits up too, his elbows resting on his

legs, fingers curled in exasperation. But that doesn't matter. Not here. Not in a place where politics is merely a fast pass to government megaprojects and creaming off public coffers. It doesn't matter what one really wants. Just toe the line and, above all, be Malay. Never question the leader: it gets you everywhere. And those at the top of the ladder are always trying to push the rest off.

'Are you sure you won't even consider it?'

He looks at her hard, incredulous. 'Sometimes I wonder what you actually think of me. Or maybe I shouldn't ask. Fuck, I probably deserve it.'

She is sorry. She wishes love weren't so complicated. Maybe it's why she stays, the thought of starting over just too overwhelming. The sorting, the picking, the tidying of feelings before the jagged pattern of love is revealed takes time, years perhaps. At least with him, she doesn't have to deal with the other things, like in-laws and relatives. The house of their loving is sparse, furnished to a Scandinavian degree of minimalist utility. Function before form. Need before want. The dream purposely omitted from its walls and floors.

'Do you even love me?' His words cause tears to well in the corner of her eyes. She remains silent, thinking about all the time she has spent loving him while apart. Not calling, not seeking, not trying to make his life more difficult than it is, settling instead for small snatches of time. The moments she orchestrates in her head when he is away, lining up the fragments of her separate life, picking the most important bits so she can arrange them neatly for when he arrives. How does she tell him that he is like a ghost, his presence a constant unseen beside her? Every funny thing someone says, each shiny object, an exciting new possibility, all of it weighed for its importance, its capability to make him feel thought of, missed, adored, all considered and measured for their value to please. Does she love him? She doesn't know how not to.

'Loving you is all I've got outside of work and Poh Poh. It's the one thing I truly own all to myself. So even if it's a small part of you, I'll take what I can get,' she says. The hurt crawls out of her core, up her throat, blooming in hollow sobs.

He starts to cry too. 'I should never have left you.'

But there is no place on the map of this country for them. Perhaps elsewhere, but not here. Except here is where the rest of them resides, in the folds of their suffocating families, where the fine leaf veins of rules keep scoring the lines of separation between her and him, as if determined to make them choose. Love over blood and money. One love of a lifetime over generations of others. Leaving before staying. Self before others. Him over them – the only people who gave her a home when her own parents disappeared.

'Iska, you could never leave your family either. Neither of us can.'

The carriage of her life is already full, its doors barely able to close, open–shut, open–shut, stalled. She is in the doorway, one hand on the outside, clinging to him, not wanting to let go, while the familiar crowd inside holds on to her collar, her elbow, her ankle. Her hair comes undone from its twisted chignon, its tumble a weight causing her to look back.

She doesn't know how not to love him. And she doesn't know how to leave him. Her body is bruised from the constant banging of train doors that threaten to someday close shut.

But when has that ever mattered?

'This can't be all there is.' He is rubbing his face with his palm, his cheeks wet. 'We just keep getting carried away by the current of our parents and families, and when does it stop? When do we get to jump out of the goddamn river, and . . . and take that hike into the woods, or climb a mountain, or just freakin' pitch a tent and do nothing if we feel like it? When?'

'Maybe never,' she whispers. But then again, she hadn't stopped to consider it before. Life puts one thing after another in front of her, like a magic pavement built by a knowing hand. Poh Poh always has plans.

6

She wakes to a persistent ringing. Fifteen missed calls. 'Kevin?' She is breathless, heart pounding, sensing disaster.

'You have to come to Ipoh. Now.'

'I know. Your mum and Seh Gu, they paid me a visit yesterday. Have they spoken to Poh Poh? Did you hear?'

'She's gone, Jasmine.'

'What – who? Who's . . . what do you mean gone, did, did someone go somewhere?'

'Poh Poh. A heart attack . . . last night. She's dead.'

The End. Forever. Full stop.

While Iskandar and she were asleep with their private sorrow.

Poh Poh didn't even wait for all of them in the end. Just slipped away like a suspect house guest, or a runaway bride and her one suitcase, trailing unfinished business behind her. She left in her sleep when no one was looking. It was Seh Gu who found her this morning when she stopped by with a packet of fishball noodles from the market – Poh Poh's favourite breakfast.

Jasmine wakes Iskandar in a panic, his startled eyes confused at first by his surroundings. They dress in a hurry. She packs a small bag and grabs her car keys. There is no time to ring for the chauffeur.

But he takes the keys from her hand. 'You're not driving, not like this. I can't let you.' She starts to protest, but he kisses her silent. 'Let me. It's the least I can do. I'll just get you there and leave the car with you. I can catch the train back here. I'll be waiting when you return. I promise.'

It is a regular Saturday, so traffic is light. Leaving the city, they stop at a petrol station to grab breakfast. Back in the car, she feeds him mouthfuls of curry puffs, wiping the crumbs from the corners of his lips. He glances at her now and again, as if they are new lovers.

They have not done this since returning from London, where they took a weekend trip to the Cotswolds the winter they first met. The roads there were winding and narrow, hedged by old stone walls on either side. They were almost crashed into by an old lady in her Morris Minor.

Here, they are on the wide expressway, heading north. She notices that he is speeding, and she places her hand on his thigh. 'Slow down.' After all, Poh Poh isn't going anywhere. And Jasmine is in no hurry to face her aunts.

'You're thinking,' he says, catching the faraway look in her eyes.

'I just realized I am alone now in this world. Without my Poh Poh, I don't have anyone.'

He frowns. 'I'm here. You've got me.'

She knew he wouldn't understand. 'Do I?'

He lets out a sigh, tightening his grip on the steering wheel. 'I wasn't kidding when I said I was leaving her.'

But still. 'I don't have any family besides my Poh Poh. I mean, yes, I have my aunts, but it's not the same. Poh Poh was the only one who ever fought in my corner. Now that she's gone, I have no one.' Things with her grandmother had never been easy, Jasmine always feeling like she came up short. The debt of a lifetime isn't easy to repay. But at least Poh Poh had never been her enemy.

Iskandar pulls in at a rest stop, turning off the engine next to a waqaf. He walks round and opens her door. 'Come with me.' He leads her to the small gazebo and pulls out a pack of cigarettes.

For a while, they say nothing, the whoosh of cars whizzing by filling the silence. They sit side by side on a concrete bench. Looking round, he takes her hand and raises it to his lips. A quick kiss while no one is watching.

'I love you,' he whispers.

'I know,' she replies.

'Marry me.'

She is quiet. If she says yes now, at least there will no longer be Poh Poh's scorn to contend with. But what about Phoenix? Marrying him would mean giving up one dream for another. A life with him over her life's work. Now, with Poh Poh gone, Jasmine is less certain she can walk away from the latter.

'Or don't. But know this: I've loved only you for half of my life. I can't remember what life before you was like. And I don't want to. No matter what. Whether or not you like it.'

Her chest tightens from the weight of his words. She pretends for a moment that they are all that count. She doesn't want to know the rest of it. Not for a while.

Later, she leans her head on his arm as he drives, her right hand interlaced with his left. She thinks about how they might actually be together. To passers-by, they probably look like a married couple. And somehow, still in love.

The highway slopes up, approaching a hill. 'Almost there,' Iskandar says. 'I finally get to see where you grew up.'

Cresting the peak, they see the humps of limestone outcrops scattered like sleeping giants, punctuating the flat green landscape. Thin clumps of mist crown the top of each hill. No matter how many times she has made the drive, the first glimpse of her home town always makes her pause. It is pretty, almost magical. Like a secret uncovered.

Iskandar lets out a slow whistle. A thick mass of clouds hangs in the distance. 'Looks like a storm is brewing over Ipoh.'

She is almost home. With him by her side.

As they turn off the expressway, Iskandar and Jasmine grow silent. The rain slashes the air in thick silver ropes, its loud pounding on the car roof making it impossible not to shout. They inch through Ipoh town, the storm obscuring most of the buildings from view.

At the house, the front gate is open, swinging in the whipping wind. This is the place where Jasmine grew up: a two-storey nineteenth-century building set back from the bustle of Treacher Road. Iskandar pulls into the driveway already littered with cars parked in a hurry. Jasmine will have to dash to the porte cochère. She reaches for her bag from the back seat.

'Wait.' Iskandar wraps his arm round her neck, pulling her close.

She plants a quick peck on his lips, one eye on the entryway. A white curtain of water rushes down the windshield, but she is still afraid someone will see.

'Call me, okay? I'll come pick you up, whenever you're ready.' His eyes are searching, afraid he will never see her again.

The rain shows no sign of abating. 'Maybe stay. There's a

couple of new hotels in town. But I don't know if I can see you.'

There is a hint of a wistful smile at the corners of his lips. 'Yes, maybe. Might be a good idea. Gives me time to think before heading back. Don't worry about me. You go take care of things.'

'Okay. I love you.'

'Always. And hey' – he grabs her hand as she turns to the door – 'be good.'

Jasmine opens the car door and sprints to the porte cochère. In a few seconds, she is drenched. She watches him reverse out of the driveway. She wants to cry, but doesn't. Or perhaps she does. Maybe she is just wiping the rain from her eyes.

Kevin is standing in the doorway, towel in hand, cheeky glint in his stare. 'Is that who I think it is?'

Jasmine nods as she flips her hair, bending over to pat it dry. 'I'm a mess. This is pointless.'

They slip through the foyer, passing a few people talking in hushed tones, and go upstairs to her old bedroom. She unpacks, retrieving a black blouse and trousers, before changing in the bathroom.

Kevin flops onto the bed, slouching his shoulders over a bolster. The bed is an antique four-poster made of rosewood. Jasmine climbs in, yanking the pillow from him, and lies down, wrapping her limbs around it.

'I don't want to go downstairs.' She is suddenly weary.

'Fine. Move aside then.'

She rolls over, making room as Kevin stretches out next to her. They are ten again, pretending her bed is the belly of a giant ship. Stowaways off on an unknown adventure.

'She just left, Kev. Just like that.' She fans her hair out on the pillow, running her fingers through the tangles. 'No warning, no goodbyes. Nothing. Just . . . gone.'

'I haven't cried yet. Have you?' He turns his head to face her. 'I'm not sure I can.'

'I don't know what to feel. I mean, it's Poh Poh.'

It wasn't like she was Jasmine's mother. Not that Jasmine would know what that feels like. The old lady was the only constant in Jasmine's life. Sparse with affection, but generous with advice. Jasmine never wanted for material things. Just the kind that didn't come off store shelves, like hugs, bedtime stories, or the clucking, fussing, smothering love she saw her aunts dispense every time one of her cousins tripped or cried.

The closest she has come to that is Iskandar. But now with Poh Poh gone, she wonders whether he alone will be enough.

Kevin sits up. Reaching under the bed, he pulls out a bottle of single malt. 'I heard about my mum and Seh Gu's meeting with you.' He unscrews the cap, taking a swig.

She crawls out of bed. Taking a pack of cigarettes from her bag, she cracks a window open.

'You brazen hussy, you wouldn't dare . . .' Kevin waves a hand to his mouth, feigning shock.

'Screw it. Poh Poh's gone. She can't do a thing about it.'

'This is Poh Poh we're talking about. She might haunt you with a can of Baygon.'

The memory, of their grandmother rushing in one afternoon when they were fourteen, makes them howl with laughter. Kevin had nicked a cigarette from old Uncle Boon. Thinking Poh Poh was away, they tried to smoke it in Jasmine's room, only for the old lady to burst in after sprinting up the stairs (according to Ah Tin), brandishing a can of mosquito spray. The cousins shut themselves in the bathroom, too terrified to come out till morning.

Jasmine lights a cigarette.

'I don't want it, you know,' Kevin finally says. 'Phoenix.'

She exhales, watching the stream of smoke disappear in the rain. 'Why not, Kev? I mean, you have a right.'

'To be Bak Kwa Princess? I have my reputation to think about, Miss Piggy.' He moves to her side and pokes her middle.

'Oi! These extra curves are what made you those millions of dollars, Wonder Woman. All those nights stuck in the damned office, eating junk food with those boring merchant bankers.'

'Well, they haven't exactly stopped someone from wanting you,' he says, his own cigarette now in hand.

'He wants me to marry him. He's leaving his wife.'

'For real?'

'I don't know.' Her voice is quiet, uncertain. 'A part of me wants to believe it.' But most of her is too afraid. Life has never been in the habit of granting her those sorts of wishes. And right now, she isn't even sure it is what she wants any more. The window abruptly blows wide open, sprinkling her face with mist.

Kevin leans against the sill, staring out into the dark. 'You know, now that Poh Poh's gone, I figure you can finally pretty much do what you want.'

'What makes you say that?'

'She probably left everything to you. Okay, minus some titbits to keep her daughters quiet. At least for a while, until you gather your armour and line up the cavalry.'

'You never know with Poh Poh. I mean, even after all these years, I still don't know a thing about my own mother.'

'Would knowing make a difference at this stage, Che?'

'Maybe then I wouldn't be alone.'

'The thing about mums,' he says, exhaling the last of his cigarette, 'is they come with a no-return policy.'

Someone knocks on the door. The cousins exchange a look of mild panic. But before they can fling their cigarettes out the window, the door opens to reveal Ah Tin.

'Aiyoh, if your aunties find out!' Ah Tin slips in, shutting the door in a hurry behind her. She is softer now around the edges, the angles of her youth smoothed out by motherhood and time. 'The goldsmith's son is here. I thought you'd like to know.' Glancing at Kevin, she waggles her finger. 'You naughty boy! Always getting little miss into trouble!'

'What lies!' Kevin laughs. 'Shoo! We have to get pretty now.' He gives Ah Tin a gentle shove out the door. Turning to Jasmine, he says, 'Put on your war paint. We're gonna need it, so slap on some extra on my behalf.'

*

Downstairs, the house has filled with people in rain-speckled clothes. The air is damp with hushed grief and respect.

The living room is set up for the funeral service: chairs from the caterer arranged in rows facing the coffin, a lectern up front and a buffet table at the back with stacks of prayer books. Rosewood chaise longues are pushed against a side wall.

Seh Gu is the first to spot the cousins. Her face is puffy from crying, her nose grown slightly bulbous and red at the tip. She draws the two into an embrace. 'I cannot believe Ma Ma left just like that,' she whispers through her sobs.

Tai Gu stands watch over the casket, her body curved over

its top, fingers splayed on the clear plastic cover. Her face is a mixture of sorrow and leftover fear. She dabs the corner of an eye with a white handkerchief. Seeing the children, she steps away. 'I have never seen her look so peaceful.'

Jasmine holds on to Kevin's arm, her grip tightening as they move towards the coffin. Poh Poh is dressed in a white sheath, fingers clasped. Her hair is pulled back in a hard shell of a bun, its surface a shiny, lacquered silver. In life, she wore very little make-up, except perhaps a thin swipe of coral lipstick. But now, her closed eyes are two dark lines of kohl, with equally striking eyebrows. The coral lipstick is much bolder, as if applied to last longer than one dinner. Alive, Poh Poh would have been mortified. In death, she has become the absurd.

'Good lord,' Kevin whispers. Jasmine can feel his arm twitching beneath her grasp.

Her own eyes widen, her hand at her mouth, concealing a laugh that is threatening to spill out. Jasmine draws a long, deep breath and yanks Kevin away, through the small mill of mourners and into the darkened porte cochère.

They collapse against the wall, their bodies now shaking, their suppressed giggles coming out in keening gasps. Jasmine rains tiny slaps on Kevin's arm. 'Stop it, stop it, stop it. Oh crap, oh Jesus Christ.'

Kevin's eyes are rimmed with wet, one hand fanning his face. 'Oh, I don't think she's going to go gentle into that good night, poor Poh Poh.'

Jasmine catches her breath at last. 'Kev, we have to do something. We can't leave her like this.'

'Hell, I am not meddling. My mother would kill me. Who

do you think is responsible for that? Don't you recognize the eyebrows?'

The realization sends Jasmine into another fit of giggles. Kevin holds his palms up, shaking his head.

Someone clearing his throat instantly silences the cousins. Kuan Yew is standing in the doorway, his face hidden by the light from the house. 'I hope I am not interrupting. My condolences on your loss.' He takes their hands, shaking each in turn. 'So sorry.' The two cousins nod, wiping tears from the corners of their eyes.

Jasmine's phone buzzes in her pocket with an SMS:

Sayang, I've checked into a hotel. All good. Hope you're holding up all right.

At once, the thought of going back into the house seems too much for Jasmine. 'Let's get out of here. Please.'

They decide against the fluorescent glare of the Chinese coffee shops and the cloying smell of nasi kandar joints. Instead, Kuan Yew drives them to a small Italian place tucked into the middle of a row of shophouses on Concubine Lane.

The restaurant is quiet and lit in a low, yellow glow. Old-fashioned posters decorate the place, of pizzas and platters of bolognese held aloft by rotund Italian chefs. The comforting scent of garlic bread hangs in the air. Suddenly, Jasmine is ravenous, her hunger overcoming any guilt she has of stealing away from Poh Poh's wake. The aunties should be able to hold things down for a bit. Maybe they won't even notice her absence.

To her surprise, she spots Iskandar – the familiar hairline that tapers into his slender neck, bent over a newspaper. As they take their seats, she watches him for a moment, conjuring the scent of his skin. She wonders what he is thinking, and whether those thoughts are of her. Slipping her phone out of her pocket, she texts him:

Dining alone? Wanna join us?

Iskandar's head jerks up after reading her message and he swivels round, catching her eye. She feigns surprise. He walks over, throwing a curious glance at Kuan Yew.

'I thought that was you.' She stands to offer him her cheek. 'Won't you join us?'

The men are introduced, Jasmine passing off Iskandar as a KL acquaintance. He tells the group he is here for a quick break and is heading out to Kellie's Castle tomorrow if the weather cooperates.

They ease into conversation about the weather, the town, the restaurant and the stock market. Jasmine and her recent success. Their work. The rain. The hotel where Iskandar is staying. Tips on where to find tomorrow's breakfast for Iskandar's benefit. The fact that the other three all went to school together. Small world. Imagine that.

Seated next to Jasmine, Kuan Yew is attentive, pouring her wine, flagging the waitress for Jasmine's every need. A fork because she dropped hers. An extra plate for the mussel shells from her vongole. Some water.

Meanwhile, Iskandar watches, the flow of his speech barely showing a hint, while his eyes never stray from the pair across from him.

By the time they finish dinner, the rain has stopped. They

step out onto the quiet street, its black asphalt silvered by a thin sheet of water.

'Gimme a ride to my mum's?' Kevin asks Kuan Yew. 'Everyone's left your house, Jasmine Che.' A signal. All clear.

Kuan Yew gives Jasmine a quick peck goodbye with apologies. He is heading back to KL in the morning, unable to attend the funeral.

Iskandar offers to take her home.

Her childhood abode is shrouded in darkness when they reach it, except for the entryway light that emits its weak, orange smoulder, surrounded by a scourge of rain ants.

'Come in.' She unlocks the door.

'You sure?'

'I'm not going to risk you never knowing where I come from. Not when I've waited this long.'

She takes his hand and leads him to the staircase.

'Wait. I should at least pay my respects.' He is standing still, taking in the shadows of the house, his eyes straining to discern its outlines. She leads him to the living room, where a lamp has been left on next to her grandmother's coffin. The room smells of the slow rot of flowers from wreaths wilting in the humid heat.

'Iskandar, meet my Poh Poh.'

He places a hand on the coffin lid, leaning in till his breath mists its cover. He whispers, hands quivering, 'I'm sorry, ma'am. I never meant to hurt her. I promise to take care of her for you, if she'll let me.'

Jasmine looks at him in surprise. She did not expect an apology. In the thousands of imagined instances where Iskandar might have met her grandmother, Jasmine only dared to think of the obvious: Poh Poh greeting him with churlish scorn, leaden words like the tyres of a hitman's car, rolling over centimetre after centimetre of his cracking bones. Iskandar unable to defend himself, extending a hand in greeting, only to be ignored.

In the end, there is this. Only a silent witness to a grand-daughter's betrayal. Poh Poh powerless, except for the ghost of her disdain that seeps through the walls, circling Jasmine like rain ants, stinging.

'Where is everybody?' Iskandar scans the room, not compre-hending the weight of its unexpected desolation.

Everyone has gone, the aunts home to sleep at Tai Gu's house, the servants scurried away and tucked in their own abodes. They stopped having live-in staff some ten years ago; Ah Tin was the last to leave when she married, her possessions crammed into one large blue IKEA tote and a fistful of plastic bags. There was no point to zippers or locks on her baggage; Poh Poh insisted on a final inspection. It was customary, just in case the help got ideas.

The aunts decided against a church service, a compromise to accommodate their separate faiths. While Seh Gu converted to Christianity after marrying, Tai Gu remains a devout Buddhist. Or as devout as a Chinese Buddhist can be in this country, where religion gets muddled in practice.

So, there are no crying ladies hired to mourn Poh Poh's death. Only Jasmine is left, carrying the burden of everyone's grief for the night.

'Stay with me a little longer, Iska?'

'As long as you want, babe.'

She takes him on a grand tour of the house, their bare feet silent as they move from room to room. Jasmine flips light switches on and off, pointing out spots she used to occupy. The living room where she wore scratchy dresses as a child to greet strangers and far-flung relatives. The great dining table where she seldom ate, its use reserved only for special occasions. The kitchen with its hotchpotch of crockery and containers, all coated with a thin film of grease. The rough kitchen table with its rickety stools, where she spent many hours with Ah Tin. A quick peek into Poh Poh's bedroom, its bed unmade. The sunroom that smells like Lysol.

She leads him to her own room at last.

'That's some bed.' He fingers the edges of its carved posts, pokes his head under the wooden canopy, breathing in its musty scent.

She never gave it much thought before. The bed is a hand-me-down – a remnant of her grandparents' marriage. It was shipped from Guangdong as a wedding gift from Jasmine's great-grandfather. Jasmine inherited it when she was eleven. Poh Poh turned fifty that year and opted for a modern replacement, the old one's mattress grown too firm for her liking.

'May I? I've always wanted to know what this feels like.'

'You're full of surprises all of a sudden.' Jasmine pulls him onto the bed. They both land on the mattress with a sudden, soft thud.

She laughs at the small spark of shock in Iskandar's eyes. 'Sorry, I forgot. This thing is like sleeping on old wet planks. Very little give, lots of damp.'

He cradles her in his arms, his gaze sweeping across the bed's wooden marquee. 'It's like being in a cabin, shut off from the world. I could like this, I think.' Something catches his eye on the underside of the canopy. He kneels up to examine it.

'I used to scribble my name in secret all over the house,' Jasmine explains. 'In corners, underneath chair seats, tables.'

He traces the faded letters with his finger. 'I drew robots. And monsters. Although they weren't very good. And I was never smart enough to hide them. Always on walls where Mak would find them. And then I would get a spanking.'

'I guess you had no need to hide anything.'

'Except you.' He lies on his side, head propped up with one hand, the other brushing a lock of hair off her face. He runs a finger down her jawline, lifting her chin. He kisses her, their lips barely brushing. 'I always thought that when I finally stepped through these doors, it would be to marry you.'

But her life and his don't have straight-lined trajectories.

'Now it looks like I might have some competition.' He cocks his head, stroking her neck. 'From a certain banker.'

'Kuan Yew?' Jasmine laughs, curling onto her side.

'He was mighty attentive at dinner. Kevin dropped a meatball on his lap and the bugger didn't even notice.' There is mirth in his voice.

But Jasmine senses that he is disconcerted. 'Well, his daddy's a goldsmith. He can probably afford a dowry of my weight in ingots.'

'That's that then, I am defeated. I am merely the son of a civil servant.' A rich one, thanks to being in the right politician's favour.

At dawn, she sees him off at the front door. 'Don't drive back to KL just yet. You need sleep.'

Having him at the funeral would raise too many eyebrows. Yet she wants him close, because the prospect of sleeping alone in a big, silent house is too daunting. 'Stay in Ipoh for one more night. I can probably do a late dinner. Please?'

She has never asked this of him before. Not since they resumed their affair some years ago.

'It's a date then.' He grins, yawning, stretching his arms overhead. Behind him, the sky is losing its indigo hue, the sun beginning to wake up the birds. The heady scent of frangipani flowers fills the garden. She twists a corner of her shirt from last night round her finger, wishing he didn't have to leave.

But first, she has to say goodbye to Poh Poh. Closing the front door, Jasmine walks up to her grandmother's casket. Poh Poh looks as fearsome as she did last night. Jasmine imagines her grandmother's spirit frowning in disapproval at her own final makeover.

'What do I do now, Poh Poh? Tai Gu wants Kevin to run Phoenix. Iskandar wants us to get married. But I'm not sure I want that any more.'

With Poh Poh gone, there is no longer any impediment to Iskandar and Jasmine being together. Even his wife will no longer be an issue. Except now, Jasmine's own ambition of heading Phoenix has also become an immediate possibility – one she cannot jeopardize by marrying Iskandar.

For once, she wishes Poh Poh was there to tell her what to do. Her spine stiffens at the realization. Perhaps this is how she will miss her grandmother most.

'I hope you've left instructions about Phoenix, Poh Poh. And I hope you picked me. Tai Gu is going to be trouble, even if Kevin doesn't want to come home and take over.' Not that she intends to give in to Tai Gu without a fight. 'I won't let her get away with it,' she says through gritted teeth. 'In fact, I'm not going to let her get away with this either.'

Minutes later, armed with cotton swabs and her make-up kit, Jasmine lifts the clear lid of the casket. Her fingertips stroke the side of her grandmother's cheek. The matriarch's skin is cool to the touch. Gently, Jasmine removes most of the coral lipstick from Poh Poh's lips, leaving just a trace of colour. Using a fresh swab she gingerly swipes at the thick kohl lines around her grandmother's eyes. She even manages to fix the startling brows, blotting off the excess.

'Sorry, Poh Poh, I don't think I can manage the hair. At least maybe the angels won't be so afraid of you now.' Despite the small laugh that escapes Jasmine's lips, she is crying. The tears trickle down her cheeks, salting her lips.

She has run out of time. The others will be here soon. Jasmine shuts the casket lid firmly and takes one last look at her grandmother.

'Thank you, Poh Poh. For everything. I promise I will make you proud.'

7

The day breaks with grey skies. The weather seems unfinished with its assault, the rain saved for another day, or perhaps later in the night.

The downpour from the day before has left the town water-logged, its ancient drains clogged despite development. The sludge is ankle-deep on some streets, hints of things left behind and settled in their new places peeping just beneath the surface. Butchers' black galoshes overtake the newspaper as the fastest-selling item at the Sin Fatt sundry shop on the main road. Everyone seems to be wearing them, clump-clumping on stairs and wading through the swirl. But at least their feet stay dry enough for the pruned skin to smoothen out.

At the cemetery, Jasmine stands fast beneath a jacaranda tree, one arm on Kevin, who holds a shared wax umbrella, staring into Poh Poh's grave. If Tai Gu noticed anything about Poh Poh's altered countenance earlier, she has not said a word to Jasmine. A fat bird above twitters, flapping its wings. A squirrel jumps and a monkey leaps from branch to branch, sprinkling the mourners below with leftover rain resting on leaves.

The grave is still empty, the preacher droning on. Even he wears the black galoshes. The hem of his white robe is tinged with mud. From time to time, the crowd mumbles 'Amen'.

Jasmine looks out beyond the graveyard, its gentle slope dotted with crosses and stone angels. Across the road, another hill rises, its tombstones large, ornate and curved: the Chinese graveyard, the place non-believers rest. It's where her grandmother's grave would have been, except Madam Leong had long given up on those ways. 'Too many gods to please,' she said, shortly after becoming a Christian. Yet her final resting place is at the highest possible point, even in a Christian cemetery, just in case.

They lower the coffin into the yawning hole; a pool of water has collected at its bottom. Mourners throw in flowers after it. Chrysanthemums in many colours – the cheapest from the sundry shop. An occasional rose or two – from Tai Gu and Seh Gu. Jasmine holds tight to her rose, a yellow bud, until the last of the mourners walks away.

'Safe travels, Poh Poh. And be nice to the angels.' She tosses the rose into the grave, one hand still on Kevin. As they turn, a sucking noise draws them back, the *hroook-hrook-hrook* of a child's desperate straw draining the last of an almost-empty glass. Jasmine glances at Kevin, alarmed. The slurping sound continues, then stops. Peering over the edge, they see that Poh Poh's casket is now barely visible, Jasmine's sunny rose the only thing above the sludge. The earth has swallowed their grandmother.

In the car, they smoke cigarettes, Kevin bumming one from her pack.

'You really think I'll get anything?' Jasmine finally says. Although chances are slim that Poh Poh has left her with nothing, a small part of her is still on edge. After all, she is the child who was abandoned, the one Poh Poh didn't figure on having to take care of all those years ago.

'Of course. Poh Poh won't let her daughters get their hands on her precious son's inheritance.'

Jasmine chokes on the last drag of her cigarette. 'What, the house?'

'Ah, but you forget the family jewels.'

Jasmine chuckles at first, trailing into a sigh. 'Kev, the only thing I don't know about in that house is the trunk.' A battered wooden box, lock rusted but still firmly in place. A chest of unknown things whose contents over the years have been wondered about, debated, imagined and flipped over in their minds. A place where Superman could find capes that made her fly and where Wonder Woman's magic belt was really stashed. A mountain of cold hard cash. Japanese banana money. Family heirlooms. Yesterday's plastic jewellery bought from the Indian news stand.

The trunk.

'Suits on?' Jasmine said.

'Gets harder every time. I don't know how you do it, Superman. They don't have phone booths any more.' Kevin throws her a cheeky smirk.

'Don't spin too fast in the mud, Wonder Woman, or you might get stuck.'

The engine of her four-wheel drive revs, tyres grinding in the wet earth. She turns on the gravel and heads back to the house.

*

People are funny around funerals. By the time they return from Poh Poh's burial, only a small clutch of mourners is left. The rest have scattered, making their excuses. Sons to be dropped off at tuition classes. Husbands to be fed. Laundry to be washed and aired in the sun that has finally come out. Staying too long could lead to unwanted attention from a wandering spirit, and few dare to brave the possibility of its bad luck.

Someone has placed a large ceramic basin filled with water at the entrance to the house. Tai Gu insists that Kevin and Jasmine rinse their feet before entering, in case there are traces of Poh Poh's spirit on their soles.

The crowd is predictable, made up mainly of distant relatives. Mr Chew hovers like a small winged insect near the buffet table, nibbling on bits of sweet local kueh. There is fried bee hoon and weak Chinese tea. Ah Tin has thrown in some crispy anchovies with the noodles. It must be her way of mourning. Poh Poh relished those tiny, crackling things, their fine bones often getting stuck between her teeth.

Tunku Mahmud is seated on an armchair in the living room, nodding to some tale Seh Gu is telling him. Jasmine walks over, bending down to hug him, cheek to cheek.

'Tunku, thank you for coming.'

He gestures for her to sit on the chaise longue next to him. Seh Gu breathes a sigh of relief. She needs to go to the wash-room.

Tunku Mahmud leans forward and lowers his voice. 'Jasmine, my dear, you and I need to talk. But not here. Come see me this evening, after Isya prayers.' She is puzzled and moves to ask him why, but he stops her, placing his hand on her forearm. 'This is a matter that doesn't involve your family.' He raises a finger to his lips and winks.

After the last of the mourners have left, the Leong sisters take tea in the sunroom. Several leftover wreaths have been placed in the corners; there was no more space in the hearse to fit them. A bouquet of stargazers on a tall stand wilts, the blooms bowing in the heat, pollen staining the floor a lurid mustard. A lone bee flits from flower to flower, hoping to gather remnants of nectar.

Jasmine and Kevin are summoned to join the aunts. Mr Chew is there too, his back soaked with sweat, Brylcreemed hair jutting out in apprehension. He is holding a sheaf of papers.

'It – it's pretty straightforward, madams.' He is transfixed by the bony knobs of his knuckles, the yellowing of his small fingernails. 'Madam Leong left her son's share of everything to Miss Jasmine. She split her own shares in three – forty per cent of it to Miss Jasmine and the rest equally between the two of you.'

Jasmine now owns twenty-four per cent of Phoenix. Her aunts have eighteen apiece. Combined, their shareholdings are now larger than hers. Just shy of the forty per cent held by public investors. Even though Jasmine individually holds more shares than either of her aunts, she can only control the company if at least one of them sides with her. Poh Poh's permission never came without strings. Jasmine will always have to answer to the family.

'The house, though, it . . .' Mr Chew shuffles the papers. 'Miss Jasmine now owns it. Madam Leong wanted to make sure her granddaughter always has a place to call home.'

Tai Gu sniffs, smoothing the front of her blouse, tugging its ends. 'You can keep this old place. Not that you'll ever live here. Though I hope you don't sell it.'

Seh Gu Treasure throws her niece a look. 'I think Ma Ma has been more than fair, Che. David was, after all, her only son.'

A last gift from her dead father. The one she never met. Tai Gu Ruth now has a new bone to pick with her brother's child.

'Before you get any ideas, Ma, I don't want to run Phoenix,' Kevin says, staring at his mother. 'Let Jasmine do it. Please.'

'You never want to come back from Singapore!' Tai Gu snarls, her words writhing snakes. 'I don't know why you hate us so much. You're all I have, and you won't even come home.' Her anger seeps into her eyes, threatening to spill over.

Kevin shakes his head, his shoulders drooping. 'Please don't cry, Ma. It's not you. I just . . . I have a life there.' He glances sideways and catches Jasmine's gaze.

Tai Gu makes a sharp move to stand. Her chair topples to the floor with a crash. 'Mei Mei, are you coming?'

Seh Gu rises from her seat, gathering handbags in haste. 'Yes, Che Che, of course, of course.'

The other three remain seated in silence. They catch Seh Gu's voice, soft as if soothing a child, clutching her sister in case Tai Gu trips down the stairs. The older Leong sister is screaming all kinds of profanities, her wrath echoing off the walls, trailing her to the front door. Once the car has pulled out of the driveway, Mr Chew swipes his damp brow. He looks tired and beaten, even his shirt pocket is sagging from sweat. 'There is one more thing.' Of late, there always seems to be. 'It's not a big thing, I think. But your grandmother insisted.' He reaches into the battered bag at his feet and pulls out a yellow envelope no larger than an ang pow packet. 'Something about a trunk. In her room. To be given to Jasmine. Privately.' His eyes dart towards Kevin. 'Well, you're practically siblings.'

Jasmine turns to Kevin, her brow wrinkling and her mouth falling open in minor astonishment. Poh Poh's intentions with Phoenix were already clear. What else could she have in store?

*

It is dark when Jasmine arrives at Tunku Mahmud's sprawling home. Set on a small slope overlooking the town, its white-washed exterior reflects the moonlight. The house is even older than Poh Poh's. The eaves of its front porch sag beneath the woody weight of a Rangoon creeper whose white and pink blooms emit a sickly perfume.

The plump old housekeeper leads Jasmine to Tunku's study where he is smoking a pipe, clad in a sarong and a well-worn white shirt. The room is cavernous and cluttered with books and papers piled on heavy wooden tables. Bookcases with glass doors line the walls, filled with bric-a-brac from the old man's travels and years working in the Ministry of Foreign Affairs. Jasmine never tires of Tunku Mahmud's study; there is always something new and intriguing to be unearthed from its chaos.

The old man pours her a snifter of whisky from a crystal decanter on a drinks trolley. She settles into a worn leather armchair next to his, its cushions giving way with a sigh of stale tobacco and past lives.

Tunku Mahmud clears his throat. 'I wouldn't normally do this, but I've known you both since you were children.' The smoke from his pipe snakes upwards in a languorous dance.

'If this is about Phoenix, Tunku, I think I understand my Poh Poh's intentions quite clearly. She wants me to run it, but only if I can get at least one of my aunts to support me. And Kevin, he's not interested.'

83

He watches her for a moment, his face partially obscured by the fumes. 'My dear, this is about you and Iskandar Ismail.'

Jasmine feels the flush rising to her cheeks. Of all the subjects she had anticipated discussing with the Tunku this evening, her love life certainly had not been one of them. She feels like kicking Iskandar for being absent yet again. Somehow, he is always missing when it counts. Gathering herself, Jasmine inhales deeply. 'I'm sorry, Tunku, I don't mean any disrespect, but how is my relationship with Iskandar of any interest to you?' She manages a small smile, despite her racing heart.

The old man reaches out and gives her hand a kind pat. 'Relax, my dear, this isn't an inquisition. I am merely trying to offer some friendly advice. And, perhaps, pass on a message, from his family.'

Iskandar's parents and the Tunku are old friends. Just like Poh Poh. Jasmine should have remembered this. She and Iskandar exist only in shadows, cracks of time, places no one is supposed to notice. Behind closed windows with curtains drawn. Locked doors. No spectators. They never connect the dots, the attempt to draw lines between their lives something they cannot afford.

She now realizes their folly. Locked doors make people curious, drawing them to the slice of light that slips through the gaps beneath. In a country where so much is unspoken, secrets are salves, especially other people's. You fill the hole in your heart with someone else's shortcomings so you forget what you are lacking. You soothe your guilt with other people's guilt so yours looks no worse in the reckoning. And news travels fast in a small city of millions. Someone you know will always know the someone else you seek. K-Hell's dark corners only serve to shine light.

Tunku Mahmud leans forward, drawing a long, slow breath. 'His parents are upset and asked me to speak to you. I am told he is leaving his wife.'

'Yes, but you must know I didn't tell him to do it. They – they've been having problems, you see, and Iskandar—'

'I've known him since he was a child. Iskandar has always been one to complicate things, since he was a little boy. Somehow, he has a knack for getting entangled. I'm just sorry you got caught up in all of it this time. If only I had known earlier, I could have warned you about him. But ah, such is life. And now here we are.'

Jasmine feels like a child caught playing outside past her bedtime. She wants to run, but instead stays rooted to her chair, aware she has little choice but to face the situation and the Tunku head-on. Again, she wishes Iskandar were here. She wants to wring his neck. 'I – I don't know what to say, Tunku. I'm sorry if I've disappointed you. Did my Poh Poh know all this too? If she did, she never said anything to me.'

Tunku Mahmud shifts his gaze away from her for a moment, eyes narrowed. 'I don't know if she knew. But there's no point fretting about that now she's gone. We need to sort out your life now. You're the one who's still here, and Phoenix needs you. So, one thing at a time.'

Jasmine nods. 'Yes, but I – I'm not quite sure now what I should do.'

'So, you and Iskandar . . . I understand you've known each other since college. I should have realized you weren't actually alone all this time. His wife is threatening to tell the whole town about your affair. And if I know Iskandar, he has probably already rushed to your side, and asked you to marry him.' A wan smile crosses Tunku Mahmud's lips. 'In a way, I am glad. Although I am not sure this is the best situation for either of you. But I am guessing you already realize that. I am of course on your side, but have you both really thought about this? The matter needs to be handled, and quick. KL loves good gossip, but has a short attention span. Soon, everyone will forget.'

If only she could fast-forward to that part, although at this juncture, she has no inkling what it will look like. Should she marry Iskandar?

'Tunku, do you think Iskandar and I even stand a chance? Even though Poh Poh is gone, there's still my aunts to think of. And I don't want to give up Phoenix, although I know I would have to if I married him. It's just that I've worked so hard all these years, and Poh Poh would kill me if I turned my back on the family business. Then there's Iskandar's own family. Will they even accept me?'

Tunku Mahmud takes a deep pull on his pipe. Exhaling, he says, 'Either way, you will have to decide. His parents don't mind, even though you're Chinese; they are a fairly progressive family. Iskandar will have to divorce first, however. There is no question of him taking a second wife while staying married to the first one, even if Islam allows four. His mother would not hear of it.' The old gentleman pauses, placing both hands on Jasmine's. 'But, of course, you would have to convert.'

Her head is spinning. She is exhausted, wishing the armchair would consume her. She contemplates spending the rest of her life among the ghosts of its rotting springs and stuffing, only emerging sometimes at night to poke and wonder at the things in the Tunku's bookcases. It wouldn't be such a bad existence. The housekeeper could be persuaded to feed her. And she was sure the Tunku wouldn't mind her company.

'Do you want to marry him?' Tunku Mahmud leans back in his chair, pipe raised to his lips.

Jasmine stares at her ringless fingers, spreading them out on her lap. He doesn't ask her the real question. The one that comes before that.

*

Reaching her grandmother's house, Jasmine narrowly misses the neighbour's runaway dog as she turns her car into the driveway. She wants to vomit. It feels like someone is making teh tarik with her brain, stretching the nerves to the point of breaking, then muddling them into a foamy brew. Upstairs, she strips and lies on her bed in the dark, naked. Must be a migraine. She hasn't had one in years. She shuts her eyes and tries to ignore the dull throbbing behind her lids. Soon, she succumbs to a fitful sleep.

The sounds of the muezzin's dawn azan wake her and she sits up. In the half-light, she startles as she spies a figure sprawled on the floor beside her bed, his hands tucked beneath his tousled head. 'Iskandar?' she murmurs, leaning down to stroke his hair. She forgot to ring him about dinner when she got home.

He opens his sleep-crusted eyes and a sob escapes his lips. The words tumble out in staccato. She didn't answer his calls. He rushed over and found the front door ajar, the house dark. He called out for her, but she didn't reply, and he went from room to room, lost, opening doors, colliding with ghosts lurking in the dark, the unfamiliar shapes of furniture, growing more frantic by the minute as he raced up the stairs, only to find her lying in bed, stripped bare. For a moment, he wasn't sure what he was seeing, and his chest constricted from the possibility that was so unbearable, especially now, not now, not when he has finally decided. He couldn't breathe as he slowly went up to her and placed his fingers on her neck to check for a pulse. She didn't stir, not through all that. But she was still breathing and looked worried in her sleep, her brow furrowed. So he covered her with a thin blanket, and lay down to wait for her to awaken.

He must have fallen asleep himself. The traces of fear still linger in his eyes. 'I have never been so terrified of losing you.'

Jasmine answers in small kisses on his face, neck, hair, hands. She pulls him close, her body pressed against his, head buried in his chest. They cry in great sobs of relief and sorrow and confusion, tears mingling on each other's faces and fingers until the fear is driven away, made small, laughter bubbling up from their lips, hands entwined.

'What the hell are we going to do now?' Jasmine whispers.

'Whatever the hell you want,' he murmurs back, a tender light in his eyes.

She still feels tiny, gentle tugs on her nerves. 'Get dressed. I owe you a proper Ipoh breakfast.'

They seldom eat out, but when they do, it is in places most Malays will not frequent. Anywhere liquor or pork is served, out of sight of Allah and his ummah. Even in Ipoh, their habits persist. She takes him to a fishball noodle shop, the kind that has been around for decades. It is Chinese – all the best ones are.

She orders a large bowl of fishball soup for them to share. A plate of dry noodles tossed in soy sauce for him, another with roast pork for herself. Outside, the sky turns a deep Prussian blue, the streets quiet except for the occasional crash of a shophouse shutter opening for the day. They eat balanced on round plastic stools, their shoulders hunched over the steaming food. The Formica table is covered in an explosive pattern of garish red roses. Around them, the shop staff continue to set up for the morning.

She can still sense the terror beneath his skin. It is in the slight tremble of his jaw, his wanting to cry every time she looks up from her plate. His fisted fright, clenching and unclenching. His quick, shallow breaths. His darting eyes.

She tells him about her encounter with Tunku Mahmud, and what his parents have to say about the whole affair. But she leaves out the parts about herself and Phoenix. Already, it is all too much.

She reaches out to touch him, her hand staying his. 'Do you understand what you are asking of me? If I say yes?'

'I wish there was another way . . .'

'If I do this, you'll expect me to change. But I don't want to.'

'It's not me that will. It's the rest.' He buries his hands in his hair.

At first, everyone will be patient. But it will only take one sidelong glance from an auntie or uncle for things to unravel. *When will she stop drinking?* (Never mind that he does.) *Will she go to mengaji classes and learn the Quran?* Then, *You need to teach her how to pray.* (Never mind that he doesn't.) And at Ramadan, he will fast because they all do.

There would be no question of bacon for breakfast. Or bak kut teh. Or pork crackling. Or going to places like this. Or most of her childhood favourites. An entire lifetime of eating wiped out. Her Chineseness relegated to nostalgic recollections or the remembering of vivid dreams. She has asked herself many times before. The whys and why-nots, the who-cares and why-should-I's, why-me's. She knows it is not his fault – he was born a Muslim – but neither does he question it, the thought of having a choice in his faith never arising because it is forbidden. Forbidden and assumed. That is just the way it is. Neither of them can change that. So, they live their lives in loops, circling back on the same, disagreeable versions of God. As the Almighties sulk in their corners, their followers stumble and trip, hanging onto fragments of faith that make sense and confound at the same time, rending minute tears in the hems of their little lives.

8

Two days pass. Iskandar goes back to the city by train. Jasmine stays, sifting through the house, stacking throw-aways and keep-sakes. In death, Poh Poh left too much behind.

Alone, Jasmine wanders from room to room, her hand sliding down the smooth wooden doorways and across windowsills, reacquainting herself with the worn surfaces of her childhood. She looks for signs of her past existence – a timid nick on the leg of her grandmother's prized antique altar table, her childish scrawl on the seat of a chair in the sunroom, the one she used to sit in when she was a child; her name is written with blue-black ballpoint ink, barely noticeable on the mahogany.

My place is in this house, she thinks. *No one is going to take it away from me.*

Kevin arrives in a floral print shirt and white shorts, bran-dishing a bottle of tequila. She is on the floor, sorting old magazines.

'Don't move.' He waggles a finger at the kneeling Jasmine. 'I'm going to make us some margaritas. We're gonna be here for a while.'

She stops to flip through an old issue of *Vogue* from the eighties. She misses the intensity of those days. Despite the whirling mirror balls and ridiculous amounts of hair gel, even celebrities wore plastic jewellery. Madonna's bangles. Yamamoto fashion that made everyone look like bag ladies. Ridiculous rainbow eyeshadow. It was pretentious, but everyone knew it.

'Whoa, thank God they didn't have social media then.' Kevin is back with a plastic jug that is already sweating. He looks over Jasmine's shoulder at a photograph of a model in shoulder pads and big hair. 'We'd have to pay someone to scrub our internet selves clean.' He pours her a drink.

They clink their glasses. A toast. 'To . . . our superhero selves!' Kevin says.

By the time the jug has been emptied, they've finished sorting, magazines now in neat stacks and tied together with raffia string. She fishes the small yellow envelope from her pocket. One last thing to be done.

The cousins enter Poh Poh's room. The bed has been stripped bare, the stained pillows naked of their laundered coverings. The trunk is in a corner, next to Poh Poh's dressing table.

They sit side by side, knees touching, just like they used to when they were children. Except this time, the momentous occasion isn't a new Shaun Cassidy cassette tape or the issue of *Tiger Beat* magazine with the Rick Springfield poster.

The trunk looks a little smaller now in their adulthood, but the smooth planes of its surface still retain a dull sheen. Jasmine runs her fingers across its carved rosewood top. The trunk's lid tells the tale of how a princess came to a new, strange land and bore children to her new husband, a king. Poh Poh told her the story once, but she has forgotten the details.

'Wait, wait!' Kevin lights a cigarette. 'Take a minute. We've waited so long, a bit more won't hurt.'

She understands his trepidation. When they open the trunk,

it will all be over. The mysteries of their childhood and past – all the things they have never known – will become finite and clear. The no-longer-secret secrets will have to be dealt with. What isn't in there will remain unknown. The trunk is the full stop to the old shadows of their lives.

Or perhaps it is just more meaningless junk.

Jasmine decides she won't wait any longer. She takes her cousin's cigarette and flings it out the window. 'We're doing this,' she says, determined.

She turns the key in the lock. It gives at her first attempt, despite its rusted appearance. Lifting the lid, they both recoil, the sting of camphor causing their eyes to water.

'Aiyoh, it's enough to chase away all the ghosts in Ipoh!' Kevin fans his face, frantic. They scoot backwards on their palms and bums, laughing.

Seconds later, they peer inside.

The trunk is filled with a woman's things. Thick, heavy bangles and anklets of gold. A fiery silk qipao with a phoenix curling down its back. A pair of ruby-red velvet slippers, a lotus bloom embroidered with gold thread on each one. A golden headdress that fans out in tiny branches, with miniature flowers and double strands of round beads cascading on either side.

'It's Poh Poh's wedding trousseau. See these?' Kevin picks up a pair of earrings that are at least twelve centimetres in length. Strings of little diamond-shaped gold leaves chink softly when he shakes them. 'I've heard about these. They came all the way from China. Even the qipao. In fact, even Poh Poh.'

Jasmine's eyes narrow, sensing a secret. 'Wasn't she born here?'

'Noooo,' says Kevin, eyebrow arched. 'She came directly from China.'

'How is it that you live in Singapore and know more than I do?'

'Weekend mahjong sessions. Don't speak a word and listen, listen, listen. They forget you're there after a while.' Kevin grins and winks his left eye. 'Of course, it made things worse that Poh Poh wasn't supposed to marry Kung Kung,' he continues. 'His aunts, they were all trying to matchmake their nephew to Jade Tong.'

Jade Tong, daughter of an old Ipoh tycoon who lost his fortune in the Second World War, as most of them did. Poh Poh was a usurper. 'But Kung Kung's father would hear nothing of it. He handpicked Poh Poh himself in China. Went to visit her family and everything. And . . .' His voice trails into silence.

'And . . . what? There's more? How come you never told me any of this before?'

Kevin clucks, hand tapping his cousin's knee. 'You . . .' He points a slender finger at Jasmine's heart. 'You disappeared. After you were whisked off to England, I hardly heard from you till you came back from university, all grown-up with your Paula Abdul hair. For a while, I thought you didn't love me any more.' His lips are pursed in a playful moue.

'I just, well, there was Iskandar . . . I didn't want anyone to find out about us.'

'Ha! Turns out you're not the only one in this house with secrets.' Leaning back on his hands, Kevin reaches for another cigarette. 'My Ma Ma told me Poh Poh got here a month late for the wedding. Something to do with the monsoon. The ceremony took place almost as soon as she arrived in Ipoh, and not

long after, your father was born. More than a month early . . .'
Kevin is pensive, tapping his cigarette ash into a used paper cup
still bearing traces of a margarita. 'My mum thinks Kung Kung's
father must have taken a shine to Poh Poh when he first met
her in China. Probably got her pregnant, which is why he rushed
the wedding once they arrived. What a dick.'

Jasmine looks up from a silk scarf she had pulled from the
chest and stares at Kevin, mouth agape. 'What? You think my
father . . .'

'Was actually my mum and Seh Gu's uncle, not their brother.
He was Kung Kung's half-brother, whom Kung Kung raised as
his son.'

'That's outrageous! Kevin, do you realize what you're saying?'

Jasmine's father was probably a bastard. Born out of wedlock.
And passed off as his brother's son. Suddenly, Tai Gu Ruth's
bitterness makes sense. It isn't just Jasmine she resents, but her
own brother – or uncle, if Kevin is correct. But there is no way
of knowing the truth now. Not with Poh Poh gone.

Jasmine shakes her head in disbelief. 'Can you imagine what
Poh Poh must have gone through then?'

'Maybe that's why she was such a tough cookie,' Kevin muses.
He takes a long drag of his cigarette, exhales, and watches the
stream of smoke from his lips rise before dissipating into the
air.

Jasmine regards her cousin in silence for a moment, eyes
narrowing. 'How did your mum find out about all this anyway?
Surely Poh Poh didn't tell her.'

'Ah Tin's mother. You know their family has been in our
household for generations. The cook let it slip one day after
my mum had picked a fight with your dad. Said my mother

was disrespectful for smacking her uncle. According to Mum, the cook's face went white for a second right after she said it. She denied it all immediately, of course. But you know my mum, nothing gets past her.' Kevin lets out a soft chuckle, one brow raised in an elegant arch.

Jasmine recalls how Tai Gu and Seh Gu often spoke about growing up with the cook as children. They had all been play-mates when young. Until it came time for their paths to diverge. 'I don't know how any of us would have survived our childhoods without Ah Tin's family. Even Ah Tin was more like a mother to me sometimes. Did you know I asked her once?'

'To be your mother?' Kevin laughs.

'Yeah.'

'Doesn't surprise me. You two were always as thick as thieves.'

*

In Standard Six, when Jasmine and Kevin turned twelve, their singing teacher announced that the school was staging *Grease*. Everyone jumped at the chance to be in it. Even Kevin got cast, as a T-Bird. Only Jasmine was left out, too afraid to broach the subject with Poh Poh.

On the night of the play, Tai Gu secured seats in the very centre of the front row. The school hall's drab walls were now festooned with fifties posters. A huge hand-painted sign saying 'Rydell High' hung above the stage.

Even Ah Tin took extra care to dress nicely for the occasion. The maid wore a cheongsam that fell just below her knee, her shoulder-length hair set in large waves. She was actually rather pretty, Jasmine thought. She could almost be someone's mother.

The hall was filling up, parents and siblings filing in. The air grew thick with the crush of Old Spice and Cuticura talcum powder mixed with sweat. Ah Tin wanted to look at the posters on the wall while waiting for the curtain to rise. Jasmine accompanied her, grasping Ah Tin's hand to avoid being smothered in the crowd.

The school had spared no expense with the decorations. The ambitious new headmistress, Puan Rogayah, was a University Malaya graduate from Kuala Lumpur with no intentions of rooting herself in the sleepy town of Ipoh. Her place was in the city, where everything happened – not this tattered tin-mine enclave with its crumbling old buildings.

A reproduction of the original *Grease* movie poster was Sellotaped to a wall. Jasmine could tell from the horizontal crease running through its middle that it had come from a magazine. In the poster John Travolta stood on the hood of a car, Olivia Newton-John at his feet, one hand curled around his leg.

'Wah, John Travolta is so handsome,' sighed Ah Tin. 'If he was my boyfriend, I would marry him, even though he is a gwai loh.'

'Ah Wan will kill you lah!' retorted Jasmine.

'It's okay, John Travolta is macho. My mother can throw all her woks at him, he will just pick me up in his arms and carry me away. I'm Chinese! So small! Not like this big gwai loh girl.' She jabbed Olivia Newton-John with her forefinger.

The image Ah Tin's words conjured made Jasmine double over with laughter, her knees buckling.

'Eh, eh, get up!' Ah Tin giggled. 'Don't dirty your new clothes.' Pulling the child to her feet, Ah Tin straightened Jasmine's dress, smoothing a palm down her charge's wavy bob.

'So, you finally brought your mother to school.' It was Puan Rogayah. The headmistress extended a meaty hand to Ah Tin. 'Very happy to meet you, Mrs . . .'

'Leong,' Jasmine snapped.

The stunned maid shook the headmistress's hand, her eyes wide with shock.

'We should go find our seats. Excuse us, teacher.' Jasmine pulled Ah Tin away.

'Hah, there you are, where did you go?' From the frantic flutter of her fan, Tai Gu appeared annoyed. Her husband, the wide Uncle Edward, was seated next to her, his girth encroaching on her elbow room.

'Your uncle made it at the last minute. Ah Tin, sorry ah, you'll have to stand outside.' Tai Gu waved at the large double doors at the end of the hall.

'Yes, Madam,' Ah Tin replied, hands clasped. As she left, she leaned down towards Jasmine, whispering, 'At least from there that goldsmith's son might actually look a little more like John Travolta on stage.'

The lights dimmed. Ah Tin slipped away into the dark.

The curtain rose. The audience of parents and siblings applauded. Kuan Yew's large family was out in full force. All nine of them cheered when he first appeared. Kuan Yew paused in the middle of his dialogue and turned towards them with a toothy grin.

Not to be outdone, Uncle Edward shouted words of encouragement every time Kevin so much as twitched. 'That's my son!' 'Woohoo! Brilliant!' 'All riiiight boy!!' He was on his feet, sweat beading his brow.

'Aiyoh, Edward, this isn't a football match lah!' Tai Gu

smacked his buttocks with her fan, tugging her husband's shirt. Onstage, Kevin turned as red as a ripe lychee.

By the interval, Uncle Edward was about to combust with pride. His chest strained against his shirt even more. His belly jiggled with a continuous slow laugh. 'Wah, my son, he's such a good actor. So proud, so proud,' he said, shaking his head.

Tai Gu was less enthused. 'If you think your son's so brilliant, why didn't you speak to the school like I told you to, hah? Kevin should have been the male lead, not that goldsmith's son! We are Leongs. We don't do supporting roles.'

Jasmine wondered whether Tai Gu knew how much the stage terrified Kevin. Despite his initial joy at being cast as a T-Bird, the boy had had night sweats about the whole thing. Even though he only had a measly ten lines in the show, he fretted about them all month, constantly mumbling dialogue under his breath for fear of bungling on the big night.

'You never try hard enough.' Tai Gu poked her fan into her husband's chest. 'Next year, Kevin will still be stuck here. Grow up a small-town boy. At least Jasmine is going to the UK.'

Jasmine must have gasped because Tai Gu turned, thrusting her fan weapon in her niece's direction. 'Your Poh Poh didn't tell you ah? You're going to boarding school next year. Lucky girl, not like my poor Kevin. He deserves so much more. But then again, what to do? Kevin is only her daughter's son.'

When the play's second half commenced, Jasmine mumbled an excuse and crept out of the hall, her eyes hot with tears. She found Ah Tin among the nest of maids and drivers, craning her neck through the doors to get a glimpse of the show.

They made their way to the canteen, Jasmine leading in the dark. Once there, they sat at one of the long wooden tables,

Jasmine slouched, her chin propped up on her hands. The air still smelled of yesterday's food, its greasy remains clinging to the canteen walls.

Ah Tin was massaging her bare feet. 'Aiyoh, Uncle Boon is so tall. I couldn't see from behind him, even on tiptoe.'

'Did you ever meet my parents, Ah Tin?' A small, towering question only bold enough to find air under cover of night, away from the ears of home.

The maid lifted her head, trying to make out her young charge's expression. 'Just your father. I was only a little girl when he went away to university. He was very handsome. Gentle, like your grandpa. He used to buy me goreng pisang sometimes. We would sneak out on to the swing and sit. He told me stories. Lots of stories. He wished he had brothers and sisters. But he only had me.'

'Like me,' Jasmine replied. 'I only have you too.'

'No, you have Kevin lah. Some more he's a T-Bird.' Ah Tin elbowed the young girl, fishing for a giggle.

But Jasmine didn't even smile. Her eyes were swollen from crying. 'Poh Poh is sending me away. To the UK. You know where that is, Ah Tin?'

The maid's face softened. 'My mother told me you were going to a new school. Very far away. It will be an adventure!'

'I wish you were my mother,' uttered the girl into the night.

Ah Tin let out a small laugh. 'I am your friend. Not good enough to be your mother. But it's okay, your teacher doesn't need to know.'

Jasmine wondered then if she was ever good enough to be anyone's child. But she held her doubt like a secret, tucked in the corner of her pocket, a forgotten cold glass marble, smooth and hard, that she occasionally reached for when she wasn't thinking.

A year later, she left for boarding school. After hugging Ah Tin and Kevin goodbye, she got into the back seat of the car, turning only once to glimpse them running down the driveway after her. The salty remnants of the silky sar hor fun noodles from breakfast lingered on her tongue, or perhaps it was a trail of childish tears. She waved and waved, laugh-crying at Kevin's gangly figure and Ah Tin trailing him, trousers flapping, until the car turned onto the road, the house now hidden by its bamboo wall.

The marble of doubt formed a lump in her throat as the car sped on its four-hour journey along the narrow trunk road towards Kuala Lumpur. Poh Poh had booked them into the Petaling Jaya Hilton for the night before their morning flight to the UK. Poh Poh sat in front on account of her motion sickness, dozing. Jasmine, alone in the back seat with her thoughts, felt invisible.

But as she stared out the window at the trees, shophouses, dusty towns and villages that whizzed past, the prospect of being somewhere else began to form flashes of colour at the edge of her sight. Perhaps there, she would be seen. Away from the shadow of her grandmother, on her own, she could forge a different Jasmine who never faded into walls or hovered in doorways.

She swallowed, the marble now a stone in her gut, nestled amidst the sour of her grief, her simmering fright of the unknown ahead, and a flicker of hope that she might be better than good enough for someone on the other side.

*

The sound of Kevin's low whistle snaps Jasmine back to the present. 'Oh hullo, what do we have here?'

Beneath the wedding paraphernalia lie two stacks of papers and books. Kevin reaches in, but Jasmine restrains him.

'Wait, this is Poh Poh's doing. All of this was done on purpose.' They start with the ones on the left and look through the things in order.

They are an account of Poh Poh's life in notebooks crammed with old receipts, ticket stubs, programmes from shows, cuttings from newspapers and blank postcards from around the world glued fast to the pages. Istanbul. Rio de Janeiro. Mombasa. But Poh Poh never spoke of visiting those places.

'Why do you think she kept these?' Kevin has peeled one of the postcards off the page and turns it in his hands, searching for clues. It is a picture of a decorated camel with big, dark eyes and a jewelled head; in the background is a crude sketch of the pyramids. Cairo.

'And why would she want me to have them?' Jasmine's instincts brace for a recoil. This was no accident, no mere sentimental squirrelling of memorabilia.

She reaches in for the second bundle. A photo album, its leather cover dotted with green blooms of fungus, sits on top. There are pictures of her father, taken when he was perhaps ten years old. She recognizes the embossed logo in the corner of most of them: Cherry Blossom Studio, Ipoh. The same place to which she and Kevin were dragged every Lunar New Year as children, to have their photos taken in fancy clothes.

Growing up, she had only ever seen three photographs of her father, taken during his university graduation. In one, Kung Kung is seated in a suit, his hands resting gently on a wooden cane, a younger Poh Poh next to him, a worried expression in her eyes. Jasmine's father is standing behind them, still boyish, slim and tall, lips pressed in a dutiful smile. The second was from a dinner the same night, her aunties mere diffident young women, the bright angles of their teenage selves beaming, with their brother between them, his arms slung around his siblings, his mouth a wide grin. The third photo is of her father looking down, studious and earnest, as if reading a psalm in church.

She turns the sticky pages of the album, drinking in the images. The photos are all in black and white. The last few are less formal, as if taken by someone carefree and unworried. Her father sitting on a beach, squinting, the wind slanting his hair sideways. Him and a woman, backs turned to the camera, looking out to sea. A close shot of the woman's face, obscured by black cat-eye sunglasses and a broad hat. Seascapes. Picnic baskets. A boxy convertible. Then a full-front photograph of the two at last, sitting side by side on a terrazzo bench, hands entwined. Her head is tilted up towards him, laughing, a hand pressed against his chest. He wears a comical expression on his face, eyes widened, mouth curved downwards, questioning.

'This must be my mother,' Jasmine whispers. There is a resemblance. As if the woman's portrait painter had swept the remnants on his brush over another canvas and made Jasmine. The smile is close-mouthed, lips full and wide. The hair falling in waves down her back. The gentle curve and angle of her chin. Eyes double-lidded, fringed by long, dark lashes.

'I always wondered why my hair isn't straight.' Jasmine pulls at her own tresses, their soft, springy curls at last making sense. 'And my eyes, I got them from her.'

She looks to Kevin, but he is preoccupied, the album spread

out on his cross-legged lap. He slides a fingernail under the thin film of plastic on the last page. It peels back with a small crackle. Beneath it is an old certificate, written in Jawi.

The cousins peer at the piece of brittle paper, trying to make out its meaning. The certificate is criss-crossed with creases and wrinkles, as if it had a long journey before settling into the album's page.

She and Kevin both learned the Arabic script a long time ago, in primary school, but neither can recall it now. Even if they could find an alphabet chart, deciphering it would be impossible. Arabic letters, when joined to form words, are abbreviated and unrecognizable from their individual shapes.

Jasmine whips out her phone and takes a photo, sending the image to Iskandar. He is the only one she trusts who could perhaps shed some light on the document.

She lifts her gaze towards the window. The afternoon sun blazes across the blue sky, silvering the tops of trees. A tiny brown pipit chirps on a branch nearby. Nothing looks unfamiliar, yet there is a sense that things have shifted, in the hue of the waxy, yellowing leaves, the mould that now hides the clay of roof tiles, the roti man's screaming ditty that blares on speakers as he travels through town. He used to ring a fat, heavy bell. Growing up, she listened out for it every afternoon and raced down the stairs, hoping to bribe Ah Tin into buying her a forbidden sweet bun or butter-cream loaf.

A stray thread now pokes out from the tangled web of her history. Secrets, when spoken out loud, have power and throw light into dark corners, revealing things that want to be forgotten.

*

104

Iskandar doesn't ring back till close to midnight. He has just reached her condo in KL. He had dinner with his parents. He is seeing his wife tomorrow about the divorce.

Jasmine doesn't want to ask. But she is tired of not knowing.

'What did they say?' She feels queasy, her stomach rumbling. It must be the clams from her char kway teow dinner. She rubs her belly in circular motions, waddling to her grandmother's room in search of a remedy.

'What the Tunku told you: get it over with, as fast as possible. "Clean up this mess", that's what Bapak said. He still wants me to run for office, says he's lined up a meeting with the party officials next week. Unbelievable. The man only thinks of himself.'

'And your mum?'

Iskandar sighs. 'Thank God I'm not an only child, or even her favourite. As long as her precious eldest son doesn't screw up, the rest of us are pretty much negligible. I mean, she's pissed, of course, that a son of hers is having an affair. But beyond that, the same: sort this out quickly, before everyone talks.'

Jasmine is silent for a moment. 'Well,' she says in the end, 'at least no one told you to go plant potatoes . . .'

He lets out a belly laugh, her joke unexpected. 'That's true. But get this. I know why I was thrown out. Not that I don't deserve it. The wife has another man. Some trainer she met in her gym.'

Iskandar, the unfaithful cuckold.

It is Jasmine's turn to laugh. 'Oh, I'm sorry, honey, I didn't mean to . . . shit . . . you two are . . .'

'Please, don't say it . . .'

'Really, unmade for each other.' She quietens, the sick feeling returning to her stomach. She scrabbles in Poh Poh's dressing table drawers and finds a half-empty bottle of mentholated oil. She unscrews the cap and sniffs it, subduing her nausea. 'Ugh.' She sits, catching her breath.

'What's the matter? You okay?'

'It's nothing. Just a little tummy upset. It'll pass.'

'Whose marriage papers did you send me?'

'Marriage papers? Is that what it is?' She had thought it was maybe a birth certificate, or land deed, or something else.

'Yes, well, an old one, obviously. Nowadays they're not written in Jawi any more. So it says that the couple married on 10 May 1969 in the Kuala Lumpur mosque. His name was Daud Abdullah. Hers was Salmah Ibrahim.

'And there's something else,' he adds. 'The man has an alias: David Leong Boon Chee. I didn't know you had a Muslim relative.'

She abruptly feels the need to throw up. 'Hang on,' she says. 'Hang on.'

She runs to Poh Poh's bathroom, lifting the toilet seat. Bending over, she retches, but nothing comes out except bile.

'Iska, let me call you back.' She hangs up and leans against the toilet bowl, her breathing shallow, tattered. After rinsing out her mouth at the sink, she makes her way out of the bathroom in a slow stumble and lies down on Poh Poh's bare bed.

She punches in Iskandar's name on her phone. 'Sorry.'

'Are you sure you're okay? You were sick the other day too.'

'Yes, yes, I'm all right. Just a little . . . stressed, that's all. Probably nothing. Probably dinner. I'm okay.'

'Yeah, well, get some rest. Do you want to come back

tomorrow? I'll come get you. I don't want you travelling all by yourself. Not like this.'

She is silent for a moment, not used to the care. He has never been so available before, not this second time round. In London, he walked on the outer edge of the pavement, his hand gripping her upper arm when they stepped out into the road. In KL, they rarely meet outside her condo. If she was ill, he would see her eventually, but not before sorting out his day, his wife, his work. By the time he arrived, fevers would have broken, sore throats would be soothed with honey and lemon, pills swallowed, a tumbler of water and tissues by her bed. He would plant a dry kiss on her cheek, placing his hand on her forehead, regret churning in his eyes.

She takes a deep breath, curling on her side, legs pulled into a foetal position. She can hear his gentle breaths over the phone line.

'Sayang.' There is hesitation in his voice. 'Jasmine . . . is Leong Boon Chee your father?'

She swallows, hard. 'Yes.' She tells him about the trunk.

'And you didn't find anything else?'

She doesn't tell him about Poh Poh's wedding trousseau. Or the mystery about her father's early birth. 'It's Poh Poh. This is . . . I don't know how to explain it to you, but this is exactly the kind of thing she did. Half-stories, she always just . . . why do you think I know nothing about everything?'

'But if this is true, then . . .'

'I know. I know what this means.'

'On your birth certificate, what does it say?'

Jasmine does not respond.

'Sayang, who are your parents, legally?'

She takes a deep breath, exhales. 'My grandmother.'

'You mean . . .'

'Yes,' she replies in a small voice. 'My grandmother registered me as hers when I was brought back to Ipoh. That was what I have always been told, what Poh Poh told everyone. She registered me as her child, father unknown. Officially, I was born here, in our house in Ipoh.'

'So you don't actually know who your parents are.'

'I don't know. I don't know anything any more. Poh Poh kept everything close to her chest. I don't think even Tai Gu knows. Except I figure Poh Poh must have spoken to someone about this. Someone must have helped her . . .'

She remembers the bunch of pristine, blank postcards in the chest.

9

Tunku Mahmud's house looks less imposing in daylight. The white honeycomb walls show mossy stains, discolouring its exterior a dirty green-grey. She finds the elderly gentleman on the long, low veranda outside his living room. A strip of lawn runs parallel to it before slanting down into a grove of fruit trees. On seeing her, Tunku Mahmud folds his newspaper with a snap, his face breaking into a grin.

His wife, Raja Aminah, greets Jasmine with a stiff smile before making her excuses and slipping away to supervise the cook, who is making some kuehs for tea.

'I'll be locked up in my study again this afternoon,' Tunku Mahmud says, lips pursed. 'Her Quran reading group's coming. And I suppose you're off to KL? Otherwise, we could go to the club . . .'

Jasmine shows him the marriage certificate, laying it carefully on the coffee table. 'I was hoping you could tell me about this.'

He doesn't pick it up to examine it. Instead, he peers at a tree whose leaves jut out from just above where the garden slopes down. 'I think I may have a musang in my rambutan tree.'

She catches a glimpse of a furry brown tail scuffling in the leaves.

He turns to Jasmine. 'Actually, he's been there a while now. I just haven't told anyone. My wife will have the gardener chopping off branches if she knew. She's terrified of them.'

Jasmine stands and walks to the lawn's edge, shading her eyes with her hand. 'He's probably harmless.'

'Oh, he'll get to the fruit before I do when it ripens.'

She walks back and sits down. A sharp crescendo of cicadas drying their wings drowns the silence between them.

He is still staring into the distance when he finally speaks. 'You were only a week old when I first met you. Such a wee baby. But your tiny fingers had an iron grip. You refused to let go.' He waggles his little finger, and a soft laugh escapes his lips. 'It was a bad time. KL was a mess. The riots, you know. They were over by the time I got there, but things were still very unsettled. Your father had died, you see. Your grandmother sent me . . . well, I offered to go, to bring his body home. Except there you were, when I got there.'

Jasmine knows about her father's death. Poh Poh told her he was killed by a group of Malay men who were ransacking Petaling Street the day she was born. 13 May 1969. A day when the dam broke. When suddenly it was no longer okay not to talk about things; except words, by that time, had fled people's mouths, replaced by the blind rage of parangs and broken bottles. Both Chinese and Malay people had run amok, pulling one another's children out of cinemas and homes, beating each other senseless and leaving strangers to die on the banks of the mud-clogged river and the sides of roads. The official death toll was 196, although other estimates run to tenfold. Her father's life ended, a national statistic.

Three days of mayhem, KL burning itself down from within, leaving an indelible stain on the back of its citizens for decades.

'And my mother?'

'Your parents were staying with your father's old friend; I forget his name. His father owned a coffin shop on Petaling Street. She was young, had no money, nowhere to go. She asked me to take you with me. She was in a bad state. Your father had gone out to find some medicine; you were running a fever the day you were born. She gave birth to you there, you see, in the coffin shop, just imagine. They couldn't get a doctor. It was just too dangerous. He got caught right outside the hospital walls. Beaten up. Probably by a bunch of Malay men. Or the police. Who knows. His friend finally traced him days later. By that time, his body had been taken to the General Hospital morgue. It was horrible, just horrible.'

The Tunku takes a napkin from the table, swiping it in rough circles over his eyes. He lifts his teacup, hands trembling.

'All of us just wanted to forget. We were terrified. Of each other, of ourselves. We didn't know we had it in us, this violence. The anger, yes, that was the fault of the British. Divide and conquer, they said. But there was always kindness too, even then. Your mother wasn't the only one. I heard stories of other people, Chinese folks hiding under Malay beds, Malays huddled in the Hindu and Buddhist temples. We're not all bad, we never were. Most of us were just trying to get by. The country was still so young, so new. And well, maybe we were all just too impatient.'

When you build a dam in a hurry, you ignore how strong

the undertow is below. At some point, it breaks, its currents sweeping small humans, like insects, into the swirl.

She was born in a coffin shop, on Petaling Street. 'Where is my mother now?'

'I don't know. I never heard from her after that. Your grandmother was scared. Too scared someone would find out. I had an old schoolmate in the Registry Department. You weren't registered yet, you see. The riots. So I helped your grandmother get your birth certificate done, except we changed some details. We thought it was probably the best thing to do. Otherwise, who knew? The Islamic department could have taken you away if they found out you were a Malay baby. We couldn't risk that. You were the only thing left that your grandmother had of her son. She wasn't about to lose you.'

A single tear rolls down Jasmine's cheek and she sweeps it away.

The old man looks at her, his face drawn with grief. 'Please, don't blame your grandmother. At the time, she was about the age you are now. And she'd lost her husband the year before. Then her son. Your grandfather's illness took a huge toll on her. He was sick for three years before he died. All that time, she cared for him and your father and aunts, and ran his business. She probably did better than he ever could have, really. Your grandfather was never a determined man. She was his backbone. She never let anything break her. But I think that losing your father did.'

He stares directly into Jasmine's eyes. 'I have never met anyone like your grandmother.'

Mombasa. Rio. Istanbul. David. Salmah. Jasmine.

*

When Jasmine was ten, after weeks of careful practice, she finally perfected her name in cursive. She spent days filling page after page of her notebooks with it. Jasmine Leong Lin Li, over and over again, on book covers and blank pages, in the margins and in between printed texts. By the time Uncle Foo the becha man fetched her from school one day, her fingers were stained a dark blue from the ink of her fountain pen. Ah Tin rushed Jasmine to the bathroom upstairs in a desperate attempt to wash the indigo ink from her charge's fingers in time for lunch.

'Ah Lin Li, what have you done?' Ah Tin scrubbed Jasmine's fingers with her own coarse ones.

'Wah, your skin so sharp!' shrieked Jasmine.

'Shhhh!' Ah Tin clapped a hand over Jasmine's mouth. 'You crazy or what? Your grandma sees this, and we'll all lose our jobs. She's in a bad mood today. You better keep quiet. Just eat your lunch. Don't say anything. Afterwards, I'll make you banana fritters for tea. Okay? Okay?'

At lunch, Jasmine curled her fingers around her fork and spoon in an attempt to hide her inky digits from Poh Poh's piercing gaze. For once, she was thankful she still had not mastered the acrobatics of chopsticks.

A man, someone she had never seen before, sat across the table from Jasmine. She stole furtive glances at him from time to time. He had a crooked smile and friendly mischief in his eyes. The kind that would probably sneak her a sweet or two when Poh Poh was not looking.

'Ah, this chicken very spicy, Madam, but very good.' Sweat rose on his brow like droplets condensing on a glass of ice water.

Poh Poh only sniffed at the compliment. The chicken was nothing special in her books, made hurriedly in a wok over stinging high heat and a handful of spices thrown in for flavour. Jasmine knew this was not the sort of visitor one wasted a whole afternoon over, double-boiling herbs and meat on a simmering stove.

The stranger tried again, undaunted. 'Madam, is the Hotel Melaka still in town ah?'

'Why? You thinking of staying the night? What for? I wouldn't advise it. There's nothing much to do here.' Poh Poh's voice was stony and sharp.

'Well, I thought since I've come here, why not—'

'Ah Tin! Take Jasmine down to the kitchen. She can finish her meal there.'

Jasmine was used to these occurrences by then. Meals were always a tenuous affair. She was summoned and dismissed at her grandmother's will, and it didn't matter whether Jasmine was just beginning, or had only a mouthful left to finish.

She got up, Ah Tin trailing behind her. Once out of sight, she crept upstairs to her grandmother's bedroom. Beneath the bed, she slid a panel of wood in the floor open a tiny crack. It was a common feature in old houses. Wives used them to keep track of their husbands' deals or mine secrets, to use later for leverage. The Leong home was littered with peep-holes, but this was by far the most useful. It overlooked the formal dining area, where most business and important matters were discussed. Where contracts were negotiated, daughters bartered, and inheritances lost or gained. Ah Tin had shown it to Jasmine one Saturday morning while tidying Madam Leong's room.

Poh Poh and the stranger were now in full sight.

'I think you'd better get to the point of your visit, Mr Woo.'

The stranger swallowed and put down his chopsticks in haste. But one slipped from its tiny porcelain holder, teetering for a moment before clattering to the floor.

'Well?' It was the voice Poh Poh used when she was especially vexed, its rising tone punctuated by the raised arch of an eyebrow.

'It's about the girl. Her mother.' A tremor rose in the visitor's voice.

'What mother? The child is an orphan. She has no one but me,' Poh Poh growled.

'But Madam, you need to know, in case someone tries—'

'You think you know everything ah, Mr Woo? Just because my son and that wretched woman stayed with you in KL? What, above some coffin shop? The only thing you need to know is that no one is going to get past me for as long as I am alive. She is my grandchild and that's all there is to it. She is a Leong. She is the only thing I have left of my son. You see, Mr Woo, despite my apparent well-being, I am a beggar. And beggars cannot be choosers. So I take what I can get. If it's a girl, then it's a girl.' In a snap, Poh Poh rose, toppling her wooden chair to the floor with a crash.

'Mr Woo, everything in this house belongs to me. The child owns nothing. You go tell that to anyone who thinks they can get at my possessions. They will get nothing, and neither will Jasmine, not unless I give it to her. We're Chinese, and that's the way it works.'

The vanquished Mr Woo, by now already on his feet, head bowed, took his leave. By the time he said his hurried goodbyes and slipped his feet into dusty, well-worn shoes, a becha was already in the porte cochère. Jasmine stuck her head out the window and watched the becha bumping down the driveway, out the gates and onto the road, where it turned into a tiny speck, lost among the crowd of buildings, cars and people.

That night, when the house had settled, joint and beam softly creaking, Jasmine crept out to the darkened dining room. The moon shone its weak light through the slanted windows that were shut fast.

She slid under the table, crawling away from Poh Poh's seat at its head, to the opposite end. The chair that was usually reserved for only the most special of visitors. Lying on her back, breath held tight, she wrote with care in blue ink on the underside of the chair: 'This belongs to Jasmine Leong Lin Li.'

*

It is light when Jasmine opens her eyes. She fell asleep on the living room floor last night, her head propped up on a porcelain pillow from her grandmother's collection. At her side, a dozen or more Russian nesting dolls lie strewn in disarray.

After seeing Tunku Mahmud yesterday, she returned to her empty childhood home, her mind swirling with the revelations from her meeting with the old gentleman. Despite his explanations, Jasmine couldn't help feeling angry and cheated, but about what she wasn't quite certain. Is it the fact that she is not who she thought she was? And did the aunties know? If they did, Tai Gu would surely have used Jasmine's real heritage to push her out of Phoenix already. But what about this mother of hers? Who was she? And is she alive?

As evening crept in, the heavy wooden furniture conjured its old silhouettes on the walls. She rang Iskandar several times, but her calls went unanswered. A part of her wondered again if it was even worth having him in her life. Someone who is never present when it really matters, only there to celebrate after the fact, in secret, once the dust has settled. Jasmine curled into a foetal position on the chaise longue, tears wetting her face. Her weeping loosened a tangled ball of dark, long-buried fears, a mass wound so tightly around its core that she had never dared unravel it before this.

Old questions niggled at her insides. She opened her grand-mother's cupboards in the living room, turning over every souvenir from faraway places in search of answers. Tiny gold-plated spoons from Luxembourg. Miniature crystal bells that tinkled, piercing the silence of the house. She swept her arms under furniture, rolled up carpets and pulled open drawers.

All that rose from the darkness was dust, until, exhausted, she fell asleep while staring at the ceiling, her neck against the chilling porcelain pillow retrieved from the coffee table.

Now she walks through the house, letting its comforting, familiar scents seep into her bones. The musty cushions on the couch, still holding lingering traces of Poh Poh's talcum powder. The damp of the smooth wooden chairs in the sunroom. Poh Poh's bedroom that always smells like clean, ironed laundry.

Her own bed, the sheets a little sour from her sweat. There are leftover marks on the walls from peeling Sellotape where her Duran Duran posters used to be, prised from the centrefolds of *Tiger Beat* magazines. A collage of photos from school: Kuan Yew and his gang of athletes; Kevin and her, arms slung around each other, grinning with missing front teeth; a snapshot from her English boarding school days, big eighties hair and shoulder pads, gussied up for a rare school dance with the boys from St Anthony's. The dance where she got her first kiss under the moonlight, from Navin, St Anthony's maths club captain, against an exterior wall covered with old creepers.

The days when she thought she knew who she was. Unlike now, her own being a perplexing morass – its muddy landscape pierced by the trunks of dead people, stubborn mangrove trees of the living showing leaves, their roots poking up from the swamp.

*

By late afternoon, she arrives in KL and pulls up to the gates of her condominium, certain of where she comes from, but unsure of who she is.

The condo is dark and empty. She opens the curtains, the sultry afternoon light flooding her living room. She checks her phone: there are five missed calls from Kuan Yew. He wants to meet her about Hong Kong, their next target for Phoenix's expansion. But she doesn't have the headspace for that yet.

Instead, she opens her laptop and goes through her emails. Mr Chew needs her in the office as soon as possible. The *Market Watch* reporter is badgering him for a response to some follow-up questions, especially now Poh Poh is gone. Jasmine has no answers.

An email pops into her inbox – a summary of headlines from today's news. The opposition leader has won a by-election, placing him back in the game. An independent, alternative news portal is heckling for change. The market is jittery with consternation. Phoenix's stock price is down ten per cent.

Her phone rings. It is Kevin.

'Hey, I'm leaving tomorrow for Singapore. In KL at the moment, and Matthias is with me. I want you to meet him. Please? I've met yours, now it's your turn to meet mine.'

Her instincts recoil; she wants to remain cocooned for a while, yesterday's revelations still churning in her head. But this is Kevin, so she relents. It isn't as if he can invite the man to dinner with his mother.

Besides, they have a lot to catch up on.

'Okay, Luccio's on Changkat at eight,' she replies. 'And Kev, he's not mine. Not really.'

'Oh, details,' he shoots back. 'The man was never anyone else's. It's just you who doesn't want to see it. You know how they say when you love someone, it's like an invisible thread binds you to that person? Well, there are some chains between you two. The heavy-duty kind. You just need to take the plunge.'

If only it were that simple. But perhaps now it is. She's Malay, after all, at least half of her. If Poh Poh hadn't intervened, Jasmine would have been brought up a Muslim. And probably married Iskandar already. Three kids and a house in a gated community. A lifetime of birthday parties and weddings. Of interminable hours spent making small talk with meddling relatives and his father's political allies. Years of watching her back and fake smiling, all the while wondering why she feels something is still missing.

Maybe she should just stop resisting. After all, she isn't the first Leong, it turns out, who has fallen in love with someone not Chinese. Her father, and maybe even Poh Poh, whose love life now appears almost tabloid-worthy. As if something in their genes wants to rebel against the rules of their ancestry. Her father dared to buck tradition in the end, except he died and didn't have to deal with the consequences. She wonders how he would have fared had he survived. How Muslim he would have become. How not. How Poh Poh would have accepted his choice. If Jasmine would even have known Poh Poh at all.

She phones Iskandar. This time he picks up on the second ring.

'Sayang, I can't talk now. Sorry I've not called back before. Something's come up. My father needs me to have dinner with him. I tried to get out of it, but it's with some cabinet minister.'

Jasmine suppresses her irritation, only letting out a small sigh of discontent. 'That friend of his? The scumbag? You're really running for office?'

He groans. 'They're all assholes. My bloody dad. He thinks I should, but God knows it's the last thing on my mind right now. He's just . . . he's nervous. Things are not going well. We need this project, or his business might go under.'

'But what about Kamal?'

'That idiot brother of mine? Too busy running around town, chasing some actress. He's the CEO anyway. He doesn't have time to be a politician. I'll see you later when I get home, okay? We'll talk then. I gotta go. Love you.'

The scrambled secrets she wants to share hang in the silence, untold. Again, she will have to wait. By then, her frazzled thoughts will have unwound, been put in order and filed. The honey and lemon drunk, the pills swallowed without him. Their life in KL back to its old rhythm, of big things crammed into small snatches of conversation. Of the two of them pulled in different directions, straining to hold on to the tenuous tie of their togetherness.

She wonders if marrying him would change anything at all. And whether a life with him is worth the sacrifice she would have to make. Giving up her dream of becoming Phoenix's CEO. Turning her back on her family's legacy and instead becoming a bystander to its future.

10

Jasmine is on edge by the time she gets to Luccio's, her manicured nails leaving faint half-moons on her palms. If Iskandar becomes a politician, things will get worse. All eyes will be trained on him even more. She will have to decide one way or another. Again. Except this time, the stakes will be higher. And there is no turning back.

Kevin is already there when she arrives, a beautiful, slender man with shining green eyes at his side. No wonder her cousin doesn't want to come home.

'Jesus, Kev, he's hot,' she yells over the music. 'Where on earth did you find him?'

'Grindr! I know, right? Who would've thought? And he cooks! Chinese food!' Kevin grins with clenched teeth, his fists balled up. She hasn't seen him like this since they were eight, when his father bought him a talking Luke Skywalker doll, complete with glowing lightsaber. The bar is too crowded, so they elbow their way upstairs to the dining tables, where things are less chaotic. They sit at a table on the balcony, overlooking the street crawling with cars and people, valets waving tickets to drivers pulling up outside restaurants and drinking joints.

'It's a bit like Lan Kwai Fong, minus the hills,' Matthias

122

remarks. He works in Hong Kong. Kevin met him there while on a work trip.

They order a bottle of wine, then another. Kevin is in a jocular mood, Matthias is eager to please. Jasmine drinks too much, wanting to numb the thoughts in her head. By this time, the notion of marrying Iskandar has turned sour, like milk left out too long on the counter. The two boys provide enough distraction. Matthias is funny, with a dry sense of humour, just the kind to keep her entertained and laughing wildly. Or perhaps it's the drink. Kevin is just plain chuffed, so he titters along, lips pressed in smiles that tell her his heart is swelling with joy. Or lust. She can't tell the difference, because she has never met any of his other conquests.

After dinner, they head downstairs. The crush of people has swelled, bodies swaying in their spots to the DJ spinning garage music from a raised platform at the back of the room. They make their way to the bar. Matthias secures Jasmine a high stool. She orders a double shot of gin and soda and starts to wiggle on her perch, wanting to dance. Her limbs feel loose and she gives in to the familiar, boozy elasticity. Things are starting to smooth out and recede when her phone buzzes.

She staggers off her stool, phone to her ear, as she squeezes through the throng to the outside. Her heels almost slip on the slick pavement.

'Iskandar, what time are you coming back?'

'Sayang, I'm still stuck here. All the way in Putrajaya. So I might just crash at my parents' tonight. They're still in discussions. I can't get away. I just phoned to make sure you're okay.'

She wants to tell him how her world has just turned upside down. How she isn't who they both thought she was, but maybe he'll like who she actually is, even if she doesn't. Or that she's confused and has no idea what to think, isn't sure if she hates herself or her parents or her grandmother. Or maybe she shouldn't hate anyone at all because it's not really that big a problem, really, it isn't. But she doesn't know. And she wants to talk to him properly, not with the interruptions of his parents and his wife and her mad grandmother who has always controlled her life for as long as she can recall. Except she's waited all afternoon, for years. And right now, she's too drunk. Plus, he can't talk anyway, as usual, and maybe they should just forget everything. Because things are already bad now, and if she says yes, it would all probably get worse, both of them ending up hating each other. She wants to tell him that it's over, that she will never marry him. Because doing so would mean giving up too much.

Her legs feel like rubber. Right now, all she wants is to scream and rip off his clothes, and have zipless sex, toes curled against sheets, fingernails scratching fine welts down his back.

Instead, because the music pouring out of Luccio's is too loud, and the revellers on the pavement are rowdy, she replies, her voice curt, shouting through the din, 'Sure. Fine. See you tomorrow.'

Back inside, the air is thick with cigarette smoke and bodies sidling up to one another. She stumbles back to her stool. Kevin and Matthias are wrapped in their shared lust, discreet hands around one another's waists, swaying to the beat. She orders another drink.

Someone next to her hails the bartender. 'Put theirs on my tab.'

The barman shoots Jasmine a look. She turns to see Kuan

Yew at her side. She throws her arms around him, her face just centimetres from his, head tilted.

'You . . .' she slurs. 'You always just . . . turn up at the right time.'

He is wearing a lopsided smile, amused. 'Either that or you're following me. Except you've been avoiding me all day.'

He is teasing her, she knows, and right now she doesn't care.

He watches her for a while. Her body sways in small, languorous arcs to the music. She lets out a long laugh, leaning back, almost toppling. He moves behind her, his body stopping her fall, arms round her waist. He leans in close. 'It's nice to see you've finally decided to celebrate.'

She wraps her arm around his, pulling him closer. His bulk is comforting, the smell of his aftershave making her think things she shouldn't be thinking, but then again, she is drunk and her goddamn lover is nowhere in sight. Nowhere.

So, she turns around and kisses Kuan Yew full on the lips. A long, searching, hungry, open-mouthed kiss, while pressing her breasts into his broad chest. He makes her feel tiny and delicate, like he could sweep her up in his arms and take her out the door. Away from everything, even her old life.

'Do you wanna get out of here?' His voice is hoarse and deep. She nods. He helps her off the stool, her heels wobbling on the floor.

As she leaves, Kevin grabs her arm, glancing at Kuan Yew. 'Jasmine Che, what are you doing?'

But she is feeling reckless. 'Whatever the fuck I want tonight. Just this once.' She raises a finger to her lips in silence, blowing him a clumsy kiss as she walks out the door.

She clasps Kuan Yew's hand, letting him lead as they weave

through the mob. His black Bentley is waiting at the kerb. He pays the valet and opens the passenger door, making sure she is safely strapped in before he enters the driver's side. No chauffeur, she notes. His car smells like polished leather and is quiet, except for a lounge track drifting low from the speakers.

'I don't know where you live. You'll have to tell me where to go.' He manoeuvres the car through the crush of partying pedestrians.

'Yours. I don't feel like going home yet.' She takes off her shoes, drawing her legs up to her chest, leaning into the plush seat that smells like the inside of an expensive handbag.

'You sure?' He reaches out and catches her hand, his fingers tickling her palm.

She swerves her head round, laughing. 'Don't tell me you'd rather not.'

His condominium in the heart of KL is on the thirty-third floor, close to the Twin Towers, their ghostly heights gleaming into his living room. The lights are turned down. She stretches out on his couch, barefoot. It is huge, the kind you can just fall asleep on, sinking into the cushions.

He offers her a glass of something. She gets up, half-sitting, and motions for him to join her on the couch. He obliges and she takes a gulp.

'Ugh, water. I want a real drink.' She pushes the glass back into his waiting hand and falls back on the couch.

He laughs a little, pulling her head onto his lap, stroking her hair. 'I think you've had enough for the night. I need you to bring your A-game for our meeting tomorrow.'

She grabs a throw cushion and covers her face. 'Nooo . . . no work talk. Please.'

He removes the cushion, casting it aside. 'Okay, okay.'

They are silent for a while, him caressing her hair, watching the reflection of the city lights in the switched-off screen of his large TV.

'Jasmine Leong Lin Li,' he murmurs. 'What the hell are we going to do with you?'

But she has drifted off to sleep, her mind overtaken with dreams of Poh Poh, the parents she doesn't know, Iskandar, Tunku Mahmud, a civet in a rambutan tree. She is chasing the musang away, brandishing a parang, threatening to cut the fire ant-filled branches down, making it rain with their stinging, angry bites that leave raised red welts on her skin and face.

*

She wakes to find herself in a strange bed. Her phone is on the bedside table. There are missed calls and messages from Kevin:

> Che, are you okay??!
> I just rang your house. You're not picking up. Che, PICK UP!!!
> You better not be in a gutter somewhere. CALL ME!!!

She groans, slapping her phone face down on the table, and pulls the covers over her head.

Kuan Yew sits down on the bed next to her. 'You must be feeling a little dusty.'

She peers out from under the duvet, nose wrinkled. 'Dusty? How long have I been sleeping?'

'Ah, sorry, it's Aussie speak for not quite a full-blown hangover. Just, you know, when your brain's a little, well, dusty.'

She massages her temples. 'I think it's worse. Might need to hire a professional cleaner.'

He laughs. 'Well, there's breakfast when you're ready. I've got a spare toothbrush in the bathroom, towels if you want to take a shower. I'm afraid I don't own any dresses in your size, though. I'll be outside.' He strokes her face with the back of his palm.

Alone, she peeks beneath the covers. She is still fully clothed.

Later, she emerges fresh-faced from a shower but in yesterday's dress.

Her hair is piled high in a loose bun, held by an elastic band she found in the bottom of her handbag.

The table is laid out with a spread of pastries, fruit, juice and coffee.

Yoghurt. How grown-up.

Kuan Yew pours her a cup of the black, steaming brew, his eyes never leaving her face, a faint smile on his lips.

'You must think I'm a complete idiot.' She stirs her coffee, her gaze fixed on the swirling, black liquid. Her cheeks feel wet. She's crying.

His face softens. 'Hey . . . hey, what's wrong? Look, nothing happened. Okay?' He reaches out and lifts her chin with his hand. 'Look at me. I know you. I've known you for a million years. There's nothing the world can throw at you that you can't handle. Nothing.'

She breaks into sobs, pushing the cup away, burying her head in her hands. 'Not this time, Kuan Yew. I can't fix this shit. It's not even anything I've done. I'm so tired.'

He comes round, wrapping her in his arms from behind. 'Shhh . . . tell me what's wrong.'

And because he is the only one who has asked, she tells him everything. Even Poh Poh's suspected secrets. Everything except about Iskandar. By the time she finishes, her sobs have stopped, her face now sticky from the remnants of tears.

'Crikey. You should write a novel.'

His suggestion elicits a small half-giggle. She wipes her face with a serviette, blowing her nose. 'I feel like Bozo the Clown.'

'Hey, if Bozo looked like you, I'd reconsider my preferences.' He taps the tip of her nose. 'Right, that's it. Back to bed. You're in no shape to be out there.' He bends down, scoops her up in his arms and carries her to his room. She is too drained to protest.

In bed, they lie on top of the covers, she on her side, his body curved round hers. She switches her phone to silent.

His room is quiet, his apartment too high up for the traffic noise to reach it. She thinks how it would be so easy to remain here and pretend the world outside doesn't exist. As if she is somewhere else altogether, far from the madding people in her life. Her past, Iskandar, her aunts, Phoenix. She wills herself to stop thinking of them, slowing her breath, snuggling closer into Kuan Yew. He smells like coffee and the promise of meals laid out in advance, a refrigerator well stocked with fresh food instead of leftover takeaway. A lifetime of waking up together, her dozing off at nights as he reads in bed. Where she never has to awaken alone.

He feels like certainty.

Jasmine turns around, pushing him onto his back, laying her head on his chest. She can hear the strong beat of his heart. He curls his arm around her frame, and her leg drapes across his.

'Why are you so kind to me, Kuan Yew?'

His fingers run up and down her arm in feather strokes. 'Why wouldn't I be? I like you. I always have.'

She lifts her head to look at him, questioning.

He only smiles back, yearning in his eyes, then shifts his glance up to the ceiling. 'For a long time, I envied you. You and Kevin. But not in a malicious sort of way. Just, I guess, I wished I was like you guys. Your lives seemed so easy, so comfortable to me. Our family never had much. Well, there were a lot of mouths to feed.'

Recalling his seven siblings, Jasmine giggles. 'You realize the whole town used to stop and stare every time you lot went out all together, right?'

'No shit,' he says with a laugh. 'Ba Ba always had to make two trips every time we drove to the cinema. Thank God we didn't live too far away from it. Most of the time we just cycled there or walked.'

'You guys always looked so happy. I mean, sure, there were always one or two of you shoving each other in the back, but you all looked like you actually wanted to be around one another.'

'We did. Well, most of the time.'

She can feel him breathe, his every exhale ruffling her fringe. She plays with the buttons on his shirt, undoing them, her fingers trailing down the centre of his smooth, broad chest. 'And look where you are now . . .'

His breath grows ragged, but he doesn't stop her. She straddles him, reaching behind to unzip her dress.

'Are you sure about this?' he whispers, gripping her waist.

She answers him with a kiss, her tongue and lips searching,

one hand yanking the elastic from her hair, which cascades down in black waves.

She doesn't know why she does it. He is tender and safe and surprising in turn, his hands unfamiliar but seeking and eager to please. The sex is slow, unhurried, no deadline grinding its clock down until they have to part. There is time to finish everything they start.

He is considerate, his kisses long and deep, as if searching for something still hidden from him. Even when they lie skin to skin. Each time she rushes, he slows her down, lingering over each caress, each move, each breath, till the room fills with the musky scent of them, the air growing thick from the heat.

When he enters her, she thinks of nothing but the feel of his broad back beneath her fingers, the thin sheen of sweat on his skin, the strangely pleasant metallic taste of his neck as she nibbles it, him moaning with pleasure, yielding to her every sigh.

'I feel drunk,' she laughs, when it is over. She stretches, cat-like, her body still thrumming. Her skin glows from the warmth of him, fingertips tingling as she slides them across the satin-smooth sheets. 'Where on earth did you get these from? They're awesome.'

He nuzzles her neck. 'Trust you to notice.'

Afterwards, they eat lunch on his couch. She is wearing his shirt, her dress a crumpled heap on his bedroom floor. He feeds her french fries, two or three at a time, her mouth sucking his fingers, licking the sweet tang of tomato sauce. Flaked fragments from their croissant sandwiches scatter like confetti all over their clothes and the sofa.

'Oh my God, what a mess,' she says, gathering the crumbs onto an empty plate.

She feels like a giddy schoolgirl.

By late afternoon, the sun slips behind the Twin Towers, its rays reflecting pink and orange on the building's glassy facade.

'I wish I could just stay here and not leave.' Jasmine takes in the city from Kuan Yew's balcony. She is once more wearing her dress, which he has ironed, her hair neatly twisted into a chignon. His grassy cologne clings to her skin.

He leads her back to the dining table, a sharp intent in his eyes. 'This is probably not a good time,' he says, 'but since you're here, I might as well say it. I think this could get difficult for you, Jasmine. If word gets out about your parents . . . you know how people are here.'

Selfish. Selfish and blind. They don't give a shit whose lives they destroy.

'I mean, the Chinese are not gonna care, not really. Your customers only want what they want, whoever makes it. But things are getting hotter round here, politically. If the wrong people get ahold of this information, it could blow up in your face.'

Wrong people. Tai Gu. The media. The public. Iskandar? The thought of him makes her insides lurch. He is probably wondering where she is. He might be waiting for her at home.

'It's unfair,' she replies. 'Why should anyone care? It's haram anyway, our bak kwa. Not like they're gonna eat it.'

Kuan Yew takes her hands, holding them firm. 'Precisely why it will matter. They won't want one of their own having anything to do with some haram business. They're gonna try and' – he crooks his fingers into air quotes – 'save you.'

Not if this doesn't get out.

Maybe she shouldn't have wished to be noticed. Oblivion can be a powerful defence. If there is anything she needs saving from, it is probably her whole history at this point. The choices made by those who came before her.

At once, she is angry, rage burning in her gut. At her parents for loving her to life, at Poh Poh for keeping her from it. At the Malays for possibly forcing her hand. At Tai Gu with her hardened resolve.

'My aunt is going to use this to get rid of me, I just know it.'

Kuan Yew is thinking, lips slightly pursed. 'There might be a way . . . Actually, it's what I was going to talk to you about today. Except now, maybe there's a different argument, one that could benefit you directly instead. But I need some time to tweak a few details.'

They promise to meet again next week, once he's back from a meeting in Europe.

*

Iskandar is watching TV on the couch when she returns to her condo. 'Sayang, where were you? I called the office, but they said you didn't go in. Did you even come home last night?' He eyes her, curious, taking in her little black dress.

'I stayed over at Kevin's hotel room. It got late. I was drunk.' She heads straight for the bathroom, locking the door behind her.

Whipping out her phone, she types a text:

Kev, I was with you all last night. Okay? Call you later.

Staring into the mirror, she notices a slight red bruise above her collarbone. She turns on the shower, letting the hot water

133

run over her body and her hair, the traces of Kuan Yew's after-shave dissipating.

Afterwards, she chooses a collared T-shirt and a pair of shorts. Iskandar is still sitting on the couch, the *Market Daily* open on the table.

'Have you seen this?' He points to a story.

She picks up the paper, scanning the headline: 'Phoenix Rising: A change on the horizon?'

That perky reporter has written a piece about Poh Poh's passing, questioning the future of the company and suggesting that Jasmine is expected to take the helm.

'This should help you, won't it? With your aunts?'

Jasmine baulks at the expectation in Iskandar's eyes. She hasn't kissed him yet, she can't. Instead, she gets up, retrieving a tea towel from the kitchen, and wipes the coffee table clean of cigarette ash.

'Use the fucking balcony,' she says, her voice gruff with discontent. 'We're not college kids any more.'

He is confused, his body stiffening, sensing a fight. He tries to reach for her, but she pushes him away.

'Don't,' she says. 'Don't try and get out of this.'

'What did I do?' He shoves his hand through his hair, gripping it.

'I'm tired, Iskandar. I've wanted to talk to you since I left Ipoh, but I haven't been able to, not really. It's always like this. You're wrapped up in your mess of a life, and I have to wait till you've sorted it all out before I can even get a piece of you for myself.' Her eyes flash with anger.

'I'm sorry,' he says, dejected. 'I know this must be hard for you, and it's my fault, I know. But my father, he needs me.

We're in bad shape, sayang. Really bad. He's over-extended. I told him not to take on that last project, but he and my brother wouldn't listen. Now they need this new deal, so . . .'

'So you're running for office?' she screams, her fury now a flood. 'Just like that. Again! You're gonna just give in, after all that crap you gave me about us running away and starting over and leaving all of this bullshit behind? What the fuck, Iskandar, what the fuck?' She shoves him, hard.

He is stunned, his eyes wide with fear and anger. 'What do you expect me to do? Just leave them in the lurch? My family? You of all people should understand.'

A life debt is a hard thing to account for. Jasmine realizes once again how alike they both are, with their ledgers full of debits untallied. There is no end to the repayment scheme, interest mounting every second that ticks by. She feels suffocated, the breath sucked out of her.

'We're never going to be enough for you, are we?' she says, collapsing onto the couch. And a life with him will never be enough for her. Not after all the years she has spent building Phoenix into the company it is today. Plus, Poh Poh would never approve. She imagines her grandmother turning away at the news of Jasmine marrying Iskandar. Perhaps never speaking to Jasmine again. Phoenix is all that matters now. It is how she will keep Poh Poh's legacy alive. She owes at least that much to her grandmother.

Iskandar tries to hold her, but she resists.

'Go,' she says, her voice small and low. 'Just go, Iskandar. Please. I don't think I can do this right now. And leave your key card behind.'

Now that he is gone again, she feels little guilt. She sits on her bed, clenching Iskandar's copy of her condo key card, drapes drawn shut.

The doorbell buzzes. It's Kevin.

She lets him in without a word and flops onto the sofa. He observes her in equal silence.

Minutes tick by.

The azan pierces the air. Thelonious Monk is back.

The familiar sound of the muezzin's call to prayer makes her want to cry. She chokes back a sob, stifling it with the back of her hand against her mouth.

Kevin hands her a Kleenex. 'How much of that have you been doing since last night?'

She tries to laugh, but it gets stuck in her throat. 'Go away!'

He relaxes, stretching out his slim legs. 'Yeah, sure. I was meant to be on a plane to Singapore. Called in sick. Suspected pneumonia.'

She lifts her head, curious and worried.

'I couldn't leave my best girl,' he says, waving his hand. 'They're big boys, they can do without my brilliance for a bit.'

She laughs, finally, chucking her used tissue at him. She misses. Kevin raises an eyebrow, sizing her up. 'So . . . last night . . .'

He doesn't ask where Iskandar is. She tells him about Kuan Yew. And Iskandar, his wife, his father.

Kevin lets out a loud guffaw. 'You're shitting me. The poor sod's got both his women cheating on him now? Is there such a thing as a double-cuckold?'

She shoots him a sideways glance, eyes narrowed, arms crossed across her chest. 'Well, he deserves it.'

'Of course he does. Karma's a bitch. But he loves you, you know. I can see it.'

She draws a long breath, exhales. 'But it's never going to be enough, Kev. I've called it off. For good this time.'

She tells him about her visit to Tunku Mahmud, his eyes widening with every revelation.

'You want to find your mother, don't you?'

The truth is, Jasmine is unsure. After all this time not knowing, she is now hesitant, afraid of what else she might learn.

'I don't know if I can take any more surprises, Kev. As it is, I'm barely treading water. Look at the mess I'm in. The shit I can't undo. Like you said, mothers don't come with return policies.'

And her wardrobe is already crammed full of skeletons, their rattling bones growing louder each day, threatening to spill out into the light.

11

It is Jasmine's first day back at work since Poh Poh's passing. She gets there before dawn, eager to settle herself in before anyone else arrives. For a moment, she hesitates in front of her own room, before pushing open the large doors to Poh Poh's office. Everything appears to be in its place. Poh Poh's customary tea caddy in the left-hand corner of her expansive teak desk, custom-made in Myanmar. Files stacked neatly on the right-hand side. Only a large bouquet of birds of paradise seems the worse for wear.

Jasmine sits in her grandmother's plush wing-backed chair, its moss-green arms a little worn. Turning round with her back to the desk, she gazes out through the floor-to-ceiling glass panel at the view below. Over the years, Damansara Heights – a previously residential enclave of the monied – has become more commercial. Its low rolling hills used to be drawn with undulating rows of homes, punctuated every so often by some rich family's bungalow. Today, the houses are almost concealed from view by the numerous skyscrapers that seem to pop up like mushrooms after a heavy rain.

Her aunts and the board have yet to name Poh Poh's successor. In the meantime, the market has grown nervous, its uncertainty reflected in the downward trend of Phoenix's stock price over the last few days. Jasmine knows she must force a decision, if only a temporary one, to stem the ebbing tide.

Determined, she rises from Poh Poh's chair and stacks her grandmother's things into a neat pile. She strides to the supply room, returns with a cardboard box and places Poh Poh's things inside. Before long, the room is emptied of her grandmother's possessions, leaving only the contents that remain in the locked filing cabinet Poh Poh has always kept in the corner of her office. 'These are the most important ones,' her grandmother used to say. 'In case anything ever happens to me.' Jasmine already knows what the cabinet contains: copies of Phoenix's major contracts that are still in force.

By the time the staff trickle in to work, Jasmine's old office is merely a shell, her belongings firmly installed in Poh Poh's office. She has left the giant doors open, the carved phoenixes framing Jasmine's figure in her grandmother's wing-backed chair. She watches the workers as they walk in and hesitate with a start at the unfamiliar sight.

Mr Chew arrives at a quarter to nine, his small eyes widening as he bends to put down his briefcase beneath his desk. Five minutes later, he knocks at the door. 'Miss Leong?'

She beckons him to sit in one of two chairs facing her across the wide desk. 'We need to appoint a new CEO.'

'Y-yes, I am aware of that, Miss Leong, but I thought I'd speak to you first. Because your aunt, Ruth Leong . . . I assumed at first you would become the CEO, naturally, but I understand your aunt has, er, other ideas.'

'Well, maybe she'll change her mind when she understands how much her own fortune has decreased over the last few days. The market needs answers. And they can't wait for the whims of an old woman.'

By lunchtime, Phoenix's stock price has dipped five more points. Frustrated, Jasmine tries to ring Kevin, but he is away at a company retreat in Batam. Iskandar is no longer an option. Besides, the chances of him answering her call even on a good day are slim. On a whim, she dials Kuan Yew's number. He picks up on the second ring.

'Oh, good, you're still in town. I took a chance. I still owe you lunch, from our char kway teow date all those years ago.'

His laughter sends a small thrill down her spine. 'I leave tonight. But I can meet you for a quick one. It's not every day I get asked out on a date.'

They meet at a ramen place not far from her office. The restaurant is in Bangsar Shopping Complex, a popular meeting spot for the well-heeled crowd. At lunch it is bustling with suited executives and coiffed tai-tais in their designer casual wear. Unlike Iskandar, there is no need for subterfuge with Kuan Yew. She doesn't have to worry about being seen with him.

Nevertheless, he gives her a quick peck on the cheek when he arrives, careful not to draw too much attention. Bangsaratis love a good gossip. And the sight of her and Kuan Yew could set tongues wagging. Since Poh Poh's passing, the media have been carrying stories about Phoenix and its potential successor. Many will now recognize Jasmine.

'Are you okay?' he enquires as he settles in his chair. She is touched by the concern in his eyes and manages a small nod.

Over lunch, she tells him how she has taken possession of Poh Poh's office.

Kuan Yew guffaws, shaking his head in amusement. 'You sure don't waste any time, Jasmine Leong.'

'Well, I figured I might as well, since I don't know how long I'll get to sit in that chair.'

His forehead wrinkles into a frown. 'What do you mean? Who else would it be, if not you?'

She tells him about Tai Gu's insistence on installing Kevin as CEO, despite her cousin's resistance to the idea. 'The problem is, we need to name someone now, even if it's temporary. To calm down the market, at least. Plus, with all I've found out about myself and my real parents, if news gets out . . .'

Kuan Yew nods, adjusting his tie. 'What does your Seh Gu Treasure think?'

At the mention of her second aunt, Jasmine smiles. Seh Gu has always been a pacifist. But Jasmine also knows her aunt has a soft spot for her. 'You're right, actually, I should call her. Except she's not often one for rattling tiger Tai Gu's cage.'

'So, tell them this is all just temporary. Ask them to make you acting CEO. At least till all of you can sort things out internally. And Kevin can finally tell his mother to her face that he's not keen. Again. And insist that they make you CEO.'

'But what if eventually—'

'One step at a time, Jasmine.'

She sighs. 'You're right. Poh Poh always said that battles are often won in inches, not miles. I guess I was just trying to not get into another fight with Tai Gu.'

'Oh, I don't know. I reckon you can be quite persuasive when you want to be,' Kuan Yew says, laughing softly. 'Now let me drop you off at the office. I'd like to see these legendary phoenix doors for myself.' He rises from his chair and with a lopsided grin, offers Jasmine a hand.

By evening, she has managed to get everyone onside. Even Tai Gu is pacified, comforted by the notion that Jasmine's appointment is not a permanent thing. The announcement is made to the stock exchange after its closing. Tomorrow, the world will know Jasmine is now Phoenix's acting CEO.

As she stands in the lift vestibule, Jasmine traces her fingers over her lips. She recalls the warmth of the quick stolen kiss Kuan Yew gave her when he left earlier. There is something in the immediacy of his presence that feels new and unfamiliar to Jasmine. He is there, whenever she seeks him out. No need for her to wait, storing away little nuggets of her frustration or joy until he is ready for her to put them on display for his review. Already he has sent her text messages with witty obser-vations of the airport chauffeur and other travellers waiting in the airport lounge. She has responded almost immediately, unafraid of being intrusive.

This is something she could get used to, she thinks. It wouldn't be hard at all. And perhaps, she realizes, it is what she deserves.

*

Their first board meeting post-listing has just ended, and the conference room is freezing. Tai Gu sits on one side of the massive table, Kevin and Jasmine on the other, trying not to catch Tai Gu's eyes. Now that her position is safe for the moment, there is no need to antagonize the old lady. The other board members have left. The food technologist and the lawyer are old Ipoh connections Poh Poh appointed before the listing.

Seh Gu conferenced in earlier, flashing a proud smile at the sight of her niece seated just to the right of Phoenix's chairman, an old friend of the family who is a retired army general.

The agenda of the meeting was to discuss the new bak kwa packaging and Phoenix's planned expansion abroad. If the old folk had any misgivings, Jasmine hopes her presentation has dispelled them. The data looks promising. Consumers are ready for something more modern. Kevin, only there at his mother's insistence, had helped Jasmine with the legalities earlier. His input has at least managed to push the board into finally trade-marking their new brand name and logo. With the expansion, they can't afford any avoidable risks.

'We need one more board member, in case of a vote.' Jasmine knows odd numbers are crucial, in the event of a deadlock.

'What are you afraid of?' Tai Gu Ruth barks, disdain in her downturned mouth.

'Ma!' Kevin looks up, aghast. 'Stop!'

'Stop what? You'll thank me later. I'm not like your father, happy to let you be content with scraps of whatever life shoves at you. You only deserve the best. You're my son.' Her jaw muscles ripple. 'Besides,' she continues, 'who knows where she comes from, really?' Tai Gu raises a pointed finger at Jasmine.

'Ma! Enough! You don't know anything about her mother!'

'Exactly! No one knows! Your Poh Poh might have, but she buried that secret with her, didn't she? All because this one is her son's daughter.' Tai Gu turns to stare directly at Jasmine. 'I told that reporter, nothing is certain. I told her that if I had my way, things would be different. She called me, yes, she did. I bet you didn't think I would be so clever, did you? I'm not just some old woman you can push aside, Jasmine. There's a lot more at stake now, especially with our plans to expand our property development arm further in Ipoh. I need to make sure all this doesn't jeopardize our latest project. I am not going to let anything stand in the way of realizing your grandmother's final dream. Not even you.'

Jasmine is enraged. In her mind, she stabs Tai Gu in the eyes with a hairpin from her own chignon, her aunt stumbling round the room, screaming with horror from her going-blind eyes. Beneath the table, Jasmine jiggles her left foot, biting her tongue, her right hand gripping a blue ballpoint pen.

Kevin is mumbling, shaking his head. 'Don't don't don't . . . shut the hell up, Ma . . . oh my God . . .'

But his mother does not relent. 'The difference, Jasmine, is that Kevin is a man. He can still marry some younger woman and have babies. Heirs. You can't. Not really, at your age. And then what will happen? No one to take over after you're gone! What, your Seh Gu's children who are whiter than baos? There are things that last longer than you.'

Tai Gu stands and advances towards Jasmine. Unable to stave off her anger any longer, Jasmine rises from her chair, leaning against the table with tented fingers. 'You can't just get rid of me, Tai Gu! I have just as much right to be here, even more maybe, given all the years I've put into making Phoenix what it is today. If not for all the work Poh Poh and I put in . . .'

'You and your Poh Poh?' Tai Gu hisses through gritted teeth. 'Your Poh Poh is just like all the rest before her. Never wanted to give me or Seh Gu a chance. The only reason she let you get so far is because your father died.' Tai Gu takes another step closer to her niece.

Alarmed, Kevin gets up from his chair, holding his hands out to stay his mother.

Sensing her cousin's imminent confession, Jasmine pleads, 'Kevin, stop, it's okay, please don't . . .'

But Kevin is beyond caring, a determined set to his jaw. 'Good God, Ma, don't you get it? I'm gay! I don't want to come home. Not here! Because God knows, I might just embarrass you. And then what? And . . . and babies? I can't even marry, not in this country.'

His mother is holding a palm to her cheek, mouth open. The other hand flutters to her breast, her breathing ragged. Jasmine sinks down into her chair, her gaze flitting between Tai Gu and Kevin. She is terrified now for her cousin, afraid of what his mother might say that could rend an irreparable tear in their already fragile relationship.

Kevin eyes his mother intently. 'Oh, don't tell me you didn't know, Ma. It's why you push so hard, isn't it? Well, I'm not perfect. At least, not the way you want me to be. But you just refuse to see it or accept me for who I am.'

Tai Gu takes a step back, hands trembling by her side. Her eyes glitter with tears. 'You're all selfish, all of you. Your lives could be so simple. But you choose the hard paths on purpose to hurt us – the ones who came before you. Years of putting ourselves aside, for you to just throw it all away on a whim.' Glaring at her son, she hisses: 'Men, you say. You like men. No one gets to choose who they like. Let alone love.'

Kevin softens, his voice now tender. 'I didn't choose this on purpose, Ma. No one is out to get you. Not Dad, not me, not Poh Poh even. Let go of it, Ma. Let everyone live their lives. And you live yours too, but let go.'

Tai Gu is stuffing board papers into her bag. Loose sheets flutter to the ground, ignored. She raises her head, her eyes dark as garnets. 'You can take all your lives and shove them. But I will not let go, not ever! This family will be what it should be, for once. Not what you people think is fair. Life isn't fair. It is what it is. And I'm going to put things right if it kills me.'

They watch her storm out of the room. Her wedge shoes clomp across the tiled floor of the corridor outside before receding into silence.

Jasmine walks up to the conference room door and shuts it. She drops back into her seat, still stunned. Then, glancing at Kevin, she murmurs, 'Shit, Wonder Woman, that took some guts.'

Kevin drops down into his own chair, loosening his tie. 'Well, damn, I didn't see that coming. Not even from me. But she was going to hit you or . . . or something.'

Jasmine reaches out for his hand. 'Kev, I'm sorry. You really didn't have to. I mean, she is off the rails, but she's still your mother . . .'

He lets out a small laugh. 'It's been a long time coming anyway. There was probably never a good way to do it. Wait till I tell Matthias his boyfriend just came out to his mother. Accidentally, but maybe on purpose.'

Jasmine throws him a quizzical look.

'He's moving to Singapore to be with me.' Kevin stares at an ink stain on his palm. 'It's serious this time, Jasmine. I think I'm in love.'

'You sneaky bastard! When's the wedding?'

'Whoa, can we just let him move in first?'

'Move in? To your place? Shit, this is serious. When?'

146

'Next month.' Kevin stands up and hoists his backpack onto his shoulder.

Jasmine walks over and places her hands on her cousin's shoulders, taking a deep breath. 'Hey, that's huge, Wonder Woman. I'm really happy for you. Maybe today was a good thing, after all. I mean, you can't keep that man of yours under wraps for ever. Don't make the same mistake I did.'

Her cousin nods, a wan smile crossing his face. 'You'll be okay, won't you? I'll try and come back soon. But you know where to find me in the meantime.'

She nods, giving him a big hug. Then, checking her watch, she gasps. 'Crap, it's six thirty. I gotta go.'

'Which one is it?' Kevin says with a cheeky grin.

'Kuan Yew,' she replies, laughing in return.

'Oh, you mean *Olivier.*'

'Second date. He's back from a work trip, and he's cooking.'

'Sounds like I'm not the only one getting serious,' Kevin teases.

A flush rises to Jasmine's cheeks. 'Maybe. It's nice, you know, not having to hide. Or having to sneak around behind some-one's wife.'

'So it's really over then, you and Iskandar?'

Jasmine nods, lips pressed firmly together. 'Yep. For good. Whether or not Kuan Yew and I work out. I can't give up Phoenix, Kevin. I need this. For me, for Poh Poh. For everything she's done for me.'

'Plus, I can't think of anyone else who could run the company better,' says Kevin, planting a peck on his cousin's cheek.

*

147

Kuan Yew smells like oranges and bread when she reaches up to kiss him at his front door. His scent makes her stomach growl; she skipped lunch earlier, on account of having to catch up on work. Her hand is still wrapped around his neck when he pulls away, gazing down at her.

'Good day?' He is clearly glad to see her.

She breaks out into a big laugh, kicking off her high heels once she gets inside and closes the door.

'Kevin came out to his mother.' She likes the immediacy of it. The not having to sift through a week full of happenings, being able to tell him what just occurred. He has kept in touch while away, sending messages and calling her every day. Jasmine senses no signposts where she cannot stray with him, his life open to her inquisitions. But she has remained silent about Iskandar, telling herself that he is now in her past. Kuan Yew's eyes widen in slight surprise. 'I see . . . I didn't know, I mean, I should've guessed but I, yeah, crikey.' He rubs the back of his neck. He is still in his office clothes, his shirt unbuttoned, tie tossed on the back of a chair.

Jasmine eyes the spot between his collarbones, lowering her long lashes.

She is still laughing as she undresses, letting her clothes slide down to her feet.

He is thrown off for a moment, then grins. 'Well, I missed you too.'

She raises a finger to his mouth. 'Stop talking.'

They have sex right there on the living room floor. This time, it is she who lingers, inching her way down and across his body, his torso striped by the long rays of the evening sun that creep in through the sheer white curtains. She notices a small tattoo just above his hip bone. 'This must have hurt,' she says, tracing the Chinese characters in blue ink.

'Like a bitch,' he says, 'but it was worth it.'

'Wait, isn't this Chinese for "chicken"?'

He tells her about his time as a pizza delivery guy, during his first three months in Perth. 'I landed a job in Chinatown. Yeah, pizza in Chinatown. The owner was from Hong Kong. Some ex-Triad member, probably on the run.' He turns on his side, props up his head with his hand, a lazy grin on his face. 'He dared me. Said he'd give me a raise if I got a tattoo. I guess I must have looked like some terrified fresh-off-the-boat teenager. Which I probably was.'

'No way. You and your swagger? You used to strut down the halls with that John Travolta walk all the time, especially after that *Grease* performance! And all the cool boys looked up to you too.' She recalls him in school, commanding the back row of the classroom.

'Hey, I was only a small-town boy. And suddenly, there I was, out of my element. It doesn't take much for a city full of gwai lohs to scare you shitless. He could see I needed the money, but I didn't want to do the deliveries. Only to stay in the joint, sweeping floors, cleaning toilets. The money was in the tips. So he decided to teach me a lesson.

'He called me a chicken constantly, and the other guys working there picked it up. The name started to stick. After a week, I had enough, and it was clear on my face. My boss said he'd stop if I got a tattoo. Except when we got to the tattoo parlour, he told the tattoo guy where to put it. I have never not-screamed so hard in my life!' He throws his head back, his laughter booming round the room. 'I guess, whenever I've felt scared since then, this is the reminder to suck it up.'

She pulls on his shirt and perches on a stool, watching him move around the kitchen in his undershirt and boxers. From time to time, he turns to smile at her, as if to check that she is still there.

'Let me help,' she offers, but he gestures for her to stay put.

'Pour some wine, if you want.' He decants a bottle and sets the table for two.

He slides her a plate of bruschetta to tide her over while he makes dinner. She lifts one to her mouth, her teeth sinking into the tangy tomatoes, some of it spilling onto her lap.

He watches her wolf down the food. 'Oi, save some room for dinner.' She could get used to this.

He serves up spaghetti vongole, heaping it onto their plates. She devours each mouthful, as he eats slowly, bemused.

Afterwards, she leans back, one hand on her tummy, groaning. 'I feel a bit sick now.'

He shakes his head, clearing the plates, as if amused by her little-girl self.

Jasmine eyes the dirty dishes and wonders what Kuan Yew would think of her own apartment and its constant state of disarray. She wonders how he keeps everything so spick and span. 'So, don't you have help? Who cleans?'

'Twice a week. But they only come when I'm at work. I don't really like having people around when I'm home.'

She scans the apartment, taking stock at last. The place is furnished with a restrained sense of taste. A bachelor pad, almost spartan, except softened with earthy tones. 'Who did this up for you?'

He glances back at her from the kitchen sink. 'I just picked stuff from a website and my secretary got the movers to do it. Why?'

Jasmine hesitates before answering. 'I just figured you would get someone to help you. After all, you must have plenty to do at work, not to bother with stuff like this.' She waves her hand, gesturing to the space.

He is done washing up and sits back down at the table, topping up their wine. 'I didn't grow up with housekeepers, Jasmine. I'm used to doing things by myself.'

She is more than a little embarrassed, the gap in their childhoods looming vast. His family lived in a shophouse back then, all the Laus crammed into a two-bedroom space above the goldsmith's store. They didn't have the luxury of a cook, let alone someone like Ah Tin. Or Mr Boon.

'I admire you, you know,' she says. 'I don't know how you did it.'

He shrugs, fingering the stem of his wine glass. 'You just do what you gotta do, I guess. It's life. You don't know where you're headed, maybe you have an idea. And one day, if you're lucky, you get there. Speaking of which . . .'

He fetches his laptop from his study and shows her a spreadsheet. 'About the plan I mentioned last time. I wanted to talk to you about RSE taking a stake in your company. We think you have interesting prospects, so we'd like a foot in the door.'

She straightens her spine at the mention of work. Scanning the numbers, she says, 'You've done some projections. Wait, this is the bak kwa.'

'Yep, we think it has legs. The market's just there for the taking. The Singapore players are the biggest ones right now, but Phoenix has a great story: an all-female brand, right down to your history. The other companies are all men. Plus,' he says, twirling his pen across the back of his palm, 'you're a hell of a lot better-looking than that ninety-year-old across the causeway.' He winks. 'The media will love you.'

His predictions align with Jasmine's. It's the reason she wants to take the brand regional. She narrows her eyes, her business sense kicking in. 'What's the catch?'

'I want a seat on your board. I reckon it won't hurt for you to have an ally there at this point. And you need a tie-breaker in case of a vote.'

*

It has been a while since she's had time to swim. Turning on the jets in her pool, Jasmine plunges in and starts to swim, stroke after stroke, kicking her legs at a comfortable pace. A few times, the soles of her feet touch the wall behind her, but she pushes her way back into the current. Swimming helps her think, with Kuan Yew's proposal now occupying her mind. It may be a way to keep Tai Gu at bay. But she's never mixed work with pleasure before. Doing it could make things complicated, and her life is already a tangled mess at the moment, what with these new-old secrets crawling out of the past. Still, Phoenix is the one thing she has worked on for so long, the closest thing she can call her own. Not that the other family members haven't been involved, but she knows the company inside out. She deserves to be CEO.

Without Phoenix, she will have nothing, now that Poh Poh is gone.

The realization makes her miss a stroke and she is pushed

to the far wall. Shaking her head, she surfaces, choking, swallowing a mouthful of bubbles. She pulls herself out of the pool, reaching for a towel.

The phone rings. It is Tunku Mahmud.

'My dear, Iskandar Ismail's father just rang me. He seems to think you and his son are a bit out of sorts. I wouldn't want to get involved, but I just rang to check that everything's all right with you. What with all that I've told you. Are you all right?'

She isn't sure how to respond, despite being annoyed, especially now she and Iskandar are no longer an item. Yes, she's all right, she cheated on him and doesn't really feel guilty, not when he's been sleeping with her and his wife all this time. But then again, it's not like Jasmine ever had any claim over him. Perhaps once, a long time ago, but not now, not recently. If anything, she owes his wife an apology, but hell, Jasmine doesn't own him, and now it's all over.

Over.

'I'm all right, Tunku, thanks for asking.'

'Well, that's good to hear. I'm only concerned about you, you know. These people, well, I would be the last one to get between you and that man. But I thought you should know, just in case no one's told you: his father is serious about him running for office. I gather it will happen soon. You could end up being some cabinet minister's wife in a year or two. If you must. Or not.'

'Did you love my grandmother, Tunku?' She recalls the blank postcards in Poh Poh's old trunk. Perhaps the old man has his secrets too. Ones that involve him and Poh Poh, and a love that went unfulfilled.

There is a momentary silence before the old gentleman clears his throat. 'Love, you know, is . . . it's a funny thing, love. Your grandmother was a good woman. A very good woman. She always stood up for you, no matter what. You should know that.'

A cabinet minister's wife. If she says yes to Iskandar, which she probably still could. Then she would belong to someone and something much greater than Phoenix. A world she cannot imagine being part of. Of course, it would mean a lot of interminable weddings and small talk, nodding to other ministers' wives, and biting her tongue each time they coo over some small thing, or comparing husbands and festive hampers from rich beneficiaries, shaking small children's hands and nodding, always nodding, in approval of things that don't matter. Jasmine can't imagine anything worse, the idea forming a lump in her throat. She quickly says goodbye, and rushes to the bathroom to throw up.

She wipes the back of her hand across her mouth, feeling wretched and woozy. Leaning back from the toilet bowl, she collapses against the cool, tiled bathroom wall. This has been happening a little too often of late. She calculates the days, reeling her thoughts backward to the last few times she had sex – with Iskandar, then Kuan Yew.

Her period is two weeks late.

She feels short of breath. No, no, no, no, no. This can't be, it mustn't be. Not now. Her period always arrives with clockwork precision. A fortnight's delay is terrifying, though it could just be caused by stress. Or maybe it's peri-menopause.

Tomorrow, she'll get a pregnancy test. She's got to find out as soon as possible and get things taken care of. A pregnancy has no place in her life. She's never wanted babies. She has no time for it. No motherly instinct. No desire for something clawing and pulling at her all the time, like those toddlers she sees on weekends with their mums, always needy and crying and sweaty in their prams. Or running away across shopping mall floors, their mothers tearing after them, weaving through crowds.

A baby is yet one more thing she doesn't need.

12

That night, Jasmine dreams of babies and children, her own childhood memories mingling with images of mothers, infants glued to their breasts, sucking the life out of them. Toddlers and kindergarten herds, chasing her through a corridor as she runs barefoot down a passage of squelching mud, away from their high-pitched screaming.

She wakes in a fright, her skin damp from sweat, sheets tangled round her body. It is the phone again. She wants to throw it across the damned room, but instead reaches for it by instinct. It's Kevin, an urgent edge in his voice: 'Have you seen the news? Bring up the *Market Watch*'s homepage.'

The story was written by Rebecca Tan, the snobby swan, but has now been picked up by apparently every major daily and news portal across the country: 'Phoenix heiress faces challenge over murky past.'

Jasmine feels her heartbeat quicken, bubbles of trepidation rising in her throat.

Information has surfaced that Jasmine Leong, heir apparent to Phoenix Berhad, may be challenged in her assumed appointment as the company's CEO. Our investigations have revealed that Jasmine Leong's official

*birth certificate names her as the child of the late Madam
Leong, the company's CEO, who passed away last week
after Phoenix's illustrious public listing on the Kuala
Lumpur Stock Exchange. However, sources indicate that
Miss Leong may in fact be the daughter of the late David
Leong, Madam Leong's only son, who was killed in the
KL riots on 13 May 1969. The identity of her birth
mother is unknown, although it is believed she was
Malay. David Leong allegedly converted to Islam prior to
marrying the unnamed woman.*

'The goddamn bitch,' Jasmine growls. 'How the fuck did she
find out?'

'She must have done some digging. You know how reporters
are. And this Rebecca woman has quite a reputation for
exposés.'

Jasmine's mind races. 'But she must have known to look
before she could find anything. Or somebody spoke to her. Oh
no,' she sighs, sucking her teeth. 'Iskandar.'

*

When he arrives at her condo, Iskandar looks gaunt and tired,
grey shadows beneath his eyes. Although clean-shaven, he
appears to have had very little sleep. Jasmine detects the sweet,
lingering whiff of whisky on his breath.

'What the hell, Iska? What did you tell her?' Jasmine is still in
her nightclothes, her T-shirt from last night crumpled, hair in
disarray. He came over as soon as she rang, her voice cold with
anger.

He looks at her, his face drawn, eyes wounded. 'I didn't do

it, sayang. How could you think I would do such a thing? I've never even met the woman.'

She winces, the term of endearment too familiar. This is the first time he has been to her condo since she threw him out.

He walks to the kitchen, padding across the floor with weary footsteps. She hears him open a cupboard and shut it, the soft, sticky thud of the fridge door. He returns with empty glass in hand. 'There's no ice. Your freezer's empty.'

'It's not even lunchtime. Isn't it a bit early, even for you?'

They sit on the couch, saying nothing for a few minutes, a hollow chasm between them. Yet Jasmine can feel the heat of his presence emanating from beneath his shirt. He clenches his teeth, flexing the muscles in his jaw.

'Is this why you won't marry me?' His eyes are fixed on the carpet. 'Why you are giving up on us?'

'I am not Muslim.' Her voice is heavy and leaden. 'I don't care what my parents were. They didn't bring me up. I'm not going to let other people tell me who I am.'

'But . . . it's the truth, isn't it? You can't deny it now. Whether you like it or not. I don't understand, this should make things easier for you. For us. You don't have to become something you already are. And it's not like things would change between us. No one can tell us what to do behind closed doors.'

Except now there is a door between them in the shape of Kuan Yew, a shape even more familiar to her now than Iskandar. A bright silhouette that reminds her of where she really comes from. One that doesn't require her to choose between gods or give up her own desire to make Poh Poh proud.

'Your people killed my father.' She remembers what Tunku

Mahmud told her. 'How can you think I want anything to do with that?'

He stares back, disbelief in his eyes. 'My people? Your mother was Malay, for fuck's sake, Jasmine. You can't just hate us all. That would mean hating half of yourself.'

'I was robbed of my father. I never knew him.' Her eyes brim with tears. 'I don't know that woman either. They're just shadows. They're not who I am, even if I am their blood and bone. But the parts of me that I know, these people are not that.'

He reaches for her and pulls her close, leaning back on the cushions, hands cradling her body. She lets out a long wail, her torso shaking, as he shushes her, rocking, as if soothing a child. After a while, he leans back, stretching out, willing her to lie with him on the couch, stroking her back. He lets her cry until her weeping recedes into tiny sobs.

'Marry me,' he whispers. She answers only with small, ragged gasps.

'Marry me and all this won't matter. I love you, I always have.'

As if all that mattered these days were the two of them. Not Phoenix, not all those years she has tried to make herself matter to him, to Poh Poh. The hours she has spent making do without him, putting herself together every time she cracked. The black holes in their loving that still remain, perhaps never to be filled, even if they get married. Because their togetherness might not survive it.

She realizes he is no hero, despite his name. Iskandar, Alexander: no protector of hers, anyway. He was only a reprieve all this time. A safe berth for when things got too stormy. A familiar presence that required little effort, in truth, the road of their affair long rutted with wheel tracks to follow, even with eyes half-closed. They knew which potholes to best avoid, when to veer onto the verge.

'You're only in love with the idea of us,' she says, gathering herself and sitting up. She turns to him, cupping his wan face in her hands. 'We should have ended a long time ago. Neither of us can save the other.' They never grew out of their college ways, the messy, disjointed impermanence of it, knowing that there was always somewhere else to be after this, after them.

She will always love him, in some corner of her being. The place where all good things are kept, despite the many hours and years of longing that sit between them. He is the rare happiness found in her youth. But now they have grown older without realizing it. Time has crept up and made them defunct, obsolete. A thing that has no use in their lives any more, like pagers and Pac-Man and VCRs.

Except . . . there might be a baby. A new life, something she is still unsure of. So she doesn't tell him. Not yet. One more secret between them will not hurt at this point.

*

The aunties are full of panic and outrage.

'How can this . . . this paper be so irresponsible? Oh my dear, I'm so sorry I'm so far away.' On the computer screen, Seh Gu appears incomplete, her pencilled eyebrows missing. It is early evening in Vancouver.

But here in Malaysia, Tai Gu is a stalagmite, twisted and steadfast.

'You need to resign and let Kevin take over.'

'It's horrific, they cannot do this to you. To us. This is the twenty-first century!' Seh Gu shouts, winding a tea towel around her fists. 'What do they expect us to do? If we suddenly started making chicken bak kwa, would they let up? Then it wouldn't be un-halal, would it?'

Tai Gu sucks her teeth. 'Canadians. As if we would ever give up our heritage just to appease these people. And as if they would ever believe us even if we tried. Jasmine, you need to step aside and this will all blow over. Malaysians have short memories. I will not let you ruin everything. I'll take over myself if I have to.'

'Oh, if only your Poh Poh were alive. She'd know what to do, she'd put them all in their places.' The corners of Seh Gu's eyes wrinkle with worry.

'Someone told the reporter,' Jasmine says. 'Someone who knew.' She glares at Tai Gu. 'You did this. What did you tell that reporter, Tai Gu?'

Tai Gu's cheeks start to twitch, her lips tremble. 'How little you still fail to understand. If I had found out, this would never have seen the light of day. Never. Are you mad? To risk everything and destroy us?'

Jasmine is seething with rage, but her aunt's words make sense. None of the people around her, her aunts, Iskandar, betrayed her after all.

By afternoon, things worsen. The religious right-wing polit- ical party calls for the Syariah Court's intervention. They want to claim Jasmine as one of their own, save her from the brink of eternal damnation. Liberals scream injustice. Lawyers weigh in on the constitution. Even the prime minister is asked to comment; the media catch him at a ribbon-cutting ceremony for a fish canning factory in Terengganu, the Malay heartland. The man has no principles, the vote his only concern; he is non-committal, but that could change. Jasmine is a national headline. All afternoon, she sits in her office, the doors firmly shut, away from everyone's view. Even Mr Chew knows not to approach her.

Her phone is full of messages ignored, from Kevin, her aunts, the merchant bankers, Phoenix's traders and reporters. She cannot yet bring herself to confront them all.

The only time she picks up a call is when Kuan Yew's name flashes on the screen.

'Jasmine . . .'

At the sound of his voice, she lets out a small sob and before long she is crying, small wails escaping her lips.

He listens in silence until she quietens herself, her breath now ragged. Finally, he says, 'Tell me where to be, and I'll come see you.'

'I'm sorry. I don't know what came over me.' She is embarrassed by herself. It isn't like her to cry in front of someone else, except Iskandar. And even then, it was always because of their impossible situation. Never something like this. Poh Poh didn't condone such weakness.

'Hey, it's just me, Jasmine. I've seen you cry before. Remember the time you fell off that darned swing in kindergarten?'

The memory makes her giggle. She had been trying to impress April Kamila, their school Queen Bee. The other girl had challenged her to a who-can-swing-higher competition one day during recess. Jasmine had jumped at the chance, hoping April would then become her friend. Only Jasmine's dress that day had been too slippery, and as soon as the swing arced high in the air, she found herself slipping and had to let go, landing on the ground with a thud. It was Kuan Yew who had rushed to her aid then, propping her up on her slow limp to the principal's office. She can still recall April's mocking laughter trailing her all the way across the school lawn.

'What on earth did you ever see in April Kamila, Kuan Yew?' Jasmine had heard the pair dated briefly towards the end of secondary school. But she was already abroad at the time.

'She was cute. And she liked me. Besides, you weren't around any more,' he says, chuckling.

His words make her hesitate. Kuan Yew can be more, she realizes. Someone she can possibly share a life with, unlike Iskandar. Someone who will always be there, and perhaps place her first. Someone she can call her own.

'Thank you, Kuan Yew,' she says. 'I needed that.'

'So, I'll see you later then, yes? Then at least I can hand you the Kleenex, if you feel like crying some more. Or maybe stop you from breaking all your crockery,' he teases.

She hangs up, letting out a small sigh. If things are to move forward with Kuan Yew, she must tell him the whole truth.

As the trading day closes, Phoenix's stock price falls ten per cent. Not too bad, actually, given the circumstances. Right now, there is no real threat to the company's prospects. Just Tai Gu insisting she resigns. People can think what they want, Jasmine figures. The market won't care as long as Phoenix is making money, even the Malay shareholding public. Muslim pension funds aren't invested anyway, thanks to Phoenix's non-halal bak kwa. To them, Phoenix is as unkosher as that beer brewery in Sungai Way, or the conglomerate that owns casinos across half of Southeast Asia.

But a part of her knows that the public is fickle, its temperament easily swayed. Her life is now a dry field of tinder, waiting for a spark to burn it all to the ground, leaving her exposed, stripped of her armour. Secrets may not survive its assault.

*

The swan is dressed in a muted grey trouser suit, her fiery lipstick the only dash of colour. She walks across the restaurant in short, quick strides, her gaze fixed on Jasmine.

'Thank you for meeting me.' Jasmine shifts in her seat.

Rebecca Tan scrutinizes the room. The restaurant is empty except for two other tables closer to its entrance, out of earshot.

'I figured you would call me eventually,' the reporter says.

Jasmine can tell from her restrained composure that Rebecca Tan is used to difficult conversations. The woman is stone-faced, braced for a tirade.

Jasmine gets straight to the point. 'How did you know?'

Rebecca's face breaks into a sly smile. 'It's always the jealous ones that give things away. It's not difficult to find information these days. I just put two and two together after speaking to your aunt. Look, I know this puts you in a difficult position.' Rebecca places her hands on the table, fingers interlaced. 'But I was just doing my job.'

'Difficult?' Jasmine retorts, her voice low, face twisted into a grimace. 'Difficult doesn't even cut it. But you already knew that, didn't you? What have you got against me anyway? What have I ever done to you to deserve this?'

Rebecca's eyes narrow, her smile now spreading across her face.

'Listen, you're just another story to me. For a while, I thought you might be someone I could push, you know, as a model female entrepreneur, since there aren't many out there who are up to scratch. At least, not in this country. We're hardly given a chance, unless the men give us permission.' Her face hardens.

'Your mother was a GRO,' Jasmine growls, voice full of stones. She has done her homework too. Rebecca Tan's mother used to be a famous Guest Relations Officer, the moniker used for bar girls in the top KL karaoke joints during the eighties. 'You know perfectly well what this information would do to someone like you. Like me. People are afraid of us. They admire our gumption. They think we're gutsy and smart and brave, but if we slip up, there it is. What do you expect from the daughter of a bar girl? Survivors, is it? That's what they call us?'

Rebecca lets out a derisive laugh. 'Us? What do you know about growing up like me? Kids used to call me names in the playground. All sorts of names. Daughter of a hooker, and I didn't even know what that meant. I had to look it up in the dictionary, behind some bookshelf in the school library. There's no "us", Miss Leong. My mother put a roof over my head, did the best she could. But mothers aren't perfect. Far from it. Mine was the reason I had no friends in school.'

Jasmine is quiet. This woman is like her in some ways, always on the outside looking in. She draws in a breath. 'At least you have one. I never even met mine.'

'Better none than one you're ashamed of, Miss Leong. I used to tell people mine wasn't my real mother. That I was adopted. Just so the other kids would maybe talk to me. Because their mothers told them I was a child of a whore. I used to wish my mother would die sometimes. Except I loved her. I still do. But it's never been easy between the two of us.'

Jasmine lowers her head, lips pursed. The reporter's words have unsettled her. Yet her curiosity about her own mother persists. 'I'm sorry to hear that. But I guess I still need to know about mine.'

The reporter scrawls in her notepad, tearing out a page. 'Here. She doesn't live too far away. Port Dickson. If it'll help.'

Jasmine stares at the slip of paper in the reporter's hand, hesitating for a moment. It seems life is not done yet with tossing curve balls her way. But she knows dodging this one may leave her permanently curious. So she reaches out and takes the note from the reporter, hastily stuffing it into her handbag. She'll deal with it, eventually. After that other niggling unknown in her life has become clearer.

*

Sunset is the time of day Jasmine loves most, on the rare occasion she is home for it. As she sits on her balcony, watching the sky turn rosy and violet, the world seems a kinder place in the gloaming, done with its ravages for the day.

But this evening, it is pouring, no sunset in sight. She stares out at the whiteness of rain fog through her sliding doors, the sheets of water obscuring her view of the city. It is growing dark.

She sips at a glass of red wine in her hand. The tests came back positive, all five of them. The sticks are lined up on the coffee table, all with two pink stripes each on their displays. Positive, pregnant, with child; baby, you're having a baby!

Blindsided at forty-one. This is a problem she did not antici-
pate. And also a chance she will likely never get again.

But surely the odds of her having this child are slim, given
her circumstances. She's a little too old. It would be risky. The
doctors will probably advise her against it, tell her to get an
abortion. Or maybe those . . . those tests they do with some
long needle inserted into your womb would determine some
abnormality. Because women aren't meant to be new mothers
this late in life. And if she has the baby, she will be over sixty
by the time the child graduates from college. What if she dies
before then? It wouldn't be fair to the child. After all, Poh Poh
is dead, and Tai Gu is hardly the sort who would take a child
in. Unless Kevin doesn't have kids of his own by then, which
is likely. Maybe then, maybe Tai Gu would.

But why is Jasmine even thinking about that? She's not
having this baby, she can't. The mere thought of it is just
ridiculous. She can barely cook a meal to feed herself, let alone
some wailing toddler. Nothing in her own experience has
equipped her for something like this. She has never even held
an infant, always opting to view other people's kids at arm's
length, a forced smile on her face, proclaiming their cuteness.
They all look alike to her.

And what terrible, noisy things children are. Delightful for
only a few moments before turning into screeching monsters.
She wishes they didn't allow them in Business Class. If there
were flights with no children, Jasmine would be first in the
queue.

She supposes that people have them for security. Because it
is the thing to do. So someone will take care of you in your
old age. But she doesn't need a child for that. She has enough

money to ensure a comfortable retirement at some point. An elderly community where they play canasta and bingo all day, in some foreign country where those things exist. Not here, not in Malaysia, where the elderly seem to potter around dated houses, bumping into fading furniture, waiting for their children to turn up.

Or perhaps she could end up like Poh Poh, working till her very last breath. That would be fine, she surmises. Here and then gone, the slow descent into incapacity dispensed with.

Except Jasmine doesn't plan on a life without sex. Affairs, or flings – she's good at those. She can continue to have them for at least the next, oh, fifteen or so years. Times have changed. Women no longer need to shrink into old age.

No. There is no question about it. This child is not going to happen.

And right now, there is Kuan Yew. The last thing their situation needs is a baby, especially when it's not even his. They were careful, or he was, at least. But the prospect of Kuan Yew hearing about Iskandar from someone else is a possibility she doesn't want to risk. She must tell him before she loses the courage to do so, even if it means he might walk away. They have known each other far too long for things to end because of a lie.

But when Kuan Yew arrives at her condo, he is handsome and worried, planting kisses in her hair and on her forehead as they embrace. She wants to stay enveloped in him, pretend that the rest of her, the new being inside of her, doesn't exist.

It is his first time here. She realizes how careless her life must look, with its overflowing ashtray and magazines scattered all over the coffee table. Her fridge full of takeaway containers. Shoes tossed, unshelved, just by her front door.

The rain has receded to a light drizzle, tiny clouds of mist now shrouding the tops of trees. Their outlines are still visible in the dark. Walking out onto the balcony, he takes in the view.

'KL looks so perfectly harmless from here,' he says, leaning his body over the railing. 'I should have chosen to live further out from the centre.'

She rests her head on his arm as they stand, watching the macaques play a round of tag on the brightly lit tennis court below. The primates are out late this evening; perhaps the rain thwarted their earlier plans.

He laughs. 'You could almost believe we aren't in the city. Those guys must be hazardous to players.'

It is why the court is often empty, most of the complex's residents too terrified to battle the monkeys. Instead, they drive out to the nearby Lake Club.

She leads him not to the couch, but the dining table. She doesn't know how to begin.

'You've had one hell of a day,' he says, concern in his eyes.

She stares at her tangled fingers on her lap, her nails beginning to sink into her palms. Her voice, when she finds it, is barely audible. 'I need to tell you about Iskandar Ismail.'

Half a lifetime, retold in an hour and change, the details left out, the highlights skimmed over. She does not tell him about the pregnancy. At first, there is curiosity, then disappointment, in his eyes as he sits in silence, listening. She ends with 'I know now that it is truly over.'

He is quiet, picking at the fringe of the place mat in front of him. A muscle twitches in the side of his jaw. The wind blows a gentle breeze into the living room, billowing the curtains, scattering a light spray of rain onto the floor. She gets up to shut the sliding doors. The hum of the air conditioning fills their silence. Her stomach growls. He looks up. 'You're hungry,' he says. It wasn't a question. 'I presume your fridge is empty.'

She is wide-eyed and contrite, as if caught in a lie.

He gets up and grabs his car keys. 'C'mon, let's go. You're coming for a ride.'

He takes her to the nearest grocery store and fills up a trolley with fresh produce. Things that need dicing and stewing and cooking, along with cereal, milk, fruit, yoghurt, coffee. She follows him wordlessly, only nodding in reply once or twice when asked for her preferences.

Back at the condo, he stores the shopping away, arranging things in cupboards. 'Dry goods here, canned over there, pasta . . .'

She still merely nods, confused and hopeful.

He takes out some vegetables, pork mince and noodles. 'You're gonna help me this time.'

He directs her on how to slice the spring onions, mushrooms and onions till her eyes water from the vapours. He cooks a simple dish of Hakka noodles – minced pork braised with garlic, sesame oil and fish sauce. A side of stir-fried kai lan for greens, topped with crispy fried onions for extra crunch. While he prepares the meal, he throws an occasional sidelong glance at her without saying a word. She wonders what is going through his head.

No other man has been in her apartment except Iskandar. Yet Kuan Yew's presence seems strangely natural, as if he has always belonged there. Perhaps it is the ease with which he assumes his place in a room, in the world. A man who has had to fight for his seat at every table doesn't ask for permission.

Maybe having someone always by her side isn't such a bad thing. Technically, she isn't alone any more, not with the baby now growing inside her. The one she hasn't decided to keep. She ponders the reaction Kuan Yew might have if she tells him and assumes he will probably run for the hills.

But there's no point thinking about that now. A baby is even further from her plans than a man in her life. Even though she hadn't counted on another lover so soon after Iskandar, this one seems too good to let slip away. Except she doesn't know now whether he will stay.

When dinner is served, she wolfs down her meal. This time, he does the same.

At last, he looks up, his bowl clean. He is wearing a sad, angry smile on his face. 'You're something else, you know that?'

She starts to cry in small, quiet sobs.

'You're smart, determined, successful and rich. Yet you keep running and looking over your shoulder. Just stop.'

'I've messed everything up. I . . . you've been nothing but good to me, even though it's been years since we last saw each other and I've—'

'I'm a grown man, Jasmine. I can take care of myself. No one forced me to be here. But you . . . do you know why you are?' He lifts her face to meet his gaze.

'You don't deserve this . . . this mess that I've sucked you into. I don't know why I did it, I shouldn't have, but you . . . you've been nothing but kind and sweet and so honest and, and handsome . . .' Her voice trails off, her eyes fixed on a spot she has been rubbing on the carpet with her big toe.

His laugh is slow and deep. 'You're a hot little mess. You know that?'

Wiping the tears from her eyes with a serviette, he leads her to the couch. They sit down, Jasmine curling into his lap. She realizes she knows nothing about his more recent past.

'Tell me about Australia,' she says. She feels weary yet unwilling to succumb to sleep despite the tiredness in her bones.

'It has its pluses, but it's not like being here. I stayed away from Malaysia for years. I wasn't sure about coming back at first, but I had no choice. My father's health got worse after my mother died. My siblings have cared for them all this time. Now it's my turn. It's the least I can do. So I'm here, at least for a while.'

'Is there somebody in Australia waiting for you?' She had never thought to ask before.

He hesitates for a moment before replying. 'There were women. Some more special than others. I don't know how to explain it. Even the Asian ones were . . . different. They don't understand what it feels like to sit next to a stinking drain and eat lok-lok from a plastic plate balanced on your lap, you know. Or char kway teow from a wok that looks like it hasn't been scrubbed in decades.'

She lets out a tiny laugh.

'And I always wondered how they would react if they ever came home with me. To see my family, where we grew up. I mean, yes, my parents have a proper house now, they've had one for years. But their old ways never left them. Their bathroom still has a tub with a dipper, for God's sake, despite the rain showers we installed.'

172

Jasmine remembers those cold baths as a child. The ones where Ah Tin sometimes poured a steaming kettle or two into a large basin filled with cold tap water. Jasmine used to shut her eyes tight, cringing from the deluge Ah Tin sloshed over her head. 'Aiyoh, stop your dancing!' Ah Tin would say, Jasmine doing a small jig.

'I guess my Aussie courage ran short at bringing home foreign girlfriends, even if they were Asian,' Kuan Yew says, wistfulness in his gaze.

'You could have easily found a good woman from Ipoh.'

'By the time I came back, most of them were married,' he says with a laugh. 'Even April Kamila.' The pretty girl with the long, long pigtails that every boy in their school used to covet. The original Queen Bee.

'Whatever happened to her?'

'Oh, she runs the clinic in town. Wears a hijab, has three kids. One of them interviewed with me at RSE last week. Smart fella, looks like the dad, but a little full of himself, like his mum; I think I knocked him down a gentle peg or two. Her husband left her, you know, for another woman,' Kuan Yew says. 'She refused to let him take a second wife.'

Just like Jasmine might have been.

Feeling her tense, he adds, 'I don't judge it. I can't understand it myself, but for some people, I guess it works.'

'Iskandar is divorcing his wife.'

He is quiet for a moment before he responds, his voice gentle: 'Then what's stopping you, Jasmine? Really?'

She turns to look at him, disbelief in her eyes. 'And be Muslim?'

'So what? I mean yes, it's a big deal. But is it, really? In this country? As long as you two have an understanding, just do the necessary when you're out and about. Indoors, no one can tell you what to do. This country's so elastic anyway. There are plenty of people who make that sort of thing work.'

'You mean you would do it? If you were in the same situation?'

He shrugs his shoulders. 'If I loved her, probably yes. I'm not religious. But if I loved her, I'd have to respect where she comes from. Maybe it could work, or maybe we could just go to Australia and live, where it wouldn't matter as much.'

'But what if you had kids?'

'I guess if I were ever to take that sort of leap, the woman would have to be somewhat liberal. Maybe the kid could be exposed to all religions. Decide what they wanna be when they grow up.'

'Not here, then.'

'Not here would be easier. Actually, about your situation . . .'

She lets out a sigh. 'It's gonna get worse, isn't it?'

'It could. But you've got options, luckily. If the shit hits the fan, maybe think about getting out.'

'You mean, leave Malaysia? And go where?'

He gestures with his hands, palms open. 'World's your oyster. Get a new citizenship. Somewhere it won't matter. Or where people won't care. The world's getting smaller, but it's still a big place.'

'And give up Phoenix?'

'That's the least of your worries. I told you, get me that seat on your board. I'll help you sort it out.'

What about you and me? she thinks. *And what if I'm having a baby?* Would he still want to be a part of her life then?

'It's not fair,' she whispers. 'Why do people who don't even care about me have a say in how I live my life?'

'Welcome to the real world, Jasmine Leong. The playing ground is uneven. But you've at least got money. That helps. Believe me. You just gotta find your sea legs.' He bites his lip, then continues: 'And maybe . . . learn to cook. Just in case you need to hole up on some desert island.'

13

She spends the next day at work in a daze, scarcely able to concentrate. There are meetings with the merchant bankers, their curious concern at the revelation of her past apparent in the constant tugging of their shirtsleeves, the furtive glances when they think she isn't watching. The staff are no better, their heads quick to bow when she passes them in the corridors. At 5 p.m. sharp, she switches off her computer and heads home, unable any longer to withstand the hushed wall of mounting questions whispered outside her door.

Reaching her condominium complex, Jasmine slows at the sight of a throng of people crowding the security gantry. Spotting her car, cameras flash. Reporters. She speeds past them and into the underground car park, her heart pounding in swift beats. She dials Kevin. He picks up straight away.

'Kev, the media have found out where I live.'

'I'm here, in KL. I flew in last night. Get to your condo, and don't leave. See you in twenty minutes.'

She is fortunate that her unit doesn't face the front of the complex.

On her balcony, she is away from prying eyes.

When Kevin arrives, she is already on her third bag of potato crisps.

'Whoa, no booze?' He hugs her close.

'I'm pregnant.'

'What?'

'I'm fucking pregnant. And Kuan Yew knows now about Iskandar, but didn't yell at me. He bought me groceries instead. Check my cupboards. I have tons of food. And – I'm pregnant.'

Kevin blinks, shaking his head. 'Jesus, Superman. I was gone for a week. What the hell?'

Jasmine reaches into the bottom of her bag of chips. Only crumbs left. She sucks on her salt-crusted fingers, then lifts the bag, emptying its remaining contents into her mouth.

Kevin shows her the latest news bulletin.

Someone, a stranger, is calling for Jasmine's origins to be reviewed. The man is wearing a bright red shirt, his head adorned with a matching bandana, the words 'Hidup Melayu!' emblazoned across it. Long live Malays. The crowd surrounding him chant the phrase in unison, raising their fisted arms.

'This is the work of the Chinese party! Of Satan! How can this woman refuse to acknowledge the truth? She is Muslim! Her mother is Malay! She cannot head a company that makes pork jerky! It's unhalal! What an insult this is to Islam!'

The video clip freezes on a shot of the agitator, sweat prickling his brow. He is squat and dark-skinned, with bulging eyes. A thick, bushy moustache hides his lips. His open mouth accentuates a double chin.

She is sure the ruling party is behind it, using one of their members as a proxy for the cause.

'He's your mother's husband.'

Kevin pulls up a news story on his phone. Burhanuddin Ishak is the Member of Parliament for Port Dickson. There is

177

a photo of him holding up a copy of Jasmine's parents' marriage certificate, clearly obtained from his wife.

Scrolling through the news story, Kevin reads aloud. 'It says that his wife, Salmah Ibrahim, is distraught at the knowledge of her child – you – growing up a kafir.'

Jasmine is stunned, shaking her head, her empty bag of chips dropping to the floor.

'Jasmine, we've got to get you a lawyer. One who has nothing to do with Phoenix. We don't need my mum getting involved any more than she needs to. You've got enough trouble with this man already.'

'Tunku Mahmud.' She is thinking aloud. 'He and Poh Poh got me into this mess. Maybe he'll know how to get me out of it.'

*

In Tunku Mahmud's KL office, the old man sits at the head of a long table, wearing a flagging expression. The attorney, Malik Harun, is a tiny, wizened man with close-set eyes and a tapering nose, but there is kindness in his thin smile. His slight build takes up little room on the chair.

Jasmine sits across from the lawyer, jiggling her left leg, the right one folded underneath her.

Malik Harun shuffles his papers. 'There are precedents for cases like yours, Miss Leong, ones where the defendants have won. But yours is unique.' He scans his notes, underlining sections with a red pen. 'In your case, your father was Muslim when he died. In some others, the parent converted after the child was older. So yours is a little more complicated. And there is the question of your birth certificate.'

Tunku Mahmud shifts in his seat, the springs squeaking beneath his weight.

The lawyer explains that the real problem will occur when Jasmine dies.

'Right now, in the eyes of Syariah, you are illegitimate, if they can even prove you are this Daud Abdullah and Salmah Ibrahim's child. You were conceived before your mother and father got married.'

'DNA,' Jasmine whispers.

'I'm sorry?'

'It can't be that hard these days.'

Malik Harun's eyes cloud over. 'Right. Well, let's just assume for now that they will be able to.' He clears his throat. 'As I was saying, you're illegitimate. Which means that A) you're still Muslim, and B) you don't stand to inherit anything from your father.'

'But I already have. My grandmother's will took care of that. My father's shares are already mine. And I'll be damned if I let anyone take that away from me.'

'Yes, yes, Tunku Mahmud has briefed me. So, fortunately, that's one problem we don't have to deal with. But, if you die before your mother . . .' He hesitates, entering fragile territory. 'If you die before your mother, and you are buried according to Muslim rites, she will inherit everything. Unless you have a husband and children.'

'I am Chinese, Tuan Malik. I was brought up Chinese and Christian. There is nothing Muslim about me. I run a non-halal company, for God's sake. And I've worked hard, so hard all these years . . .'

Malik Harun holds up his hand. 'Please, call me Malik. I

179

know. This whole thing would have been a non-issue if no one found out. This man, this Burhanuddin, and your mother, they obviously want something. He's a slimy bastard, excuse my language. I checked him out. A lackey with no real political prospects. Obviously using you to gain brownie points and attention. Everyone knows who he is now, overnight. And I know no one wants to talk about death, but the truth is that, the way this country is heading, if something happens to you, unless this man and your mother are dealt with, they will likely challenge your burial. Or their relatives might, later down the line. And they just might win.'

Jasmine buries her face in her hands.

'If you want me to help you, I need to know everything so we aren't blindsided.' His eyes dart from Jasmine to the Tunku. 'No secrets, or I cannot help you.'

Jasmine draws a long, deep breath before speaking. 'Well, there's the matter of Iskandar Ismail,' she says, shooting a glance at the Tunku. 'He and I . . . well, we used to see each other.'

'Will he be a problem?' Malik scribbles in his legal pad.

'I'm not sure. We've broken things off, anyway. He tried to get me to marry him. But I turned him down. I didn't want to convert, you see.'

The lawyer nods. 'Anything else?'

Jasmine swallows hard, fixing her stare on the table. 'I might be having his baby.'

Malik's little eyes widen. He exchanges looks with the Tunku. 'Oh,' he utters. 'I see. Who knows this?'

'Only Kevin, and he can be trusted.'

'You're sure the father is Iskandar Ismail?'

'I think so. Most likely.'

'Well, we need to be certain. You need to see a doctor as soon as possible. Someone who will keep this quiet. I'll give you a name. A baby will complicate matters. Even if you manage to make the problem of your mother and her husband go away somehow, your child will be Muslim on account of its father. You need to think about that. Especially given that you're worth at least a quarter of a billion ringgit.'

After their meeting, Tunku Mahmud walks Malik Harun to the door. Returning, he finds Jasmine still in her seat, her mouth set in a grim line.

'I am so sorry for everything, my dear. If we had known things would turn out this way . . .' He reaches out for her hand.

She is exhausted, a slow numbness creeping up her spine. 'Well, it wasn't as if you could make my mother disappear for ever,' she mumbles, patting the old man's hand.

*

The waiting room smells like disinfectant and judgement. Jasmine stems the bile rising in her throat, waving a bottle of mentholated oils under her nose. She sucks on a dried sour plum. Old remedies for an age-old problem.

Sitting there on the cushioned row of chairs, she flips through an issue of a fashion weekly. A wide pair of dark sunglasses conceals her eyes. Her hair is piled in a messy bun, her face bare of make-up. She is dressed in gym clothes, the ones she rarely wears. She doesn't need anyone recognizing her today.

The society pages in the back of the magazine have a story on Phoenix's gala dinner, the one after their public listing. There is a gallery of photos, the usual suspects. One picture of the Leongs, all dressed in their finery, Jasmine at the centre. How long ago now that seems. A laughing Tunku Mahmud and some other dignitary, hands behind their backs, hiding their flutes of champagne. Tai Gu and Seh Gu holding up their glasses in a toast. Rebecca Tan and a Malay man with a pompous smirk.

Jasmine lifts her sunglasses, heart beginning to pound. The man looks familiar. She has seen him somewhere. She looks up at the clock on the wall above the nurses' station. Five minutes before her doctor's appointment. Then it hits her. The man in the photo is her mother's husband. He was at the dinner.

She pulls out her phone and types a message to Rebecca Tan:

I need to see you again. Please.

The receptionist calls out her name: 'Ms Leong Lin Li.'

Jasmine grabs the magazine and shoves it into her bag. She walks in swift, short steps towards a door the nurse holds open.

'The doctor will see you now.'

In the examination room, Jasmine changes out of her clothes into a hospital gown, reaching behind to fasten its ties. It is a little chillier, a slight draught tickling her spine. She runs a hand down the front of her belly; it feels much the same as it always has, the small life inside not yet making its presence felt.

The doctor is a woman, perhaps in her mid-forties, with caramel skin: Dr Josephine Menezes. She gestures for Jasmine to get onto the examination table.

Lifting Jasmine's gown, the doctor spreads a gel on her belly, the cold making her stomach muscles contract. Dr Menezes holds an apparatus in her hand, moving it slowly across Jasmine's middle, glancing from time to time at a screen next to her head.

'There's your baby,' she says.

Jasmine peers at the display, uncertain of what she is meant to see.

'I know it doesn't look like much yet. I'd say you're about eight weeks along.'

Pinpricks tickle Jasmine's feet, crawling up her ankles. 'But that's not possible, I've only missed my last period . . .'

Dr Menezes glides the probe round Jasmine's belly. 'You're in your early forties, yes? You were probably just spotting.'

Jasmine's last period was rather light, actually. In fact, it was barely there. But she thought it was just peri-menopause. Not this. Not a baby.

Dr Menezes is looking at her now, lips drawn into her mouth. 'I take it you're not married?'

Jasmine stares at the tiny green pattern on her gown. 'No.'

The doctor is silent, nodding, as she completes the rest of her examination. After finishing, she presses a button on the machine and a printed image slides out of a slot. Dr Menezes inspects it for a short moment before handing it to Jasmine.

The image is blurry. A dark cavity surrounded by white, a tiny bean-like shape resting in its middle. A nebulous object that doesn't appear to be living.

Dr Menezes eyes her, reaching for another small probe. 'Let's see if we can hear a heartbeat. This is a Doppler.' She hands Jasmine a palm-sized speaker attached to a stick.

Holding the wand in one hand, the doctor moves it below

Jasmine's belly button. A whooshing sound rushes out of the speaker, then a faint chugging, like a train speeding down a faraway track.

'You don't often hear it at this stage, but I thought we'd give it a shot.' The doctor holds Jasmine in her steady gaze.

Jasmine raises the speaker to her left ear. The whooshing grows louder. The train continues on its rapid journey. She imagines wheels turning, a red locomotive, pulling its long column of carriages across a landscape of lush, green mountains.

'It's alive,' she whispers.

'Yes.' Dr Menezes clasps Jasmine's hands. 'Malik Harun told me about your case,' she says. 'Only because he wanted me to help you in any way that I can. I don't know what you want to do . . .'

'I can't keep it.'

'I thought you might say that.'

A hot tear trickles down Jasmine's cheek. 'I can't have this baby. Not now. Not like this. The father doesn't know. And my situation right now . . .'

The doctor nods. 'I understand. You shouldn't have to make choices like this. But if there is a way for you . . . I know this will mean uprooting your life.'

'I cannot risk having this baby. If I do, it'll be Muslim.'

'But alive,' says Dr Menezes.

'You think I'm being selfish.' Jasmine bites her lip.

'It is not my place to judge you. However, if you decide to go through with this, it is best you leave the country to have the procedure, because it is generally illegal here, except under certain circumstances. We don't let mothers decide on their own. Whatever you do, please, be safe. Remember: at your age, there is risk involved. But also, if you bring this baby to term, it may be the only chance that you get.'

The doctor talks her through pregnancy care. Pills and supplements, plenty of rest. No heavy lifting. No late nights. No booze, no caffeine. But all Jasmine can hear is the locomotive, its wheels churning against the whooping wind, hurtling its way over the sides of mountains, journeying into unknown territory.

*

She dreams of the train, a great crimson thing, spewing clouds of steam. This time, she is inside it, watching the landscape rush by, a ravine of deep emerald forest below. The passage feels perilous, the train speeding too fast, too close to the edge of the mountainside. Its rocking stirs the tea in her cup, making its milky surface swirl.

There is a rumbling ahead that grows louder, the keening screech of brakes. She looks out the window, her face pressed close to the glass, trying to see what lies ahead.

An explosion, then rolling thunder. Giant boulders spilling down the mountainside, threatening to hit the locomotive. Her carriage rocks hard, everything sliding off the tables. Jasmine braces for the collision.

She wakes in a sweat, her heart in her mouth.

It is Monday morning. The markets will open in two hours.

*

At 11 a.m., Rebecca Tan arrives at Phoenix. Jasmine welcomes the reporter into her office, a continental breakfast spread waiting.

'You didn't tell me you know my . . . stepfather,' Jasmine says. She points to the photo of Rebecca and Burhanuddin in the purloined copy of the magazine.

The other woman watches as Jasmine sips her orange juice, and skewers a piece of dragonfruit on her own plate, chewing with intent.

'What do you want from me, Ms Leong?'

'I'll give you an exclusive when this is all over. Right after we make the announcement to the stock exchange. You can publish it as soon as the market closes. But first, tell me everything you know about Burhanuddin Ishak.'

The reporter straightens, lowering her plate. 'A deal, then?'

'Yes. I'd rather it be you than anyone else.'

'Why?'

'Because, Miss Tan, you and I are alike. We can do better, were it not for some men who don't even know us. I want to give this to you. I know it will help with your bid to become editor. And I'd rather see you in that seat than some idiot reporter who only knows how to use Google.'

'What do you need to know?'

'I want to take him down.'

Rebecca Tan is silent for a minute, picking apart a Danish. She sips her tea before replying. 'The man is five-cents-two-apiece. Throw a stone in the ruling coalition's meetings and you'll hit ten more like him. Doesn't matter what race they are, they're all the same.' She lifts her gaze.

'That still doesn't give me any ammunition.'

Rebecca lets out a derisive laugh. 'Because people like you don't know where to look. You assume it needs to be complicated. Some dirty business deal, or backroom political manoeuvre that has to be exposed before you can destroy a man. When in truth, the answers are, almost always,' she says, leaning forward, 'in the bedroom. An actress, named Zizi Abdullah. The Chinese convert. You know her. Big on Instagram, loads of followers. Rumour is that he's planning to dump your mother for this young thing. But hey, one shouldn't be surprised any more. Happens every day, especially around here.'

'I suppose it would be too much to hope that there are any morals left in men like him.'

'Hah!' Rebecca sniffs. 'Morals. Those are only dragged out when they serve these bastards' purposes. Like now. The coalition knows it will lose the next election. They're desperate for anything that they think will help.'

'And that's me.'

'Unfortunately for you, yes. Look, if worst comes to worst, just leave. Seriously. I would. Leave all this behind and go build a life for yourself somewhere else.'

'But my home is here.'

'So what? It will always be here. This stinking, sinking mess of a place. If you come from the garbage dump, doesn't mean you gotta live in it. Some distance might even make it seem prettier by night.'

Jasmine reaches out in a handshake, looking Rebecca Tan in the eye. 'I owe you one.'

'Just get me that exclusive. And keep in touch after that. I have a feeling that, even if you do leave, you'll always be up to something interesting.'

*

Tai Gu is padding across the conference room carpet, her animal instincts keen. Jasmine sits at the table, mouth set in a grim line. The memory of her aunt stomping down Phoenix's corridor is still fresh in Jasmine's mind. Next to her, Kevin stares at the carpet, unable to meet his mother's glare.

'The Ipoh town councillor is not answering my calls.' Tai Gu's voice has a hard edge. 'We could lose millions, Jasmine, millions.' Their new housing project hangs in the balance. If news gets out, their stock will tank.

'But Jasmine's past has nothing to do with Phoenix,' Kevin retorts, fingers curled in frustration.

His mother's eyes flash. 'This is Malaysia, not Singapore, you idiot. It has everything to do with Phoenix. We're Chinese; we don't get to make the rules here. Until the whole fiasco about Jasmine's mother is resolved, no Muslim official is going to come near us. They don't need the controversy, especially when the party's position is shaky. This is what they've always done to us, made us pawns. And the voters are too blind to even see it.'

Jasmine knows Tai Gu is right. Still, she says, 'But what if I can find a way to shut this Burhanuddin character up?'

'You need to step down, Jasmine. I told you so already. There is no other way. Unless you don't mind being poor,' Tai Gu says with a sneer. 'I know what it's like not to have so much money. But do you? You grew up, both of you, with silver spoons in your mouths. Neither of you will survive this, not if our stock takes a beating.

'Your father was always weak. Your Poh Poh knew. But she refused to acknowledge it, even after you were born. I told her to let me help, but no. Of course not. I was not her son.'

'But none of this is Jasmine's fault,' Kevin says. 'We can't punish her, Ma, not after everything she has done for Phoenix for the last two decades. It's not fair.'

His mother stops pacing and turns on her heel. 'Son, there is nothing fair in this life. Especially not here. This is how it's been now for hundreds of years, even after independence. We got a raw deal. But what choice did we have? Return to China? No one wanted that. No one still does.'

'Maybe Kuan Yew is right,' Jasmine says, her voice determined.

Both Kevin and Tai Gu turn to look at her.

'Kuan Yew wants a stake in our company and a seat on our board. RSE will buy into Phoenix.'

Tai Gu's lips curl. 'Is he your boyfriend now? Is that it? You want your boyfriend to sit on our board? So you can gang up against me?'

'No.' Jasmine takes a deep breath. 'I will leave Phoenix, but on one condition: let me buy out the bak kwa business. It'll solve the problem, to some extent. I exit and take the non-halal business with me, maybe base it in some other country where they don't care who I am. Then the town councillor and all those other bastards won't have a leg to stand on. I am sure you can convince them to support you, Tai Gu. And Kuan Yew can help. We can trust him, I know we can.'

Her cousin and aunt stare at her.

'Jasmine, you shouldn't have to do this,' Kevin pleads.

'No, maybe she's right,' Tai Gu says. 'If we get the housing project off the ground, shareholders won't care that the bak kwa business gets carved out. The property deal is much larger. But it will cost you, Jasmine, now that we are listed. It might cost you everything that you have.'

'Then I won't have a choice but to make it work. Get some financing for the bak kwa expansion. I'm sure I can work something out. We can't let them win, Tai Gu. Not after all the work we've put in.'

'Ma, maybe we can all chip in,' Kevin offers. 'If we pool our money, we can easily take the bak kwa business abroad. Together.' He throws Jasmine a hopeful smile.

'But Kevin, I have a feeling,' Tai Gu says, turning to Jasmine, 'that your cousin may want to do this on her own.'

Jasmine meets her aunt's gaze, nodding. 'I'd like to see this through myself. For sentimental reasons. For Poh Poh. And for me. If I need to leave to save the company, I am taking a piece of it with me. On my terms. I'm not quite ready to give up on my own dreams yet. Not after all this time.'

Tai Gu grabs her bundle of papers, rapping the edges on the table into a neat stack. 'All right then, I'll agree, and I'll get the other board members to do the same, but I have my own condition: Kevin must come back.' She turns to look at her son. 'It's time you stepped up. No more living life like some bachelor. Get married, have children. You'll need heirs.'

'Tai Gu, Kevin's personal life shouldn't have anything to do with his job.' Jasmine places a protective hand on her cousin's arm. 'Shit, I shouldn't even have to do what I am about to, all because of these stupid rules made up by some men decades ago. Don't do this to your own son.'

'Ma, I'm sorry. I can't be who you want me to be.' A tear trickles down Kevin's cheek.

His mother walks to the door and pauses, hand on the handle. 'None of us can ever have everything we want, son. Life doesn't work like that. Especially if you want to get ahead.'

After Tai Gu leaves, Jasmine turns to her cousin, embracing him. 'I'm sorry, Wonder Woman, I'm so sorry,' she whispers.

Kevin sweeps his palm roughly over his face. 'I know I can't return her to the store, but do you think they'll entertain a request for an exchange?' He reaches for a crumpled ball of paper on the table, smoothing it out with his hands.

Jasmine drops down into a chair next to him, peering over his shoulder. 'What is that?'

'A letter. I wrote my mum a letter, about Matthias. Because I figured at least she could read it when she's ready. Except I don't think she ever will be.'

'You're her only child, Kev. She'll come round. It just might take a bit of time, that's all.'

'Did you know that my dad's met him? They get along like a house on fire.'

'Well, at least that's half your fan base taken care of.'

'The wonders of golf.'

'Well, if your mum's a true Leong, the way to her heart is through her stomach.' Jasmine lets out a soft laugh.

'Don't let them beat you, Jasmine. Fight back. You deserve to run this company.'

'Maybe. Or maybe I should just pick the battles I can win.'

14

It has been decades since Jasmine last visited Port Dickson, the seaside town long past its heyday, yet still struggling to reclaim its glory. There is an air of stagnation in the town centre, with its mid-century shophouses sporting faded signs. Most seem to be run by old people, the young nowhere in sight except for vacationers and locals huddled over picnics along the coast. The sea looks grey, mud in its swirl.

The house is a bungalow from the sixties, set back from its curled wrought-iron gate by a manicured front lawn. It is modest but tidy, its whitewashed walls only slightly discoloured with moss. Potted bougainvilleas line the front of the house with their profuse, garish blooms of fuchsia and orange.

Jasmine stands at the front gate, her car parked on the verge. A woman wearing a hijab emerges from the front door, waving at her to enter. As Jasmine walks up the short gravel path, she notices an old, gold-coloured Volvo parked there.

In the doorway the woman is holding her hands to her lips, tears threatening to fall. The likeness is slight, yet present, in her large oval eyes and full mouth. Jasmine offers her hands in a salam, clasping the woman's, bending low. She takes off her shoes at the entrance, stepping into the house.

Jasmine sits on a settee in the living room while Salmah

disappears into the kitchen. Silk flowers adorn tall vases on the floor in the corners of the room, dust collecting on their petals. The settee itself is a leaf-green Victorian knock-off, its bulky, curved proportions too big for the room, lace antimacassars on the arms. The carpet has a pattern of large flowers. The damask curtains are tied back, fringed by pom-pom tassels. A series of framed photographs sits on a side table: Salmah and Burhanuddin.

The room is stuffy and smells of stale air, its windows firmly shut.

Salmah re-enters, bearing a tray. On it is a tea service decorated with flowers and gold edging. Her husband will be coming home for dinner, and no, thank you, Jasmine will not stay. She has to be back in KL, a busy schedule ahead.

The older woman appears a little disappointed, but a small spark of relief passes across her eyes.

'Why did you leave me?' Jasmine says at last. 'Why didn't you keep me after my father died?'

'I had nothing. I could give you nothing then. A single mother in those days would have been shunned.'

'But you were married.' Jasmine's voice is cold.

'And he died. Daud and I were married and in love, yes, but we were so young. I was barely nineteen, and he was only twenty-one. We got married because of you. It was his idea.' She calls him by his Muslim name. There is a faraway quality in her voice when she speaks of him, as if recalling scenery from a long-ago holiday. Rolling hills, mountains covered in clouds, a bright bed of roses, vast paddy fields. 'He was staying with a friend, Allan Woo. Allan's father owned a coffin shop.'

'And those photographs from here? Port Dickson?' Jasmine tells her about the ones she found in her grandmother's album.

'Those were taken on the day he first proposed to me,' says Salmah. She was four weeks pregnant by then, yet it took her months to say yes. Even then, they told no one and married in secret at a kadi's office three days before the riots.

They don't speak of how her father died. The woman tells Jasmine it was years before she remarried. She became a school-teacher and moved to Port Dickson, perhaps because it reminded her of Daud. David. Eventually, she met Burhanuddin and settled down, but no children, despite their trying. Although it doesn't appear to upset her.

'Sometimes, I think, maybe, it was all for the best,' Salmah mutters.

Jasmine sets her teacup down with a sharp clink. 'You think it was better that my father died?'

'Of course not. I never meant for things to get that far, never intended to fall in love. But he was there, so patient and persistent, hesitant and shy. And gentle. Unlike the boys in Kampung Baru where I lived, always sneering and teasing as if they knew they could push me up against some wall when no one was looking. He didn't frighten me.'

'You used him.'

A shadow passes over her mother's face. 'Both of us were running away from our real lives, he from your grandmother, me from my parents and all the things that were choking us. But at some point, if he had lived, we would have had to face reality. Our families. I don't know if we would have survived that.'

'And now I don't know if I will,' Jasmine says.

Her mother reaches out, clasping Jasmine's hands. 'Yes, I heard. But this is what your father wanted. You're Muslim; it's how he wanted you to be born, to live. I couldn't bring you up the way we intended, I had nothing, but now, now the truth is out, alhamdulillah, God has shown you the path . . .'

Jasmine snaps. 'What is it you want from me? Money? I become Malay and Muslim, and you suddenly become rich, is it? Because I owe you nothing. Nothing! You hear me? You can keep your Allah. I don't need you or him or anyone else telling me what I should believe.'

'Masya Allah, please don't say these things . . .'

But Jasmine is beyond caring. 'I've gone to church all my life. Truth is, if my grandmother hadn't made me, I probably would have stopped going a long time ago. God has never been kind to me, if there even is one. I don't owe God anything.'

Her mother starts to sob. 'I couldn't even feed you, when you were born. My breasts wouldn't produce any milk. You kept crying and crying, all day and night, and I couldn't stand it any longer. I wanted it all to be over, especially after your father died. I thought I would kill myself, that's why I gave you up. I didn't think I could live.'

Of course, she could, and she did. Without Jasmine, without David, without looking back. Regrets trailing her like inconsequential pebbles, eyes fixed on the road ahead. Jasmine feels her fingers curl into the fleshy mounds of her palms. She is shaking, lips trembling, pain from her nails cutting into her skin.

The woman withdraws into her own seat. 'Allah helped me find my way again, back to Him. Someday I hope you will too. You are Muslim, whether or not you believe it.' She is hunched, her body lost in the folds of her batik kaftan.

Jasmine wants to fling the teacups across the room. Hurl

them one by one into the wall, their sickly sweet contents trickling down in brown stripes. She wants to smash the teapot, sweep the platters of kueh off the coffee table, grind their gelatinous green and pink layers into the carpet with her bare feet, break the tray in two over her knee.

She tastes blood in her mouth, from biting the inside of her lower lip.

'I have to leave now,' she says, her voice hoarse. As she puts on her shoes, Salmah hands her a paper bag, heavy with its contents. 'A small gift, from me. Please.'

Although the last thing Jasmine wants to do is to take anything this woman wants to give her, she is too weary all of a sudden to argue. Instead, she mumbles a thanks, head bowed, and trudges down Salmah's driveway without looking back, the paper bag scrunched beneath one arm.

She gets into the car, starts the engine in haste, then blindly wends her way to the coastline. Driving past the town, she reaches Cape Rachado and parks at the foot of the lighthouse hill. Unthinking, she nibbles on the fingernail of her right pinky.

She peers into the paper bag on her front passenger seat. No note, no letter, nothing except a stack of books. An instruction manual for the Muslim prayer. A Quran in English – as if it could make up for Salmah's absence from Jasmine's life all these years. A book on the life of Prophet Muhammad. A headscarf, just like the one Salmah wore to conceal her hair. A perfect starter kit for becoming a good Muslim. But nothing to shed even the slightest sliver of light on whether Salmah had any regrets giving up her daughter.

Jasmine throws the first book out the car window; she needs

no one telling her how to pray. There is a rustling in the leaves: a band of macaques descends to the ground, their beady eyes never leaving her gaze. She watches as they pick up the book, rip the pages with sharp teeth, then spit them back out.

She starts the car engine, puts it in gear. As she reverses, she chucks out the scarf, its length billowing, lifted by a small breeze. The cloth gets caught in the branch of a tree. A macaque scrambles up to it, reeling it in, then winds the scarf around its neck and gnaws its ends. It runs farther up the tree, away from its troop. In the rear-view mirror, Jasmine catches a glimpse of it, the monkey baring its teeth in warning as the others approach.

She passes the turn-off to KL and heads north, not stopping until the hills of Ipoh come into view four hours later, backlit by the setting sun. She pulls into the familiar driveway and unlocks the door to her childhood home.

Jasmine flips on the lights in the high-ceilinged foyer, the chandelier illuminating the curved wooden staircase. The house is emptier without Poh Poh's bric-a-brac, pared back to just furniture and a handful of ornaments artfully curated by Kevin during their big clean-up. It almost looks like a grand old show home from a magazine.

She flops onto the rosewood lounger, its surface hard despite the cushions. She is hungry, but the fridge is empty. She drove here unthinking, her instincts keeping her foot on the accelerator, past the big city, past the mess that lies there, drawing her towards this house where everything is familiar.

A dull, numbing pain throbs at the base of her spine. Maybe it wasn't such a good idea, taking a long drive like that in her condition. She climbs the stairs to Poh Poh's empty room, its bed still naked. Despite their fervour in cleaning things up, she and Kevin had saved some of her grandmother's unguents, giving in to their Chinese thriftiness. Jasmine finds a tube of mentholated cream and rubs some of it on her spine, the slow, burning heat easing her sore muscles. When she goes back downstairs, her phone rings.

'Jasmine ah, are you here in Ipoh? I passed by the house and the gate was open. Lights on.' It is Tai Gu.

'Yes, it's me,' Jasmine replies, uncertain, the lingering discomfort from their last exchange still fresh in her mind.

'Ah, okay, okay, I thought maybe there was a robber. Have you eaten? I'll bring you some food.'

No awkward gaps in the conversation. No hesitation. Just the promise of dinner sweeping the angry talk of last week away.

It was Iskandar who pointed it out to her one time after they had fought. 'You Chinese are funny,' he said once they'd made up. They were lying on her couch after dinner. 'Food just ends every awkward conversation. Like a turning of the page. As if what came before is finished, over.' He swiped his palms, one over the other, in sweeping strokes.

They had been arguing again about their untogetherness.

'It's how we show love, I guess,' Jasmine said. 'No matter how badly behaved I was, I always got fed in the end when I was a kid. To us, leaving someone you love hungry is the worst possible cruelty, somehow.'

Tai Gu arrives, bearing a large Tupperware container. 'Hakka noodles. I just made some this evening.' There is enough for four people.

'Who were you feeding, Tai Gu?'

'Aiyah, you know lah. Always make extra. What's the point, cooking for only myself? Same effort. If no one else eats it, I just heat it up the next day and have it for lunch.'

They sit in the kitchen, at Ah Tin's old table, under the violet-blue fluorescent light. It had not occurred to Jasmine before how lonely life must be for her aunt. No husband in her life any more, and a son too far away.

'Tai Gu, I know you're upset. About me. And Kevin. But you must know he cannot change. He is what he is.' She bites her lip, bracing for any possibility. There is no telling where this will go. It is not normal for them to talk about things like this.

Her aunt chews the last of her noodles in silence. Putting down her chopsticks, she sighs, shoulders drooping. 'I hoped he would give me some grandchildren.'

'Maybe he will,' says Jasmine. 'Times have changed. There's always adoption, and surrogacy even. I mean, he can afford it.'

'You young people and your ideas. It won't be the same. Blood is blood.'

Jasmine takes a deep breath. 'I just met my mother.'

Tai Gu looks at her niece, a shrewd light in her eyes. 'Jasmine, you and I are family, no matter what. But I have to be honest with you. We don't know what her people are like.'

She is right. The meeting was far from heart-warming for Jasmine. The Quran is still sitting on the passenger seat of her car. 'Maybe I should just go away,' says Jasmine.

Tai Gu pats her niece's hand. 'One day at a time. We will find a way around this. We Chinese always have. Whatever it is, I promise you, we won't leave you high and dry, Lin Li. That is something we will never allow, no matter what this country tries to do to us. But maybe you don't have to leave. This is home, after all. Where our roots are. This house.'

'Promise me you'll be nice to Kevin, Tai Gu, please.'

The old lady brushes Jasmine's hands away with a gentle sweep. 'Aiyah, he's my son. That's never going to change. Whether he and I like it or not. Joined at the hip, or womb, I suppose. Okay lah, son-in-law also son-in-law lah. It doesn't mean I have to like it. But if that is what it takes, who am I to tell him no? He is a grown man, after all.'

Jasmine knows the minute Tai Gu sets eyes on Matthias, she will likely change her mind. His beautiful face and green eyes will win her over. Plus, maybe, a deft rendition of a Chinese dish or two.

'But what about you?' Tai Gu softly enquires. 'That Kuan Yew fellow, he seems to like you. A lot.'

Jasmine's eyes widen at the mention of Kuan Yew. She swallows her mouthful of noodles. 'I – I, well, it's all so new. But yet not, if you know what I mean, since we knew each other as children. But now things are different. We're both older. And a lot is happening right now. I'm not sure it's a good time to even be considering anything like that,' Jasmine confesses, blushing.

Her aunt straightens her posture, shifting her gaze into the distance. 'Love isn't something that works according to our schedules, Jasmine. It comes when it does. Just make sure you don't ignore a good thing when it's right in front of you. Besides, it's not as if we haven't known his family our whole lives. They're good people. And in the long run, that can sometimes count for a lot.'

After Tai Gu leaves, Jasmine collapses on her bed, exhausted.

It is too late to drive back to KL. She stares up at the wooden canopy, thinking back to the night Iskandar was there with her. Her eyes sweep across to the corner where her name is scrawled.

This is home. This is where she belongs.

15

Kevin and Kuan Yew pore over a spreadsheet on Kevin's laptop in RSE's boardroom, huddled at a corner of the conference table. Jasmine fans herself with a file, a fine sheen of sweat building on her skin. It is after hours, and the building's central air conditioning has turned off.

She casts her gaze around the room, out to the view beyond the wide glass of the opposite wall. KL lies beneath them, bathed in the evening's rosy glow, a blanket of smog just below her eyeline. She walks to the window, her eyes picking out the hidden back lanes and coffee shops she has frequented for decades. The five-star hotels where deals are made and broken, sex and love wrought and spent in lost afternoons. This isn't a city that is easy on the eye, even from way up here. It is messy, disorganized and confounding, despite the elevated six-lane highways that now ring its outer edges.

She walks towards the air-conditioning floor unit in the room and flicks on its switch, standing for a moment in front of it, relishing the blast of cool air.

'Jasmine, what do you think of this?' Kuan Yew beckons her over.

She scans the spreadsheet. She knows he is hesitant. This was not in his plans when he suggested taking a stake in Phoenix.

She looks up from the laptop, eyes fixed on Kuan Yew. 'The bak kwa business is only twenty per cent of Phoenix's value once this new Ipoh development gets off the ground, Kuan Yew. And if the company agrees to the discount, RSE will be getting a good deal.'

The new construction project, Phoenix Village, is worth billions, part of a larger township that will keep the company profitable for the next six years. Set around a large swathe of land just outside town, the development was mooted by Poh Poh as part of a bid to save an old Buddhist temple that will lie at its heart. If successful, the temple will be refurbished and become a new historical attraction for Ipoh. Letting it fail is not an option. It is to be part of Poh Poh's lasting legacy.

'We can do it, we have the know-how,' says Jasmine. 'The town councillor knows it too. He wouldn't be able to get the old Chinese communities to agree if not for us. He needs us. It's just this whole mess that's gotten in the way. Without us, the old Chinamen won't budge. Plus, this was Poh Poh's last project before she died. I'd like to see it built.'

'Yes, but our interest is in the bak kwa business. It has the potential to go beyond Malaysia.'

'I know. And there's nothing stopping you from getting a piece of that. After I've sorted things out. I just need some time.'

Kuan Yew twirls his pen over the back of his hand. 'Give me a piece of it now, and you've got yourself a deal.' He taps his pen on the table, a sly smile on his face. 'But only if you can get the Ipoh town councillor to say yes to your development up north. Once that's in the bag . . .'

'That would be insider trading, if I tell you before I announce it to the stock exchange,' Jasmine counters. She looks at him, curious about where his thoughts are leading.

Kuan Yew's face breaks into a smile. 'Ah, but you're cashing out, Jasmine. You're gonna need a buyer for your shares. It'll be a private sale, at the discount you're suggesting.'

Kevin lifts his head, shifting his gaze from the laptop towards Jasmine. 'Are you sure you want to do this? You might be left with virtually nothing once you buy out the bak kwa business. You're gonna need capital to do the expansion you were planning.'

Jasmine will be placing all her bets on the bak kwa business. She knows it is a big risk, but one she is willing to take. She will need help with the financing for the regional expansion. But her credibility abroad and the business's track record should enable her to get some traction with regional funders. Still, there is no guarantee.

But not doing it will mean Jasmine loses all ties to Phoenix, and everything she has worked on in the last twenty or so years. All the late nights, the hours, the sacrifices she has made will come to nought. She could just remain a shareholder of Phoenix and fade quietly into the background. But what good would that be? She is not used to being a silent partner. Poh Poh always allowed her to take an active part in the business. It is what she has trained for all these years.

This way, she will still have control over a small part of her past. And, hopefully, be able to rebuild it into something bigger and better for the future. Something Poh Poh would be proud of.

Even if it means risking everything Jasmine has.

'I'll take a forty-nine per cent share in the bak kwa business, and help you buy it out,' says Kuan Yew.

This is unexpected. 'RSE?' Jasmine says.

'No,' Kuan Yew replies, staring straight at her. 'Me. Lau Kuan Yew. Through my company in Hong Kong.'

'But RSE—'

'My contract with them is only for three years, to help them set up their Malaysian office. I own a fund management outfit. I joined RSE on the condition that they would let me keep it. My own company only manages individual portfolios. So, no conflict.'

Jasmine sinks into one of the chairs and kicks off her shoes. She swivels the seat left and right in small arcs, chewing on a curry puff. This will mean that Kuan Yew remains a part of her life. Her new one. The one, perhaps, with a baby. The baby he doesn't know about yet. She wonders if knowing will change his mind. She has to tell him, and soon, before things are final.

Kevin is glaring at her. 'Please tell me that whatever you two love birds are planning, it doesn't involve me moving back here to run this ship.'

A small smile creeps across Jasmine's face. 'Well, now that cat's out of the bag, how sure are you Matthias won't want to move here?'

A look of mild terror crosses Kevin's eyes.

'Look, Wonder Woman, you've told your mother already. And she wants you here. You heard her. You've got the upper hand now. With me gone, she'll have what she's wanted all along. You, running Phoenix. Make Matthias part of the deal. She won't say no.'

Kevin purses his lips, a frown creasing his brow. 'I guess he wouldn't mind being a tai-tai. I'd have to explain to him what that means first, though.'

Jasmine cackles, slapping her thigh. 'The man works in Hong

Kong. Of course he'll know. A chauffeur, maids, a nice condo or bungalow in a gated community. He can even quit his day job. What's not to like?'

It's more than what the two of them would have in Singapore. A more than comfortable life at the centre of KL society, one where Kevin's position will cocoon him from the country's draconian laws on homosexuality. Sure, people may pass snide remarks behind his back, but they are bound to do so in Singapore too, despite its progressive facade. Here, at least, he will be sheltered from the worst of it, thanks to his CEO stature. Even cabinet ministers get away with it. What's more, he isn't involved in politics.

'You know there's only so far you can get in Singapore, Kev. You're not one of them, that's how things work over there. In Singapore, you'll always be second choice. Here, you'll be Queen,' she says with a giggle, wiggling her eyebrows. 'Plus, you know I'll always be there to help you out. Just a phone call away. Any time.'

A smile spreads across Kevin's face. 'Well, Matthias did say he wanted to take a bit of a break from work. Fine. I'll do it. At least I know this'll make Mum shut up for a bit. As long as I can get rid of those horrid doors on Poh Poh's office. Those big birds still frighten the hell out of me.'

Jasmine jumps up and hugs her cousin, squeezing him tight. She plants a sloppy kiss on his cheek, smudging her lip gloss. 'It's about time you took your place in the sun, Wonder Woman. So you'd better pick yourself a new cape. And just get Matthias to cook for your mum. Works like a charm, food, on us Chinese,' she says, looking at Kuan Yew.

They are packing up to leave the office when Kevin's and

Jasmine's phones buzz simultaneously. The cousins exchange looks, scrabbling in their bags.

News alerts, videos and text messages from Tai Gu.

Burhanuddin and a band of young men are picketing in front of Phoenix's largest store in a city centre mall. An after-work crowd has gathered at the shopfront. The demonstrators are chanting 'Hidup Islam! Hidup Melayu!' and brandishing placards with crossed-out illustrations of pigs.

The mobile phone footage viralling on social media shows news crews already assembling at the scene.

Photos arrive in quick succession. The storefront of the flagship outlet in Ipoh has been plastered with stickers saying 'Babi'. Pig. In red ink.

'Fuck.' Jasmine's phone is buzzing non-stop now, messages from news outlets and Mr Chew, asking for comments. One of them is from Rebecca Tan.

The Malay Youth Forces, a new rag-tag group helmed by Burhanuddin, is calling for Jasmine's resignation from Phoenix. 'We are deeply offended by Phoenix's blatant disregard and disrespect for Muslims in this country!' Burhanuddin is yelling into the camera, his face twisted in red anger. 'We cannot put up with this any longer! A Muslim selling pork? This is not right! And we cannot let that happen. Not over our dead bodies. Allahuakhbar! Hidup Melayu! Hidup Islam!' God is great. Long live Malays. Long live Islam.

He demands that all Muslim-owned malls in Malaysia ban non-halal businesses as their tenants.

For the next two hours, Jasmine, Kuan Yew and Kevin watch in quiet horror as the stories pile up from all sides, like a tide racing to swallow them whole. A tsunami.

Online, there is liberal pushback. The ones who believe the country is a tolerant place, where people should have the right to live as they choose. But these are outliers. Many feel Jasmine should resign. They demand she embrace her true Muslim identity and be done with Phoenix. After all, it would be a small sacrifice, wouldn't it? And who wouldn't want to be Muslim?

Kuan Yew is shaking his head. 'When will things ever change?'

'It's because this is all they've got,' says Jasmine, her voice soft. 'Us Chinese, even the Indians, we come from places much larger than this tiny peninsula. Thousands of years of history. Not like them. The Malays . . . only have this.'

Iskandar had told her this once. Deep down inside, he didn't even know who he really was any more. What was Malay when he was growing up, the traditions, are now deemed un-Islamic. Even marriage ceremonies are being questioned, having roots in Hindu heritage. Their songs from hundreds of years ago, a blend of Arabic and Indian influences, all judged as sinful indulgence. The spirit-laden practices and beliefs in shamans swept aside as wrongful kafir superstitions. Their delicate, hypnotic dances, based on the Ramayana, suppressed.

To be Malay today means to be Muslim, little else, he said. Even that is not a constant, its borders shifting according to whoever shouts loudest. The Malays are suffocating, their old histories denied. The vacuum left behind from the erasure of their past is filled only with God and His Word.

Jasmine winces, uncurling her fingers. The welts on her palm are deep and crimson. She buries them under her thighs.

Kuan Yew stands at the wide windows, staring out into the black night of the city below.

'You look any harder, you might just spot Sydney Harbour,' Jasmine says.

Kuan Yew turns, arms akimbo, hands on his waist. His face is flushed, his jaw vibrating with anger. 'If not for my dad, I wouldn't have come back. I was mad when I left for Australia. Mad at the system, the fact that a Chinese like me, despite my grades, couldn't get a scholarship. While Malay kids who barely squeaked by in secondary school were sent off to places like the UK and the US. Half of them could barely speak English, for God's sake. And the other half had fathers rich enough to send them abroad three times over.'

'Like you said, the playing ground is uneven.' Jasmine walks up to him, rubbing his back.

'Yeah, well, I wish it would tilt our way once in a while. The Malays have it so easy in this country. Government scholarships, special loans, business concessions. While we have to fight for everything we want.'

'Try being me,' Kevin says. 'So are we going to respond to this mob? Or keep silent, like Poh Poh would?'

Poh Poh, with her stubborn, steadfast, tight-lipped ways. Jasmine never thought she would miss her grandmother this much.

Suddenly, she is hungry. 'Screw it. Let things calm down. We'll issue a statement tomorrow. I need dinner. I can't think any more.'

Kevin checks his watch. 'Shit, I have to meet Ma. She's in town. You two go ahead. I'll tell her what we've discussed.'

'For once, we're ahead of the mob,' Jasmine says. Hopefully, their deal will pacify the braying hordes.

*

Jasmine opts for Luccio's. Lately, she is unable to tolerate the strong odour of local fare. Hawker stalls have become a hazard, with their heady, lard-laden noodles, steam rising in clouds from the woks. The sight of roasted ducks hanging whole on hooks makes her want to gag, and the peppery pork intestine soup, her old favourite, is now too strong for her tastebuds. She can't risk throwing up in public. Not tonight. Not with Kuan Yew at her side. Plus, at Luccio's, at least the toilets are clean. And these days, she is ruled by her bladder.

She navigates Luccio's moss-patched brick path, one hand wrapped around Kuan Yew's arm, dull pain shooting up her legs from her stiletto heels. Already, curious glances are thrown her way, recognizing her from the evening news.

As they pass through the outdoor dining area and reach the restaurant's entrance, Luccio's front doors fling open without warning. A staggering Iskandar emerges, his long arms flailing like wobbly helicopter blades. He is drunk, eyes rimmed with red. She freezes, clutching Kuan Yew's arm.

Jasmine holds her breath as Iskandar approaches, stumbling. He lifts his head, taking a clumsy swipe at his floppy fringe. His eyes turn cold at the sight of Jasmine.

'I knew you had someone else. You left me for him?'

He swivels his body, taking a large swing at Kuan Yew.

'Iskandar, stop!' Jasmine screams.

But he is not listening. Iskandar punches Kuan Yew, a blow to the eye. There is blood. Kuan Yew pushes him away. Iskandar sways but remains standing, grabbing a wine bottle from a nearby table and smashing it. Its jagged, broken edges gleam in the restaurant's lights as Iskandar holds it aloft and charges towards Kuan Yew.

It all happens in a flash. Kuan Yew sidestepping to avoid Iskandar, Jasmine pushing herself between them, her arms up, palms facing Iskandar, hoping to stay his rage. She feels the warm gush of blood on her skin, bright red seeping down her forearm, pooling at her elbow before staining the pavement.

Her body folds, knees buckling, her head hitting concrete. The last thing she hears is Kuan Yew screaming her name.

16

Jasmine awakens to blinding fluorescent lights overhead, the sharp sting of disinfectant hitting her nose. She covers her eyes with her left hand, feeling the rough scrub of bandages wrapped around it against her cheek. Someone switches off the overhead lights. The room is bathed in a soft amber glow from the lamp above her bed. Jasmine opens her eyes to see Kuan Yew at her bedside, his left eye bruised and a little swollen.

He leans over, brushing her fringe away from her forehead. 'Hey, hot little mess. You gave me quite a scare.' There is weariness in the creased corners of his mouth. He sits on a chair next to her bed.

Jasmine half-closes her eyes. She can barely face him. He must know about the baby by now.

'Go back to sleep, Jasmine. Get some rest.' He is stroking her hand, her face, her hair.

When she awakens once more, he's gone, and the sun's fierce rays are visible through a crack in the heavy curtains. Otherwise, her room is shrouded in gloom.

A door opens, a nurse's head pops in. 'Oh, you're awake. Good. The doctor's just here to see you.'

Dr Josephine Menezes appears, picking up Jasmine's charts at the foot of the bed. After examining them, she looks up.

'Good news. You both appear to have escaped unscathed. Well,' she eyes Jasmine's belly, 'perhaps her more than you.'

'H-her?'

The doctor's eyes widen, aware of the slip. 'My apologies. It's been a long day. I really shouldn't have said anything. But yes, chances are high it's a girl. You'll need to take care of those stitches on your arm, though. They should heal well, not leave any major scars. Thankfully, no concussion after you got knocked out. Although that probably saved things from escalating further.' Dr Menezes explains that Jasmine's hormonal changes were probably the cause of her fainting.

For once Jasmine is grateful for Iskandar's relative incompetence. He only managed to leave her with a bad cut on one arm. Nothing more serious. Given his inebriated state, it was probably the worst he could have managed anyway. He was never a steadfast drunk; she could drink him under the table any day. Perhaps even now.

Despite the minor injury, Dr Menezes is sternly giving her new orders. 'You need to stay home for a month, just to be sure. Not quite bed rest, but maybe don't be going shopping and to the office and the gym and whatnot. Since you seem to be attracting a fair bit of trouble these days,' she muses. 'I don't want you to get into any more scrapes, or I'll be forced to actually put you on bed rest. We can't be too careful given your age.'

'God, you make me sound old, doc.' Jasmine grimaces.

'Well, like it or not, you're considered a geriatric pregnancy,' Dr Menezes says with a chuckle. 'You and I are no spring chickens, no matter what anti-ageing products we use.'

*

213

Kevin arrives bearing a bouquet of flowers.

'Damn, Jasmine, are you all right?' He gives her a quick hug and draws the curtains open, letting in the afternoon light, then pulls a chair next to her bed. 'Ma and I have spoken to the lawyers. We'll handle the media, so don't worry. I'll sort the restructuring out with Kuan Yew. You just rest.'

At the mention of Kuan Yew, Jasmine turns her head to the window and the view beyond of square office blocks.

'What's the matter?' Kevin asks, his brow furrowing.

'I don't know if Kuan Yew will still say yes, after this.' She glances down, one hand at the base of her belly.

Kevin lifts a hand to his mouth. 'The baby. You still haven't told him?'

Jasmine shakes her head in silence, her hair rustling on the pillow. 'It was hard enough telling him about Iskandar at all.'

Kevin bites his lip. 'Well, if he already knows, he didn't let on when I spoke to him. We're meeting later to sort out the deal.'

'Don't say anything yet, please. I need some time alone, to think. Please, keep everyone else away. No Tai Gu, no phone calls, no Kuan Yew. I can't, not right now.'

Kevin nods, his head bobbing in swift movements.

'Can you take me for a spin round the hospital? Do you think they'd let me? I just need some air.'

The corridors on her floor are quiet. Kevin finds her a wheelchair and pushes her into the lift. According to the lift buttons, Jasmine's ward is two floors from the top, where there's a roof garden.

They park themselves there under a gazebo. The hospital is on the fringe of the city centre, at a busy traffic junction. The sound of cars drifts up towards them. From her room, she cannot hear anything, but out here, the honks and engine rumbles, and the smell of diesel faint in the hot air, remind her there is life outside the hospital walls. A life she has to reckon with when she gets out.

Down on the ground floor they visit the concession stand to pick up some magazines. On the way back up, the lift opens on the neonatal level and Jasmine asks Kevin to wheel her out. They sit outside the nursery, staring at rows of babies through the green-tinged glass. Next to them, a man is holding his young daughter and pointing to an infant at the very front of the window. The baby is swaddled, only its pink face showing. The child gapes at the small, still object, her palm pressed to the glass. The father is gesturing, pointing out the baby's features – its broad, flat nose, its tiny rosebud lips.

He spies the cousins and smiles. 'Congratulations,' Jasmine says.

'Thanks.' The man's eyes mist over. His daughter begins to wriggle. Bending, he lowers her till her feet touch the ground. He pulls out a doll from a plastic bag and hands it to his daughter. She grabs it, giggling, and scrambles onto a chair, one of a row set against the opposite wall.

'How old is she?' Jasmine asks, smiling at the child.

'Three. We've come to see her new baby brother.' The man's mouth is curved in a slight smile, but there is worry in his eyes.

'A pair,' says Jasmine.

'My wife is not doing too well. She's in the ICU. The boy was a difficult pregnancy.' He glances at his daughter, who is still engrossed, combing through her doll's hair with her fingers. 'I'm not sure if I can do this without her.' His tone is surprised. 'I'm sorry, I don't even know why I'm telling you this.'

Kevin steps forward with a sympathetic smile. 'Sometimes it's easier to tell a stranger.'

'I don't know if I'm going to keep mine myself,' Jasmine whispers. The words just slip out.

The man's eyes widen.

'I have to go. Good luck with your wife, I hope everything will work out for you.' She grabs the wheels of her chair and reverses. Kevin turns the wheelchair around, mumbling apologies to the man.

They return to her room in silence, Jasmine lost in her thoughts. Tai Gu's earlier words about love appearing without warning echo in her head. Perhaps losing Kuan Yew matters more than she would like to admit to herself. Except now that might not even be an issue, especially if she decides to keep the baby.

*

Alone after Kevin leaves, Jasmine flicks through the channels on the fuzzy TV mounted to the wall in her room. More news of Burhanuddin and his gang. Their little demonstration has sparked a small outrage in other towns. Members of the Malay Youth Forces are gathering outside non-halal premises in Penang, Johor Bahru, Malacca, Seremban. Chinese mall owners are upset but tight-lipped, hoping things won't spill over onto their properties. Malay ones are silent, unwilling to comment, except for the proprietor of a mall in Johor Bahru who also runs an Islamic hotel. One where there are separate swimming pools for women and men. No alcohol allowed on its premises. He thinks Burhanuddin's demands are only fair.

The police have been called in to tame the crowds. In front

of Chinese shophouses and liquor stores, uniformed officers guard the entrances. The prime minister is calling for reason, with no solution offered. Unity and tolerance, he says, stopping short of asking the demonstrators to cease their activities.

The opposition has retaliated with their own night vigils in Merdeka Square and the field in Malacca where the country's independence was proclaimed. People are lining road shoulders and roundabouts with ribbons laid out to form the Malaysian flag. Liberal Malays in upper-middle-class enclaves are slamming Burhanuddin's group on social media.

There is no winner in this battle. A slippery slope that can only lead to everyone tumbling to its bottom, mangled limbs shoved in each other's mouths and arses, eyes blinded by mud and dirt.

She turns off the TV. Pokes a spoon at the plastic cup of jelly she was given for her after-dinner dessert. Strawberry with a slice of peach suspended in the middle. A little-girl treat for a grown-up woman.

Despite the turmoil swirling outside, all Jasmine can think of is the being growing inside her. If she keeps this baby, they will have to leave the country, forge a home for themselves elsewhere, give up everything she has worked for, cash out of the family business. Divorce herself from it, so the Leong inheritance stays intact for Kevin, her Vancouver cousins and their children's children.

She won't risk doing otherwise. If something were to happen to her, Salmah and Burhanuddin could benefit. And the woman has brought her nothing but misery. The only thing she has given Jasmine is a beating heart, two arms, two legs and a complete set of features: a vessel, for Poh Poh to fill. You are a girl, you can never do enough. Poh Poh's words from so long ago ring in Jasmine's ears, coursing a fierce path through her veins.

But Poh Poh also taught her how to fight back. One time, when she was twelve, Jasmine came home dirty, her pinafore stained with green streaks from the grass, its blue fabric torn at the hem; April Kamila had wrestled her to the ground after school. In an attempt to prise herself free from her captor's grasp, Jasmine had kicked, giving April a bruise on her cheek. 'Next time, use your head, not your legs,' her grandmother said, wiping Jasmine's face with a damp washcloth.

It hadn't been an argument over a game of catch. April Kamila was furious, her envy bubbling over during recess. Bobby Kumar, April's old admirer from kindergarten, had given Jasmine a ride on his bicycle around the school field earlier that week. He was merely being nice, Jasmine had thought. April demanded a turn on the bicycle after school. Except Bobby declined, calling her mean, unlike Jasmine, who was 'smart and real kind'. The truth was that he probably still held a candle for April, and boys at that age only know how to scorn those they adore.

Poh Poh bought Jasmine a bicycle a few days later. After some persuasion, Jasmine was allowed to cycle to school, its campus only a few hundred metres from their house. The bicycle was bright red, with a basket on the front. She rang the bell, the streamers on its handlebars fluttering in the wind, as she rode through the school gates. Heads swivelled and soon a crowd gathered around her.

After school, her classmates once more huddled around Jasmine and her new bicycle. Spying April Kamila at the fringe of the group, Jasmine turned to Bobby, who was at her side. His fingers caressed the cream leather seat of Jasmine's new ride.

'You want to take it for a spin, Bobby Kumar?' Jasmine thrust the handlebars at him.

Bobby's face broke into a wide grin. 'Well, it's a girl's bike, but sure!'

Jasmine watched as Bobby mounted the bicycle and took it for a bumpy turn round the school field. He was halfway when she felt a sudden jolt, and then her face was in the grass, a slender palm gripping her neck.

'You stupid idiot. He'll always like me more. No matter what sort of trinkets you bring to school.'

Jasmine's only instinct was to break free from April. Twisting round, she hoisted her legs up, kicking against April's torso. The last strong shove landed on April's face, causing her captor to squeal and release Jasmine from her stranglehold.

Jasmine rose to her feet, shaking bits of grass off her uniform. Bobby Kumar was straddling her bike, his ride complete, gawking.

'April! Why you so mean ah?' He dismounted from Jasmine's bicycle, handing it back to her. 'C'mon, Jasmine, let's go.'

They decided to walk the distance to her house, wheeling their bicycles beside them. Jasmine was still a little shaken from her skirmish. 'That was some ninja move you did there,' Bobby Kumar said, laughing.

After that, they often rode home together from school. It was a short pedal to the front of her house, where he'd leave her with a big wave, before pushing off towards his own abode on the edge of town.

April Kamila never bothered Jasmine again. The long-haired Queen Bee turned her attention instead to Kuan Yew, but Jasmine often caught April Kamila's sneer after school, as she watched Bobby and Jasmine set off together.

Jasmine recalls the man and his daughter from the nursery that afternoon, peering at the infant through the green glass. He might lose his wife, and his children their mother. At least, in Jasmine's case, nature has allowed her a reprieve. Perhaps it is a sign.

It can't be that hard, bringing up a child. Millions have done it for millions of years. She herself survived childhood, thanks to Poh Poh. And Ah Tin. And Kevin and Tai Gu, despite the latter's uneasy affection.

If she does this, keeps the baby, she will be alone, but she can afford help. A nanny perhaps, so she can go back to work after the birth. A housekeeper and a cook, no matter where she lives. The Leongs have at least given her that, a bank account to smooth over any bumps in the road.

Surely she has dealt with things much harder than a baby and won.

A baby is midnight feedings and diapers, cooing words and rocking till it stops crying. Unlike merchant bankers and tetchy old Chinese traders who require her to put on suits of stern armour before they will listen.

A baby would give her a chance to right the sharp edges of her own childhood. A person of her own, whose bond to Jasmine would be firm and not tenuous, sure and certain, immutable. A family, even if it is just the two of them. A baby could maybe, at last, be enough.

But first, she has to make plans. Just like Poh Poh did with

Jasmine's life. This baby will always have the gift of sight. A clear vista of the possibilities that lie ahead, unfettered by the chains that want to bind her in this country.

And a fortune to secure her future. There is now a new reason for Jasmine to make her proposed bak kwa venture work. Her child. The one who will have all the freedom Jasmine never had. The one who will never need to run away from her past.

'She is mine and she is a Leong,' Jasmine whispers. 'You people will not take what is mine away from me.'

17

Three days later, Jasmine is back in her condo, in bed, propped up by pillows. Tai Gu sits at her side, clucking orders at a borrowed maid. The maid hovers from room to room, straightening cushions and vacuuming, tidying. The pungent, cloying smell of ginseng chicken boiling on the stove wafts into the bedroom.

Despite the doctor not dictating bed rest, Head Nurse Tai Gu insists.

And Jasmine is too weary to protest.

When she finally tells Tai Gu about the baby, her aunt breaks into excited squeals. 'You and Kuan Yew?' she gasps.

'No, I'm afraid not.'

The smile disappears from her aunt's lips. In its place, her face narrows, nose pinched, mouth pursed. 'That Malay fellow? The one who attacked you?'

Jasmine nods, avoiding her aunt's gaze.

Tai Gu heaves a huge sigh, shoulders sagging, head moving from side to side. 'Your Poh Poh actually mentioned him to me once. I told her it was probably nothing serious. She was worried. But she also didn't want to interfere. She was afraid if she did, it would drive you away from her. She only ever wanted what was best for you, you know. We all do.'

'I'm sorry, Tai Gu.'

Tai Gu turns to face her niece. 'If only your grandmother had not done what she did the first time round, we wouldn't be here in this mess. Aiyah, this goddamned country. Sometimes I wonder if we shouldn't just have gone back to China.'

A small laugh escapes Jasmine's lips. 'The last time you went there, you swore you would never go back.'

Tai Gu had gone in search of their family's ancestral home last year, her investigations leading a trail to an old Hakka village in the northern mountains. The traditional roundhouse had proved too rustic for her taste, despite her many preparations. The toilets with no doors, the prevalence of chicken shit underfoot in the common courtyard, the cold. In the end, her arsenal of disinfectant wipes depleted, she returned to Ipoh and proceeded to turn her own house inside out, spring cleaning with ardour, as if it were the eve of Lunar New Year. Since then, there have been no more attempts to get her son and niece to discover their roots.

'I am keeping her, the baby.' Jasmine eyes her aunt. 'I know what you're going to say.'

Tai Gu holds her hands up. 'Aiyoh, Jasmine, of course you will keep it. We Leongs don't just get rid of our children. A girl, you said? She's still a Leong, despite her father.'

Jasmine raises an eyebrow in surprise.

'But if you're going to marry him . . .'

'Nope. Not doing that. That's over and done with. I promise,' Jasmine says with a firm nod. 'I've made up my mind. I'm leaving the country, along with the bak kwa business. This way, we'll be able to put all this madness behind us.'

Her aunt's eyes cloud over. 'But where will you go? Must you leave?'

'I think I've caused enough trouble, Tai Gu. We don't need another thing threatening Phoenix and our family. And I'll be damned if I let my mother or Iskandar get their hands on any of our money.' She has spoken to the lawyer, Malik Harun. 'If I leave and get a new citizenship, it will make it harder for them to get to me. Or at least make it expensive enough that they won't be able to put up a fight.'

Tai Gu reaches out to her niece, enveloping her in a hug, her bony shoulder cutting into Jasmine's chin. 'I am sorry, girl. For all this. All that you have to do. It's not fair.'

'Life's not fair. You told me that not so long ago. We just have to make the best of it and move on. Besides, it doesn't mean I can never come home. Just maybe as a visitor instead.'

'This will always be your home. You know that. No matter what colour your passport is. I just wish you didn't have to do this alone.'

Jasmine nods.

'But I guess it's in your blood.'

Jasmine throws her aunt an enquiring gaze.

'Us Hakkas, we're nomads by origin. We're built of pioneer stock.' Tai Gu smiles, sweeping Jasmine's hair behind her ear.

In Jasmine's bones, a certainty takes shape. Of knowing that somehow, even if they are hundreds of kilometres away, there are still people in her life who will look out for her. The Hakka roundhouse of her grandmother and aunts, built on centuries of traversing unfamiliar territories, their children always in the heart of their courtyards, protected from strange winds and strangers.

*

She can smell Kuan Yew's cologne in the bedroom even before she turns on her back to face him. Kevin rang earlier to warn her, unable to keep Kuan Yew away any longer, but she is too weary to even brush her hair.

She tugs at her T-shirt as she half sits up in bed, sweeping her hair to one side. She licks her lips, rubs the sleep from her eyes. The tender ache from the stitches in her arm makes her cautious as she reaches to embrace him. She tries to steady her breathing, her heart beating fast.

'Hey.' He bends to give her a quick peck on the brow. 'You're looking a bit more rested.' The swelling around his eye has receded, leaving a faint purple bruise. He is smiling. It makes her want to cry.

'Thank you, Kuan Yew, for everything.'

'Don't thank me. You're the real hero. What were you thinking, you madwoman? You could have been seriously hurt.' He is shaking his head, patting her hand. 'First time a lady's ever come to my defence. So much for me being the big jock.' He lets out a small laugh.

'There's something I have to tell you.' She is staring at the bedcovers, clutching the edges with her fists.

He takes her hands and clasps them, leaning forward. 'I already know. When I brought you in, the doctor told me the baby was safe. Floored me for a bit. But don't worry, I haven't said a word to anyone.' His gaze is intent and clear.

She feels a tear forming at the corner of her eye. It rolls down her face, hot, stinging her lips. 'It's okay. Both Kevin and Tai Gu know now too.'

A look of relief crosses his face. 'Good. At least I know you've been properly taken care of these last few days. And the baby too.'

He is so much that she wants, but perhaps can never have. 'Kuan Yew, the baby, it's not yours. I understand if . . . if this changes everything. You really deserve better than this. Than me.'

Kuan Yew sits beside her, his head hung low. He exhales slowly, clasping his hands together. She cannot tell if it is relief or regret that is pooling in his silence, the reddening skin of his tightly clenched fingers.

When he looks up, his brow is creased with concern, a wisp of angry sorrow etched in the finely wrinkled corners of his eyes. 'Look, you and I, we've known each other for ever. But this thing between us, it's new. Neither of us knows where this is headed.' He looks directly in her eyes. 'I can't make any promises, Jasmine. God knows, I want to, but I don't think it's right. Not now. Maybe in time . . .'

His strong, square jaw, that funny, handsome face she has seen change from a boy so many years ago, now a grown man with worry lines on his forehead.

'I'm keeping her. The baby.'

'Yes, yes, of course.'

How can he not be blind with rage? She is sobbing, her fists balled into her chest. 'You have to be pissed off with me, Kuan Yew. Yell. Call me names. If I were you, I would have left already. Why are you still here?' Her eyes cloud over with dread.

He pulls a Kleenex from a box on the nightstand and wipes away her tears. He holds her close, the scent of his grassy aftershave mingling with the sourness at the back of her throat. She can still smell him on her neck and hair when he pulls away, holding her by the shoulders. He is clearly torn, hurt in his tender gaze, a tentative hope in his sad smile.

'I want you.' His voice is ragged. 'I want you to be a part of my life. I want to be a part of yours. This baby, I hadn't accounted for her. But she's yours, so she's part of the deal. I know that.'

She is scared, her lips trembling.

He rubs his wide palms over his face, his mouth. 'Jasmine, I've had time to think about it. Maybe we can just take it one day at a time. See where things go. We're not twenty-somethings any more. Anyone we love is bound to have strings attached.'

'But she's Iskandar's child.'

'And you need to tell him.'

'No.'

'He has a right to know, Jasmine. Besides, I kinda feel sorry for the guy. His life can't be peachy at the moment.'

'What do you mean?'

'He's not running for office after all.' A shadow passes over Kuan Yew's face. 'So, maybe, he might just say yes to being a father.' The fight was caught on someone's mobile phone. A customer at Luccio's filmed the whole thing, and it was all over the internet within hours. Kuan Yew doesn't show her the video, and she doesn't ask.

'Jasmine, if you and Iskandar, with the baby, if you two decide to be together, I'll understand. God knows, I'll hate it. But there's a baby to think of, so . . .'

227

She kisses him on the cheek. 'He and I are over. Iskandar and me, we're done. We're bad for each other. And bringing up this child, he and I, any child together, would be a disaster.'

She holds his face in her hands, so close she can feel the warmth of his breath on her cheeks, her lips, not knowing how she is going to say the thing she needs to say next.

'I need to leave Malaysia, Kuan Yew.' She is staring straight into his eyes, her voice barely audible. 'Even if I tell Iskandar, I can't let this baby grow up here. Not like this.'

He is quiet at first, shifting his gaze downwards, his head dipping in minute nods. When at last he looks up to reply, there is regret and a yearning in his eyes. 'I have to stay, at least for now. My father.'

'I know.' She takes in a deep breath.

'Hey, there are aeroplanes, you know. And the internet.' His mouth wears a tiny smile.

And thousands of kilometres that will come between them. Days and weeks of things they will miss in each other's lives. A million little moments that will be forgotten, left untold when they meet. That familiar feeling of emptiness and impatience she knows only too well.

She feels her insides contract, as if something is leaving her body. But then he holds her, squeezing tight, his lips pressed on her exposed neck. 'I promise, you'll never have to miss me too much,' he says. 'I'll only be a phone call away.'

She realizes he knows what loving in absence feels like.

'What was her name, Kuan Yew?' she whispers. 'The one you left behind?'

He is surprised at the question, releasing her from his

embrace, a bemused wrinkle in his brow. Then, a wistful smile. 'Sam. Samantha Smith.'

'She must miss you.'

'Nah. Married a year ago, to another Aussie Chinese. They live in Melbourne. No plastic stools next to drains there. Actually, she reminds me of you. When she eats, she forgets anyone is watching. Can't cook to save her life either.' Mischief curls in his wide smile.

There is so much they still do not know about each other. Her, perhaps more than him. Gaps in his history she may never fill. But maybe there is time to narrow the divide. Or maybe those things just don't matter. Because he is next to her, holding her hand. And if things fade away tomorrow, next month, or in a year, they will at least have had this. A lifetime of flitting in and out of each other's lives, like skittles bumping into one another when the weight of a bowling ball smacks them down, only to be righted again in the next round, one at each end of a row.

'Look, Jasmine, us aside, what we talked about – Phoenix, myself, RSE – that still stands. No matter what. Agreed?'

'But what if you and I . . .'

'We can put some iron-clad clauses in the agreements. The lawyers can take care of that. But I know you, Jasmine. And you, me. Even though it's only been a while since we've become reacquainted, we both know where each other comes from. We're hardly strangers. And our families, they've known each other for decades now, which is more than most people can say when they start a relationship. Plus, no matter what happens, we both see the opportunity. It won't be as if all this is not going to make us both some nice coin.'

Always that Chinese practicality. That put-it-right attitude that makes do with whatever situation it encounters. Emotions be damned – well, at least for the time being. There will be moments to fling plates, sweep bowls to the floor with a crash, but later. After the dust has settled, and the town has gone to sleep.

She understands this; it is in her blood. The chalky, limestone-filtered water from the white hills of her childhood. The charcoal burn of the bak kwa's caramel edges. The willingness to swallow the bitter first, and dream of the sweet.

It is possible, it is within reach. As long as one keeps putting a foot forward, progress is always better than stasis.

*

Her condo becomes a headquarters of sorts. Tai Gu, Kuan Yew and even Mr Chew flit in and out each day, Jasmine anchored to her couch. Everyone is subjected to her prenatal meals, the maid barely able to cope. No one is allowed to wear perfume, except for Kuan Yew; his grassy scent is the only thing that helps Jasmine keep her meals down. A bottle of it is installed on her coffee table, within easy reach.

Her ankles swell. Even though a baby bump is not yet apparent, Jasmine feels as if she is wearing an invisible elephant suit. Her rings no longer fit her puffy fingers. She is hot and damp all the time, despite the air conditioning being set at sixteen degrees.

Tai Gu moves into Seh Gu's unit downstairs, along with the maid. She arrives at Jasmine's door each morning wrapped in a cardigan. She makes an appointment for a hairdresser to come over, unable any longer to tolerate the sight of her niece's stringy, sweat-slicked hair. The hairdresser gives Jasmine a short bob, her waves now large curls sprung to life.

'There.' Tai Gu holds up a mirror. 'I wore my hair like that too when I was pregnant with Kevin. Couldn't stand having all that mess around my neck.'

Jasmine grins at her own reflection. She is happier than she has been in weeks, months perhaps. Her condo has never been filled with so many people. She is unused to this – the noise, the clutter of bodies, the constant opening and shutting of the front door. The smell of food cooking on the stove. The sound of pots and pans clanging in the kitchen. A well-made bed awaiting her in the evenings, her room tidied, clothes folded and put away.

And the comforting weight of Kuan Yew as she falls asleep each night, at least when he is in town. Not to mention the sex. To her surprise, the pregnancy has made her ardour even keener.

It has been three weeks since she was hospitalized. Phoenix's board of directors has approved the plans for RSE's admission into the company. Now all that is needed is to effect the transactions: RSE's buyout of Jasmine's stake in Phoenix, and Jasmine and Kuan Yew's purchase of the pork jerky business.

Meanwhile, Burhanuddin keeps shaking his rattle, his social media posts gathering ever greater attention from both sides. In the newspapers, he has become a regular walk-on in photographs featuring the prime minister. A fixture of the entourage present wherever their leader may be, jostling in the crowd at airports as the man descends from a plane, surreptitiously grabbing to kiss his hands in greeting, eyeing the public if they get too close.

231

The Ipoh town councillor, himself a party appointee, has dug in his heels. The town's Chinese Chamber of Commerce is fraught with hurt, but afraid to press on too much. The Phoenix Village development would preserve the community's historical centre, making it a natural draw for weekend tourists; it would be a win all round for the town, but politics doesn't always recognize the obvious, the knotted desire for power clouding one's vision.

Burhanuddin needs to be silenced if they are to move forward. So far, news of the Ipoh town councillor's recalcitrance has not reached the markets. The standoff must be resolved before it becomes public.

*

She and Kuan Yew are alone. Everyone else has gone home at last. He sits on the couch, Jasmine leaning against his chest, legs stretched out on the coffee table. She rubs her belly in small circles.

'I can hear them, you know,' he says.

She turns her head to look at him, enquiring.

'The wheels. In your head. I just haven't quite cracked the code yet.'

She is thinking of how it will be when he is no longer a fixture in her life. A faraway voice and image on a screen. Or perhaps only a memory. The idea of it like a sinkhole caving in the base of her ribs, stopping her breath short.

There is a ticking clock on their togetherness, the very thing that wasn't there in the beginning, the thing she ran from with Iskandar. She feels the weight of it pressing down on them and picks up his hand, intertwining their fingers.

'I don't want to leave,' she confesses.

'I don't want you to either.' His voice is soft and low. 'But Hong Kong's not that far away. Three hours on a plane. I could be there every weekend, really.'

'That's a little mad, don't you think?'

'Is it?'

She pulls herself up to sitting, facing him. 'You're not serious.'

He shoots her a look, his eyebrows raised. 'I'm about to bet a few hundred million ringgit on you. So, yeah, I'm serious. Someone's got to keep you in check. Can't have you running round Hong Kong all by yourself, breaking all those poor mates' hearts. Plus there'll be two of you too.'

'I don't need five days in a week to do that,' she retorts. 'Two. Two will more than suffice.'

'Maybe I might just send Kevin for the other five then. Or he can split the days with Matthias since the latter is gonna be a tai-tai and all. He probably won't mind a bit of weekly grocery shopping in Hong Kong.'

'You silly idiot,' she says, laughing. 'Stop it, you'll make this pregnant lady piss herself.'

'Well, what does this pregnant lady think of owning a villa in Dominica?'

She blinks, confused at the turn of the conversation. 'What – where?'

'The Caribbean. Your daughter, she's going to need a different passport, unless you plan on registering her as a Malaysian citizen. You might want another one too. In case.'

In truth, she hasn't even thought that far ahead yet, not with everything that is still swirling around them.

Kuan Yew reaches for his laptop. 'You and the baby can be

233

Dominican citizens in just three months. Well, obviously you first, I guess, then her. You don't have to live there. In fact, better that you don't, for tax purposes.'

A Caribbean home her baby will never know; a Hong Kong she will grow up in as a foreigner. Unlike Jasmine, for whom places like Ipoh and KL are part of her skin, blood and hair. Whose smells and surfaces she can sense like the pull of a magnet to the core of her being. Despite the pain some people have caused, it will always be where she belongs.

Here, a white house in Ipoh marks her childhood. A home that still stands with its green lawn and frangipani tree, its furniture vandalized by her childish scrawls. Streets and narrow lanes that hold memories. Of the time she ate char kway teow with an old school friend, sitting on plastic stools. Of a coffee shop where she shared fishball soup at dawn with a shaken Iskandar. Of the cemetery that swallowed her grandmother. Of her old school, the ghost of her childhood still ringing her bicycle bell.

A place where she doesn't need a rulebook to tell her how things work. Who to know, where to go, what you can or cannot do. Those things come as naturally to her here as breathing.

But her child will be a displaced soul wandering through Hong Kong, never really able to call it home. Instead, home will be nothing more than a passport, somewhere she may visit every couple of years to spend a vacation in a villa overlooking the sea. No different from a thousand other tropical islands that dot the globe, enticing people with their white sandy beaches and turquoise waters. A holiday home. A place where her daughter will only skim its surfaces, never scratching enough dirt to know its heart. Can someone really pledge allegiance to a territory she doesn't actually know?

The alternative is to remain in Malaysia and be Muslim. No matter how much Jasmine tries to diffuse it, her baby's destiny in this country is fixed and constant as the sun. Suddenly, any choice she makes seems a Pyrrhic victory.

'Hey, hot little mess, what's wrong?' Kuan Yew is running his fingers through her curls, his warm palm now resting on her bare neck.

'Where the hell is my daughter going to call home? What kind of a life will I be giving her, anywhere?'

He runs his thumb along her jaw, tilting her chin up towards him. 'A good one. Where she has the freedom to choose her own path. Her home will be with you. Whether that's here, Hong Kong, or some little island in the middle of the Atlantic.'

'And what about when I'm gone? Who will she have left? I don't want her to be like me.'

'She won't be alone. There's fabulous Uncle Kevin. And your family,' he replies. 'And, hopefully, me. Plus, if she's anything like her father, maybe a string of lovers scattered around the globe.' He is grinning, palms shielding his face, as Jasmine attacks it with a throw cushion.

Later, after he has fallen asleep, she creeps out of bed, making her way to the dining table. A folder with paperwork for Dominican citizenship is already partially filled out in Kuan Yew's bold hand. She cannot remember the last time someone did this for her, helped her head off a problem at the pass. Before this, she only had Poh Poh to rely on, the old lady's instincts a certain guard against enemies advancing towards the gate. Glancing at the papers, she discerns Kuan Yew's concern, and understands that perhaps she may not have to face the future alone. She takes a deep breath and completes the application, signing her name at the bottom.

She pulls out a brochure from the dossier. There is an image of a blinding white beach with turquoise waters and coconut trees on the cover. Plump white clouds hang low in the sky.

It doesn't look unfamiliar. If she switches the name on the brochure cover, it almost looks like Malaysia.

18

In the end, she calls Iskandar. Even though it is the thing she least wants to do. Not that she fears him, despite their previous encounter. It was a drunken moment of insanity. She knows injuring her has shattered him. She knows this even though they have not spoken since the attack, him staying silent and she avoiding the spectre of his shadow that lurks in the back of her mind.

She finally rings him one Sunday afternoon when Kuan Yew has left town and Tai Gu is back in Ipoh. He picks up on the first ring, Billie Holiday in the background. He is sober, but there is a frightened despair in his voice.

'Can you come over, please?' she asks.

'Jasmine,' he chokes, a sob caught in his throat.

'Just come over. Please.'

He is there within the hour, his lean body framed in her front door, his wavy fringe concealing his eyes. When he looks up at her, she sees regret, then surprise flashes across his face for a second before softening into a small smile. 'You . . . look amazing.'

She places a hand behind her bare nape, and holds the door open as he crosses the threshold. He removes his sneakers once inside, standing there for a moment, unsure.

She gestures towards the couch, but he takes the solitary chair. Jasmine stretches out on the three-seater, leaning against an armrest, propping up her aching back with cushions.

A tiny flutter rises in her throat, her fingers tingling from the trace memory of his lean, narrow torso. Because he is still a part of her sinews and bone, and maybe always will be. The ungrown-up part of her that refuses to age, caught in its own circular loop of self-indulgence, where there is no need to confront the real things, the truths that force her to take matters into her own hands instead of merely blaming circumstance.

There is a brittleness to him, but she also senses a fine strain of will in his sharp gaze that stares straight at her, unwavering.

'I am so sorry. For everything,' he finally says, his eyes not breaking contact. 'I don't expect you to forgive me, and God knows, I will never forgive myself, but you need to know that I never wanted to hurt you. I just keep managing to do it somehow, and I hate myself for it.'

'I know, Iska. I'm sorry, too, for not telling you about Kuan Yew.' She is the one who finally averts her gaze. She knows how much she has hurt him too. How her leaving has left him dazed, unmoored, with no soft embrace to fall into at the end of his discombobulated days. Because his life now cannot be in order. No wife, no lover, and a family that probably holds him responsible for jeopardizing its otherwise untarnished public reputation.

He cups a hand over his mouth, as if trying to stop himself from crying. He is shaking his head, his shoulders shuddering.

She has done this to him. And the wound he is left with will perhaps take a lot longer to heal than the stitches in her arm. Except now, she is about to deal him one more blow.

She pats a spot on the couch next to her, holding out a hand to him.

He moves to sit several centimetres away, careful not to touch. She grabs his hand and holds it in her lap, staring straight ahead at their muted reflections in the blackness of the switched-off TV screen.

Squeezing his hand, she shuts her eyes momentarily before she turns to him. 'I am having a baby, and it is yours.'

His eyes widen in shock.

'It's a girl.'

In the years they were together, there was seldom talk of children. Only holidays, imagined endless weeks of a shared life that contained just the two of them, cocooned from the rest of the world. Neither of them ever really wanted children.

Now they are three, or a pair and one extra.

She feels lighter now that she has told him, the weight of it all his to reckon with for a while. Leaning back into the sofa, she says, 'We're a right mess, you and me. Maybe we've always been.'

'Not always,' he says, shaking his head. 'Not at first. We were good in London, before the real world crashed in.'

'Before we came home.'

'But you saw it coming. You knew I needed to step up and I failed you, failed us every single time.'

'We both failed us, Iskandar. I could have said yes to you the first time. But I didn't. I guess we were both just selfish in our own ways, and blind, thinking we could bend the world to our liking. As if what we want even matters in the larger scheme of things.'

'But it should, really. It's high time it did. I know I've asked you this before, but should we get married? Now that this has happened? Except . . . I doubt you'll want to because of what it will mean, and with that Burhanuddin fellow kicking up a ruckus, and everything that's happened between us, and Kuan Yew . . .'

'I'm leaving, Iskandar. For Hong Kong.' She tells him about the plans for Phoenix and the bak kwa business, Kuan Yew's stake in it and her intention to expand. How it will all help shield her from Burhanuddin, and hopefully keep her mother at bay.

'Is Kuan Yew joining you there, then? He'd better not leave you high and dry.' There is a protective streak in his voice.

A fleeting smile crosses her lips before fading. 'When has my damn life ever been that straightforward?'

He frowns. 'You're going to move there alone? With this baby?'

She takes in a deep breath and exhales, nodding. 'Yes. Yes I am. At least, for now. I don't want to rush him, us, just because of my situation. I don't want to screw this one up, Iska.' She raises her gaze towards his. 'I don't dare think it, but I'd like this to last.' There is pain in her saying this, now that he is in front of her.

But he smiles and plants his lips on her forehead, one hand holding the back of her head. 'You deserve it. I wish it was me, but I know I have a lot to sort out myself. I'd rather see you happy. Are you?'

'It feels right. But anything can happen. I'm just gonna take it one day at a time. I think it's about all I can manage at the moment, with everything.'

'I might have to borrow some of that courage of yours,' he

says. 'My dad gave me a forced leave of absence after that . . . that episode.'

'And his business?'

'That jackass brother of mine finally stepped in. Managed to pull some strings he had lying around and call in a favour. They'll be okay. I should've known,' he says, a vein of anger in his voice.

'And you?'

'Taking a step back.' He runs a hand through his hair, pushing his fringe away from his forehead. 'First thing I did was to move out of my parents' place, since the wife is still in the house. Our divorce gets finalized next month. But yeah, I just packed up my shit and got myself an apartment in Mont Kiara. Picked up a couple more gigs with a bunch of guys I play with.'

'You left your family company?'

'On a break. Bought myself some time. Just a couple of months. Let my dad and Kamal figure it out themselves for once. My job will still be there when I want it. Those two are always too busy running round town schmoozing. Somebody's still gotta actually keep things running.'

'Look at you,' she says with a laugh. 'Maybe you should go to that jazz festival in Europe this summer. The one you've always wanted to check out.'

'Maybe.' Once, they used to dream of going there together.

'You hungry?' She gets up from the couch, stretching, a hand on the small of her back.

He grins. 'Since I eased off the booze, eating's become my new pastime.'

'The troops made sure I wouldn't starve by myself this weekend. But I have to warn you, it's all pregnant-lady food, so no chillies. Although I'm sure there's a bottle of sambal in the fridge somewhere.'

They eat on the patio, watching the evening fade in, the way they have countless times before. Except now things are different, the road ahead forked, and navigating requires attention. Yet old habits die hard, and, unthinking, they still reach across to one another's plates for a piece of vegetable, fish or chicken. He pushes carrots aside for her to take when she is ready. She leaves the fish head for him to tear apart with his teeth at the end.

'Do you think at some point, I-I could meet her?'

Jasmine casts him a glance, her spoonful of rice poised in mid-air. She swallows. 'She's your daughter too, Iska. I'll never stop you from being a part of her life. God knows, the last thing I'd want is for her to grow up without a father, like I did. We'll just have to figure out how to explain everything to her, when she's older and able to understand. Except she won't be Malaysian.'

She tells him about Dominica. 'I just need to make sure she doesn't end up trapped like us. I don't want that for her. I also don't want her to be Muslim, unless it is something she chooses to be when she grows up.'

'Me neither,' he says. 'I mean, look at me. I'm hardly a good example myself. If I weren't Muslim by default, I probably wouldn't be anything.'

Jasmine knows it is no small thing for him to admit this. It's not something most Malays contemplate, their religion an assumed part of their identity. Yet Iskandar's reticence towards his faith is not news to her. It was one of the things they used to fight about. How she would have to become a Muslim just to be with him, even though he barely observed its practices beyond what was expected of him by society.

Jasmine stacks their plates, bunching the cutlery. 'I know this must be difficult for you. It's selfish of me. I know how you Malays are with your religion.'

'We're hypocrites, is what we are. It's not the religion, it's us. Look what we've done to you, Jasmine, to you and me even. I don't think any of this is what God intended.'

If not for the rules, they might have been together, perhaps even with a pair of snotty, noisy children.

He gets up and strides towards the balcony, leaning on its railing. 'I've had enough. I can't walk away from my family. And they pretty much leave me to my own devices anyway, after what happened. But am I happy? In parts. Not that I know how to be different, without being Muslim. The Eid, the fasting, knowing I am doing something rather naughty every time I break the rules. But do I feel guilty? Not really. It's just . . . it's the only way I know how to be.'

She nods, understanding. 'It's what I always loved about you. You're a right rebel, you are. Unlike me.'

'But there were lines I still couldn't cross.'

'No. That would have been too much. I don't think we would have survived anyway, if you had turned your back on your family. No love can survive that.'

He pushes himself away from the railing and walks towards her, settling by her side on the lounger. 'This plan of yours, have you checked with the lawyers? Are you sure this will mean the baby will be safe? From my family and your mother?'

'Well, there's always some risk. But I'm making things as difficult as I can for anyone who might want to try. I doubt my mother and her husband have the means to do anything about it. It's the one thing I have on my side, money. Might as well use it.'

'And Kuan Yew?'

'He's the one who insisted I tell you.'

They are quiet for a minute, each lost in their own thoughts.

'Thank him for me, please,' Iskandar says at last. 'He's a good man. And for the record, I called it first.'

'Called what?'

'I told you that the bloke fancied you the first time I met him, that dinner in Ipoh.'

She gives him a playful shove, throwing him a coy glance.

He laughs in response, slanting his torso away from her reach.

A new familiarity between them is forming. She can feel that they are beginning to settle into it, the ties between them still present if altered. It is different, but not disconcerting. Wistful, perhaps, and, if she is being truthful, laced with a small amount of grief.

But nothing either of them cannot bear.

*

The month passes and Dr Menezes gives Jasmine the go-ahead to resume her old life. She is only too glad to finally be able to get back into the swing of things. At least it gives her an opportunity to escape Tai Gu's constant scrutiny.

Except now she suspects her aunt's presence at times has more to do with Kuan Yew than herself. In Tai Gu's eyes, the man can do no wrong.

'I think I have competition as your number-one fan,' she

says to Kuan Yew one evening. Tai Gu has just left after protracted goodbyes, and extracting a promise from Kuan Yew to try her famous pineapple tarts.

He is working on his laptop, trying to manipulate a particularly thorny spreadsheet. 'Huh?' He reaches for one of the sweet treats, popping it whole into his mouth, licking the crumbs off his fingers.

'Tai Gu doesn't make those tarts for just anyone, you know. Even Kevin has to beg her for them every Lunar New Year. One time, she made us both spring clean her whole house before she would give us a Tupperware of the stuff.' Jasmine giggles, recalling the memory.

Kuan Yew regards her with a raised eyebrow. 'You didn't think I'd limit my charms to just you now, did you? This isn't my first rodeo, Jasmine Leong. I know how to get to a girl's heart. Especially a Chinese one. It's through the old ladies. Once they approve, that's half the battle won.' He winks.

She stares at him, mouth agape. 'You sneaky bastard!' Kuan Yew is the first man Jasmine has ever introduced to any of her family. She wonders how Poh Poh would have taken to him suddenly being ever-present in her life.

As if reading her thoughts, Kuan Yew says, 'I'd like to think your Poh Poh would have approved too. Although I have to admit, she was a lot more terrifying than your Tai Gu. It would have taken a bit more work maybe, but I'm pretty sure I would have won her over at some point.'

Somehow, Jasmine believes Kuan Yew isn't far off the mark. Poh Poh always told her how the Laus were a good example of what hard work can achieve, despite the condescension they sometimes endured from other rich families in Ipoh. She would have admired Kuan Yew's grit, that's for sure. The road he has travelled to get this far has not been without its fair share of bumps. Jasmine is glad she has him on her side. Of late, things have only become more challenging, with public opinion on her situation remaining divided.

In the papers, Burhanuddin is still braying, each week firing up new Malay right-wing youth groups with the mention of Jasmine. The deadline for Phoenix Village to break ground is in two weeks, and the Ipoh town councillor remains recalcitrant. The Chinese Chamber of Commerce is growing restless.

Jasmine has hired a detective to trail Burhanuddin. Earlier today, a package arrived at her doorstep. A flash drive.

She plugs it into her laptop now.

Images of Burhanuddin and a woman getting in and out of his car, grainy close-up shots of them at a karaoke joint, the woman on his lap, arms draped around his neck. She is clad in tight, stretchy dresses and strappy high heels. She wears too much make-up, and her hair is long, with bleached highlights starting to turn a slight tinge of orange. The kind of woman that will do an about-turn within weeks of marriage, donning a stylish hijab, trading in her bodycon dresses for equally form-fitting blouses and trousers, scarf-concealed hair and neck notwithstanding.

Security camera stills of a hotel corridor show her and Burhanuddin entering a room then leaving three hours later. The photos are from last week.

There is a detailed report accompanying the snapshots, with dates and times for every sighting. Burhanuddin has met the woman almost every night, their favourite haunts listed, scattered around KL. Places where monied men are known to congregate with their secret lives and second or third wives, often in darkened corner booths.

The next day, Jasmine calls for a meeting with her aunt and Malik Harun.

'Can we use these to pressure the Ipoh town councillor?' She tosses printouts of the photos and report on the table.

The lawyer's eyes narrow. Tai Gu flips through the pictures, letting out the occasional grunt.

'So it's true, he really is having an affair with this Zizi lady.' Malik sounds disappointed. 'When will these fellas ever surprise me? Just once, I'd like one of them to not be such a stereotype.'

At first, Jasmine had thought Malik was a run-of-the-mill corporate type with a vapid, placid wife. The kind of man that keeps a mistress himself, like many do. His disdain of Burhanuddin is unexpected. Or maybe he's gay, which always throws her off. Kevin would be able to suss it out, not that it matters. But it is more fascinating than this unending Burhanuddin nonsense and his drivel that keeps entering her electronic feeds. She wants to rip off Burhanuddin's bushy moustache, like she used to with the felt picture books she had as a child.

Pregnancy has made her irritable and tetchy. Like an old lady, she often now sucks her teeth in exasperation at the smallest things. Mr Chew's crooked tie on some mornings annoys her, as does the receptionist's poor taste for accessories that clash with her shoes. The effect, in the moments when the woman emerges from behind her station, is disturbing. Maybe Jasmine should slide her a colour wheel one day, except it would be certain to confuse her even more.

But Jasmine's own standards of decorum too have begun to

slide. Her armpits are now constantly damp, despite the many variants of deodorant she has trialled the last four weeks. Nothing seems to work besides wearing sleeveless clothing, and then she worries that she smells. Her thighs are starting to rub together and chafe.

This pregnancy thing is not pleasant. She feels a far cry from any maternal glow.

Her thoughts turn to Burhanuddin's wife. 'What if I showed Salmah all this about her husband? I can't think that any woman would be able to tolerate it.'

'Do you think she's aware her husband's taken a second mortgage out on their house?' Malik looks up from the detective's report.

Tai Gu puts down the photographs. 'Is it a joint mortgage?'

'No,' says Malik.

'Then she doesn't know,' Tai Gu replies. 'You obviously don't have a wife, Tuan Malik.'

Ah, so that's what it is. The lawyer is still single. Jasmine scratches an itch on her left calf with her right big toe. Her shoes have long been kicked off under the table. She is turning into a proper slob. Thank God for her short hair, which needs little styling.

They have two weeks before their stock might plunge. But perhaps that isn't such a bad thing, if the dip is only temporary.

'Tai Gu, how badly do you think our stock price will be hit, if news gets out that our launch has hit a snag?'

Her aunt estimates a twenty per cent dip in the beginning, on the first day. With luck, it will gain half of that value back by the end of the week if the market is positive overall. But an eventual council approval would, of course, be the best outcome.

Jasmine pads barefoot to her office, a slight waddle developing in her step. She dials Kuan Yew.

'Everything okay?' His voice is husky at the end of the line.

'Sorry, I probably woke you.' He is at her condo, sleeping off his jet lag. He flew in from Zurich three nights ago, but his gruelling schedule since returning has given him little opportunity to recalibrate his sleep patterns. She hears him stifle a yawn. 'I figured I'd risk it, since you'll probably love me after hearing what I have to say,' she ventures.

He responds with a low, sleepy laugh. 'Hit me.'

'So this buyout of yours, how'd you like it at an even bigger discount?'

'What's the catch?'

'We're gonna need some extra cash if we want to expand the bak kwa market into Australia.'

'So, my money. Not RSE's.'

'If RSE gets into Phoenix at a bigger discount, you'll make a profit when the stock goes back up. I'm talking a momentary dip. You guys buy in and then just sit tight.'

'I can't know the details then. Insider trading.'

'It's me offering my shares, remember? Private sale at less than your current expected buy-in value.'

'And what has this got to do with my own money going into the bak kwa business?'

'You're going to buy some Phoenix shares off the market when the price goes down. And then sell it three weeks or so later, when it increases. On top of RSE's stake, you, Kuan Yew, are going to be a short-term shareholder. The gains go back into our bak kwa venture. But we never had this conversation. Deal?'

'You know you could have just asked me for the money, right? Instead of this?'

'Well, where's the fun in that?'

'I need a sweetener, then, in that case. And it better be personal,' he teases.

Jasmine fans herself. 'Stop making a pregnant lady go even hotter under the collar. Do we have a deal or not?'

He laughs. 'You drive a hard bargain, but yes.'

'Great, you can go back to bed now.'

'Thanks,' he says, then adds, 'and I already do, you know?'

'What?'

'Love you, Jasmine Leong Lin Li.'

In her shock, Jasmine hangs up. For a moment, she stares at the blank screen of her phone. Then she lets out a tiny squeal.

But there isn't time. Not right now, not for that.

Making her way back into the conference room, Jasmine drops into a chair, grinning.

Tai Gu glances at her, suspicious, a crease forming between her eyebrows.

'Malik, it's time we hit back,' Jasmine declares. 'I'm tired of waiting. So I might as well make some money off this bastard Burhanuddin's greed.'

*

The next day, Tai Gu and Jasmine march into the Ipoh town councillor's office, wearing their best contrite faces. Encik Fakhri Abdullah is a bush jacket sort, his wardrobe inspired by previous prime ministers. He is wearing a khaki one when the women arrive, half his face hidden by a mountain of yellowing files on his expansive desk.

Standing, he invites them to sit on the voluminous vinyl settee that seems to be a ubiquitous presence in all government officials' offices, a sign of importance.

Jasmine sits at the edge of an armchair, wary that she might not be able to get back up later from its sinking hull. Her aunt does the same, well primed from previous experience.

'Tuan Fakhri,' Tai Gu says, clearing her throat. Jasmine suppresses a giggle at the man's unfortunate name. 'Tuan Fakhri, we have come to implore you to please reconsider your position. We need to break ground on the announced date, or we run the risk of losing millions. And Ipoh will be the one that ultimately suffers.' The expression on her face is inscrutable.

Fakhri Abdullah's moustache twitches, beads of sweet teh tarik caught on its broom-bristle ends. Jasmine stays her urge to swipe it with a Kleenex.

He lets out a wheezy breath, tenting his fat fingers. 'Oh, no no no,' he retorts, a pompous edge to his voice. 'You,' he angles his hands at Jasmine, 'this is a big problem, you know. You are Muslim – your parents are Muslim, so you are Muslim. You cannot deny it.'

Jasmine grits her teeth and looks down at the carpet. There is a spot that is fraying, the cheap linoleum floor showing through beneath.

'Youuu . . .' he continues, 'it's not good, this whole problem. You have to settle it first. Otherwise, how? This is Malaysia. I cannot just pretend this is not happening, you know? Cannot, cannot, like this, oh cannot . . .'

Jasmine takes in a deep breath, exhaling loud and slow. 'Tuan Fakhri, it is unfortunate that you think so. I have never been brought up a Muslim, and I have no intentions of becoming one. This has nothing to do with Phoenix Village. It is a personal matter. I am rather disturbed at your lack of distinction between the two. This is the twenty-first century. We shouldn't be bound by such, such nonsense.'

Tai Gu claps a palm to her mouth, feigning shock. 'Oh, Tuan Fakhri, please excuse my niece. She is really stubborn. I'm sure you and I, though . . .'

But Fakhri is enraged, swaying as he stands with a sibilant inhalation. He scowls, jowls sagging. 'You are really kurang ajar, rude, you know?' He glares at Jasmine. 'Because of this, I have no choice. I am not approving your project. Not until you declare you are Muslim. Otherwise, you leave Phoenix. I don't want your scandal spoiling my good name. No, no, I will not accept this. I will tell the whole world I will not support this. Everybody will know,' he says, smirking.

'Well, in that case, I suggest you do it today,' retorts Jasmine theatrically. She thrusts her pointed finger at the man. Her toes curl in glee, hidden beneath the diaphanous folds of her floor-length skirt. 'No point keeping us all hanging. Phoenix can then move on. Perhaps to Malacca, where they may not care what I do in my own home.'

'Hah! Malacca! You go ahead and try lah. I know the chief minister. See how far you get. You think you are such a big shot. I will make the announcement this afternoon! The council is rejecting your project!'

The news hits the media outlets at 4 p.m. the same afternoon. Fakhri Abdullah makes the pronouncement on the steps of his town council office entrance, just like the prime minister does when he is doorstepped. Except this is orchestrated, judging from the number of reporters and camera crews present. Jasmine counts all five of the Northern Region media desks. The journalists wear fed-up expressions, probably having dragged themselves from a leisurely afternoon tea at the behest of their KL editors.

Within the hour, Phoenix's stock takes the predicted twenty per cent plunge. Back in KL, RSE completes its purchase, and by the market's close, it is a significant shareholder of Phoenix Berhad.

'Kuan Yew, did you manage to buy up some shares?' Jasmine is sitting at their favourite char kway teow stall in Ipoh, working her way through a plate of the steaming black noodles in one hand and holding her phone in the other.

'All done, my lady, as you ordered. You'd better make sure you help me make some money.'

'Just trust me.'

'Although I'll settle for some of that char kway teow from Uncle Kee's instead. Bring me back a packet or two, and tell Uncle Kee it's for me.'

'Wait, how the hell did you know?'

Kuan Yew's laugh thunders down the phone line. 'You still underestimate me, Jasmine Leong. I can tell the sound of the old man's wok and spatula from anywhere. That's what home sounds like. Now, careful getting up off that plastic stool, love.'

'Partner, you mean,' she retorts. They signed the papers before she left for Ipoh this morning. Jasmine and Kuan Yew are now the owners of the Leongs' oldest business, its separation from Phoenix Berhad complete.

*

By evening, she is back in KL, the char kway teow dispatched to her condo for Kuan Yew. But she isn't home, not yet.

Ryokan is bustling by the time she arrives, a kimono-clad waitress ushering her to a private dining room. Kevin is already there, tapping a pair of wooden chopsticks nervously on the side of the table.

Jasmine slides into a chair facing the room's paper sliding doors. 'Ready, Wonder Woman?' She reaches out, clasping Kevin's hands.

He throws her a tight smile. 'I still can't believe I am doing this,' he says through gritted teeth. He tendered his resignation from his old job last night. His boss, hearing of Kevin's new role, was only too glad to let him go with twenty-four hours' notice, not keen to pick a fight with a newly minted CEO of a public-listed company.

'You'll be fine. Trust me. You've got this. And you've got Kuan Yew, remember? And me. You can always call me. For anything. We can talk every day.'

He answers in slight nods as the door slides open. Rebecca Tan enters, a brief look of curiosity crossing her face.

Jasmine puts on her widest smile. 'Rebecca, here's the exclusive I promised. Meet the new CEO of Phoenix Berhad.'

If she is even the slightest bit surprised, Rebecca Tan doesn't show it. She shakes Kevin's hand, sliding straight into small talk, trying to gain footing. She finds it when he remarks on the silk scarf tied round her neck. It is vintage Hermès, a fact that would never escape Jasmine's immaculately dressed cousin.

Jasmine sits back, sipping her tea. Kevin is a natural, and a lot more cordial than her. He indulges Rebecca's questions with patience, explaining the new company structure and RSE's entry.

'We're very excited to have them on board, especially with the direction we're going in,' he explains.

'But isn't your Ipoh project in trouble?' Rebecca counters.

'Minor setback,' says Kevin with a reassuring smile. 'It's just one of three developments we're looking at. We've decided to consolidate our business, so having RSE on board makes sense. It will help strengthen our credibility with potential financiers.'

'So you think this will be enough? To help your stock bounce back?' Rebecca prods.

'I've exited Phoenix,' Jasmine replies. 'And so has the bak kwa business. It's being transferred to Hong Kong.'

Rebecca raises an eyebrow. 'Your ancestors' legacy? You sold it?'

Jasmine winks. 'Yes. To me. And my new business partner.'

A faint smile emerges on Rebecca's face. 'Ah. I didn't think you'd let them win. Not you.'

Jasmine stares at Rebecca, unblinking. 'Off the record, hell will freeze over before I let these bastards defeat me.'

The reporter scribbles in her notebook, her brow furrowing, then she looks up at the cousins. 'So you think this will be enough to shut Burhanuddin up?'

Kevin replies, 'He doesn't have any quarrel any more, at least not with Phoenix. So that should also bring the Ipoh town councillor back on board.'

'But what about with you?' Rebecca says, turning to Jasmine. 'He could still make this a problem for you. I mean, you're still a Muslim running a "babi" company.'

'It's not illegal, really.'

'No, it isn't,' Rebecca concurs. 'Just socially, shall we say, grating, where some Muslims are concerned.'

'Not if I leave,' Jasmine responds. 'To some other country.'

Rebecca snaps her notebook shut. 'Out of sight, out of mind. As if wherever you're going God doesn't exist for these assholes. So in the end, Burhanuddin gets what he wants. Just a load of free publicity at your expense. And a boost in his standing within the party.' She shakes her head.

'We'll see about that,' says Jasmine. 'At any rate, now it'll be his cross to bear. Or crescent, rather,' she concludes with a small laugh.

'Well, I look forward to chatting with you again sometime, Mr Chen.' Rebecca rises, offering her hand to Kevin.

After she leaves, Kevin kneads his right hand. 'Man, that woman has a strong grip.'

Jasmine laughs. 'She thinks you're cute, you dummy.'

19

When she gets home, Kuan Yew greets her with a bear hug, kissing the top of her head. 'Hello, hottest business partner I've ever had,' he says affectionately.

She pushes him away, intent on her awkward dash to the bathroom. 'The pregnant woman needs to pee! Hold that thought!'

Later, Jasmine groans as she leans back on the couch, her legs stretched out over the coffee table as Kuan Yew massages her aching soles. She feels larger than she looks. She is not sure if Rebecca Tan noticed, but she was careful to stay seated through dinner, and her A-line dress should have been adequate cover.

'You're going to have to leave for Hong Kong soon, at least before your second trimester ends, babe.' Kuan Yew eyes her belly, its slight bulge now showing in her supine silhouette. 'The airlines might not let you fly any later than that.'

Of late, it is he who waves things in front of her, unexpected emails bearing links to baby shops and even daycare centres in Hong Kong. Or supplements to help with her bloating and water retention. She feels like an old married lady, yet they have not even been seeing each other for two months, the romance impeded by the shadow of this being growing inside her.

There is a six-week window if she wants to play it safe. Six weeks to sort out her life here before she uproots it – at least for the foreseeable future. Kuan Yew has arranged for a low-rise apartment in Kowloon Tong, a relatively new enclave across the bay from Hong Kong. Only a quick MTR commute to his office in the city, close to international schools and in the thick of a growing expat neighbourhood.

He has shortlisted three Filipino nannies. Jasmine doesn't know how he finds the time between his own busy schedule and tending to her. Because lately, that is what it feels like, him always alert to her every need, fluffing pillows and re-arranging cushions before she even sits down. She misses the days when he sat back, lounging on the couch, his eyes trailing her with desire as she moved around the condo, or surfaced dripping from a swim in the pool.

Being pregnant is no longer sexy.

'So, there's this really hot investment director in our Edinburgh office.' Kuan Yew is running his thumb in long, firm strokes down the arch of her foot.

'Huh?'

'Well, you're either wondering if there's some other woman in the picture or you're contemplating supper.'

'I almost wouldn't blame you. I feel like an elephant most days now.'

He responds with a lopsided grin. 'Well, I never thought I'd ever say this, but you'd make a fetching elephant if ever there was one.' He swings round to join her on the couch.

'I love you,' he says, looking deep into her eyes. 'I can't wait to meet this mini-you. You're going to make a great mother. Maybe not the most conventional, but great. She might go a little hungry at times, but she'll have good taste.'

Jasmine starts to wonder if his loving her has a little to do with the baby. 'Would you still be with me if it weren't for this child, Kuan Yew? I mean, really, I don't want you to be here just because you feel sorry for me. We're business partners, and that's fantastic. I reckon you and I make a formidable pair, and will probably butt heads at some point. But other than that, you know you don't have to stick around, even though you've known me pretty much my whole life. You don't owe me anything, Kuan Yew, really you don't. You've done more than enough already.'

He wears a bemused expression as he shakes his head. 'Why don't you believe you are more than good enough?'

Perhaps because she doesn't know what it feels like, her efforts to please Poh Poh all her life always seeming to fall short. If the old lady were still alive, she would likely have things to say about Jasmine's current predicament. Choice words, spilling like sharp tacks from her mouth onto the floor, scattering as Jasmine remains rooted in her place. A snide glance at Jasmine's growing middle every time they meet. An odd gesture of disdainful concern if Jasmine shows any signs of discomfort. Although Kuan Yew's unwavering presence would undoubtedly have tempered Poh Poh's chagrin.

'Look at you,' Jasmine says, her voice a mere whisper. 'You've beaten the odds, and you could have any woman you choose. Why me? I'm a mess. My life is . . . is all over the place. And this baby, God knows what I'm going to do when she finally gets here. I can barely take care of myself. If not for you and Tai Gu and Kevin . . .'

'And you'll always have all of us, Jasmine. You just need to open your eyes and see it. This is exactly where I want to be.

You said it yourself: I could be anywhere else. But I'm not. Because, damn it, you're the most confounding thing in my life. You're a curve ball. But I've learned that when life throws you those, catching them can lead to some surprising places.'

A curve ball; she who has always dodged flying objects, preferring instead to slink into a corner until she can mount a counter-attack on her assailants. Jasmine lets out a heavy sigh, her eyes welling with tears. 'I don't want you to wake up one day and think you took a wrong turn, Kuan Yew. I know that even if you regret this one day, you won't walk away. You'll stay, because it's the responsible thing to do.'

He reaches out to tuck a stray strand of Jasmine's hair behind her ear, lifting her chin gently. 'Look at me. My life isn't what half of Ipoh thought it would turn out to be. You think I got here by playing it safe? I know what I want. And I don't give up easily once my mind is made up. I can't even explain it. Maybe it's because I've known you almost all my life. Or maybe because I've gone halfway round the world and realized that this is the first time I've found someone who feels like home.'

'But . . .'

He leans forward and plants a tender kiss on Jasmine's lips. 'Yup. Home. You're it. No matter where in the world you end up living.'

*

Salmah is wearing a fancy mauve headscarf, tied in complicated loops around her face, neck and head, ending with a flourish in a flower-like shape at the side of her head. It looks like hard work, perhaps with the intent to tempt men into wonder, in place of the sight of her hair. The bulge underneath the scarf tells Jasmine there is probably still plenty of it. They are in a private dining room of a halal Chinese restaurant in a five-star KL hotel. The walls are padded with a muted gold fabric.

Kuan Yew cautioned Jasmine against doing this, but she has pressed on.

'I don't know why you'd want to go courting trouble.' His voice was gruff for a change. 'You're leaving already. It's just not worth it. Especially in your condition.'

But Jasmine insisted, wanting at least some small satisfaction from seeing Salmah upset. 'For once, I have the upper hand. After everything she and her husband have put me through, I just want her to know what it feels like to be spat on.'

'I know you're angry. I would be too. In fact, I am livid. These people have turned your life upside down for no reason other than their own greed. You think I don't want to wring that Burhanuddin's neck? But it's not worth it, Jasmine. Please don't do this.'

The discussion escalated into their first full-blown fight, Jasmine tearing off her clothes in a tantrum and plunging into the pool, trying to swim off her anger. When she surfaced, Kuan Yew had retreated to the bedroom, a towel and bathrobe left at the pool's edge. Her anger still simmering, she wrapped herself in the robe and curled up on the couch, exhaustion finally making her eyes droop with sleep.

This morning, she woke to find herself in bed, the covers tucked neatly around her. She held her breath until she heard the bathroom door creak open, and Kuan Yew's familiar footfall as he crept round the room getting dressed.

She shut her eyes and feigned sleep as he bent down to kiss her goodbye.

He did not leave her last night. Unlike Iskandar, who would have skulked away, back to his wife and his other life, Kuan Yew didn't return to his own empty apartment.

Despite that, here she is. Maybe it's the pregnancy and her wild hormones, but this is something she needs to do.

She tosses an envelope onto the table. The photos and report from the investigator are inside.

'Tell your husband to stop his bullshit crusade,' Jasmine says, ice in her voice. 'Or I'll make sure his party friends and the media know what he's really like.'

Salmah takes the envelope and slowly opens it. She examines the photos, a blank look on her face.

'I know now why he's doing all this to me,' Jasmine says. 'He's broke. You're both broke. Well, now at least you know why too.'

Salmah looks up at her, photos dropping to the table. 'You think that is why I am letting him do this?'

Jasmine's eyes flash with anger, last night's rage re-emerging, making her fingers tremble. 'Isn't it? Money, isn't that what this is all about? You people see me as some stupid golden goose you can slaughter and throw to the crowds. Why did you have to let him do all that, Salmah?' The other woman winces at the sound of her name. 'Did you know your husband is planning to leave you? For this child-woman?'

'Th-that's not true. He would never leave me,' Salmah mutters. 'How can you have the heart to say such things?'

The heart. The one her mother didn't have when she thrust infant Jasmine into Tunku Mahmud's arms. Or the one that is still absent after her husband has ripped Jasmine's life to shreds, leaving her daughter to salvage it on her own.

'That second mortgage he took on your house? He used the money to buy his whore an apartment. In KL. He's destroyed my life here, and now he's about to destroy yours. Bravo.' *Bitch*, she would add, but doesn't.

Salmah Ibrahim is silent, tears streaming down her face, her eyes rimmed with red. Jasmine glares at the crying woman, the scarf flower jutting out like a ridiculous, polygonal antenna from her head.

When Salmah speaks, her voice is small and shaken. 'I don't know why you have told me all this. No matter what, he is still my husband.'

Jasmine wants to snap her wooden chopsticks in half with her teeth, enraged by Salmah's complicity. How can she stand her husband after this revelation? Why isn't she insulted?

Salmah eyes her daughter, her gaze straying to Jasmine's middle where a small, soft paunch is beginning to show. 'I am no young thing, Jasmine. I have to make my peace with God. That is all that matters. My husband, he has his own path. But what he does is between him and Allah.'

Jasmine wants to seize Salmah by the shoulders and shake her, hard. 'God? That's all you have to say? Even when this man has messed up my life – your daughter's life – and yours? God? Well, thank God I wasn't raised by you. Life can't be pleasant as a doormat.'

'I don't expect you to understand. Maybe someday, when you are older like me, you will.'

'If you don't call off your bastard of a husband, I will make sure he falls. I promise you that. Because no one crosses Jasmine Leong and gets away with it. Not even you. I hope I never see you again, Salmah.'

This is not a mother she can love. Not one she can call on for protection.

As soon as Salmah leaves, Jasmine phones Iskandar. He picks up on the fifth ring, music blaring in the background.

'Iska, I need a favour,' she says.

'What? Hang on, I can't hear you . . . wait.' She sucks her teeth with impatience. Some things still haven't changed between them, she always interrupting him halfway through matters more pressing in his life.

She hears a door open and shut, then silence.

'I said, can you do me a favour?'

'Yes, of course, anything, what is it?'

She tells him about the meeting with Salmah. 'Jeez, Jaz, you sure that was a wise move?'

She lets out an irritated grunt. 'What is it with you two? Kuan Yew said the same thing.'

'Yeah, well, I hate to say it, but he's right. This could back-fire, badly. This Burhanuddin's a hothead. If your mother goes home and confronts him, there's no telling what he'll do.'

Jasmine is silent for a moment. 'Well, it may be too late for that now. I've already told my lawyer to leak the photos online.'

'Shit, you should have come to me first. I could have found a more discreet way to warn the party. Use my dad's goddamn connections for some good for once.'

She bites her lip, now a little concerned. 'Well, actually that was why I rang. If you hear anything after this about Burhanuddin, please let me know. Tai Gu needs to get Fakhri to approve Phoenix Village. He still refuses, even though I've left the company.'

'Sure, sure, no problem. I'm pretty certain the gossip lines will be blazing once this shit gets out. And the party can't do with another scandal right now, what with the prime minister already under fire.' Last night, news broke in a foreign newspaper about an alleged corporate scandal involving the country's leader.

'Iska, you don't think Burhanuddin will do something stupid, do you?'

He lets out a sigh. 'I don't know, Jaz, I don't know. But these mad fools can get kinda crazy sometimes. And from what I hear, he's pretty pussy-whipped by that Zizi woman. His reputation will definitely take a hit. I'd watch my back if I were you. Please be careful.'

20

The next morning, the photos appear on social media sites, mostly opposition-controlled pages. Malik Harun has been judicious. He excluded the more intimate images of the pair, limiting the release to those of the two entering and leaving hotel rooms or getting into cars. No photos of Zizi Abdullah in Burhanuddin's lap. Not yet.

But secrets, like water trapped underground, only need a small fissure to wriggle their way out, through mud and stone, to find air.

The photos receive hundreds of comments. The ruling coalition trolls defend Burhanuddin, alleging he has been made a victim of fitnah. Slander. Others slam him for being a hypocrite.

Is this what you call a man of Allah? –Muhammad Jahil

Eh, in Islam you can marry four lah. He only has one wife at the moment . . . –Batu Api

Hahaha, the dude's a stud! –Ali Ketamines

Disgraceful. An insult to Islam. Men like him should be castrated. And look what he did to that poor Chinese woman. –Mariam Abdullah

Only Allah can judge him. We shouldn't be so quick to make assumptions. –Ustaz Ishak

Fitnah? Zizi Abdullah is pregnant lah! I know her sister! –Suzie S

Ohoho . . . plot twist, so there's a baby . . . no wonder the dude is going all-out. Got new bills to pay in a few months . . . –Steadyrock54

This is the hand of evil kafirs. Kafirs kafirs kafirs kafirs kafirs kafirs kafirs . . . –MalayMantra

Eh, whatever happened to that Chinese woman anyway? –Tun Lalang

This is the work of that Chinese Opposition party! They will do anything to destroy us Malays! –Hang Bertuah

At breakfast, Kuan Yew is grim-faced, his eyes occasionally twitching as he scrolls the news on his phone.

'Say something,' Jasmine pleads. A twinge of regret forms in her stomach.

'I hope you're happy now. That this is enough.'

It isn't; she doesn't think anything will make up for the havoc Burhanuddin has wreaked on her life. But Kuan Yew's anger is something she is not used to, and she's surprised by the hard kernel of fear it wedges in her gut.

'I just wanted to hurt him back. After all he's done to me, to us all. I can't let him get away scot-free. It's not fair.'

Kuan Yew stares at her, his gaze unflinching. 'Sometimes you act like a child, you know that?'

She is taken aback, the cold edge in his voice unfamiliar.

'Jasmine, you're going to be a mother. There are things that are larger than you. You have another person's life to worry about now, not just your own. And this? Small men like him don't know when to walk away from a fight. I had hoped you wouldn't stoop to his level.'

Shame is something she is familiar with. That heavy drag of guilt that takes hold of her shoulders, curving her back with its burden. Maybe this time, she has done too much.

'I'm just so angry still,' she whispers, fingernails starting to bruise her palms. Tears threaten to spill from the corners of her eyes. Her bottom lip quivers as she cycles through the emotions racing through her body. The residual terror of him leaving her just like Iskandar used to, the burning fury of being wronged by her own mother, and the shame of having done something she knows is less than honourable. But Kuan Yew is right. It is time Jasmine grew up.

He uncurls her fingers, spreading them out with his hands. 'Let it go, Jasmine. Look ahead, not back.' He clasps her hands gently.

'That's just it, I wish I didn't have to keep running away.'

'You're not.' He cups her face with his hands, staring intently. 'You're not running away from these people, Jasmine. You're just leaving these bastards in the dust, where they belong.'

A fierce light flashes in his gaze. She wonders if this means he is leaving her. He pulls away, straightening his spine, grabbing his phone to walk onto the balcony. A signal he doesn't want to be disturbed. Jasmine watches as he turns his back on her to face the city, his strong, stocky silhouette outlined by the sun. Perhaps he is done with her childish needs now. Ready to return to his real life before her, the one that was less complicated. Except Kuan Yew isn't Iskandar. Throughout the last few weeks, he has remained by her side, despite every curve ball life has thrown her. She isn't used to having someone other than Poh Poh to depend on. Even then, Jasmine never let her grandmother into her confidence. All these years, Jasmine has swallowed her fears whole, only allowing them the luxury of air with Iskandar from time to time, whenever they could steal a moment together. Before Kuan Yew, she fell asleep with her worries alone, her body wrapped around a cold pillow.

He is speaking in hushed tones that she cannot make out. She doesn't dare to approach, a feeling like something draining out of her through her toes willing her to stay seated, so she doesn't buckle.

Wiping away the stray tear that has traced itself down her cheek, Jasmine steels herself, steadying her breath. If she doesn't want to lose Kuan Yew, she has to stop expecting him to leave. Without him, she would probably have been even more reckless, a ship off its keel, buffeted by the turmoil that has roiled against the hull of her conscience. His presence has kept her calm on the worst days.

She rises from her chair, walking determinedly towards the balcony where he is now staring out into the distance. She wraps her arms around him from behind. 'No more, I promise. I am done with revenge.'

He doesn't respond, not even when she plants a small kiss on his back. But neither does he pull away. She releases her embrace, wedging herself between him and the balcony railing, tilting her head up to look him squarely in the eye. 'I need you to understand this. You are the first person who has ever truly been there for me. Just me. Not because I am part of some grand plan, or an escape from a bad marriage. And I don't quite know what to do with that.'

'Then why are you still afraid that I'll walk away?'

Jasmine leans back, his question unexpected.

'You need to figure out why you're still here, Jasmine. Why you haven't pushed me out of your life already. I know why I'm here. I love you, yes, despite your faults. But do you know how you truly feel about me? Or am I just someone who is convenient to have around, to make your Tai Gu laugh and hold you to sleep every night?'

She wants to tell him but cannot seem to find the words. The truth is, she no longer wants to know what life is without him. Kuan Yew feels like home. But her old instincts still don't allow it, her back stiffening with leftover fear that if she finally confesses her true feelings, she might make herself vulnerable to a deep hurt that she may not be able to bear.

Instead, she says the most honest thing she can muster. 'I need time, Kuan Yew. Please give me some time.'

He regards her for a moment, before planting a dry kiss on her forehead, nodding. Checking his watch, he says, 'You'd better get going anyway. Don't you have a meeting with your aunt and that town councillor?'

*

That afternoon, Jasmine, clad in a baju kurung, meets Tai Gu at the entrance to the Ipoh town councillor's office. The floor-length skirt and its loose, long blouse conceal the slight bump of Jasmine's belly. This time Fakhri is standing as they enter, gesturing to the coffee table where tea lies waiting.

Tai Gu wears a stern expression, her eyebrows drawn extra thick and black. 'Tuan Fakhri, I don't think I need to tell you that your last decision was a grave mistake.' Her voice is as hard as stone.

The man is defeated, remorse in his drooping posture. Burhanuddin's reputation is now in question. Several progressive members of the party, seeing an opportunity to get ahead, have called for him to be dropped from the line-up for the next general election. The prime minister has yet to decide, away on a trip to Florida to play golf with the President of the United States of America.

Fakhri shakes his head, wiping sweat from his brow with a polyester handkerchief. Jasmine's pregnant nose detects a musty, sour pong from the cloth. She is glad when he stuffs it back into his pocket.

There is a slight quiver in Fakhri's voice. 'I need a favour. A way out of this so we can move forward.'

Tai Gu lifts her chin, peering down at the man, a pencilled eyebrow lifted in disdain.

'The prime minister has asked if he can come to your groundbreaking. He thinks it will help, with appearances, with this whole matter. He wants to make things right.'

Jasmine leans back in her armchair, but she braces herself with her feet, wary that she might slide off, the chair's vinyl surface proving slightly treacherous for the folds of her silky baju kurung. Safely anchored, she wonders how she is going to get up later without instinctively holding her belly. Whatever happens, this man must not know of her condition. It will only complicate things more. Especially if he finds out it is Iskandar's baby, despite the fact that she has already exited Phoenix. She

271

is tired of being the subject of scrutiny. She and her baby don't need any more attention from prying eyes.

Tai Gu's face is inscrutable. 'Fine. But the town council will have to pay for the extra cost. And I want it done next week, no more delays. I am sure the prime minister can find time to play golf at our country club.'

'N-next week? But that is too soon,' Fakhri stutters.

'Your approval, by this evening. My stock has already taken a hit because of you. And you could probably do with the extra money once this announcement gets out, no?' Tai Gu glares at him shrewdly.

'Of course, of course, I will announce it. And I'll speak to the prime minister's office right away. You'll have my answer by the morning.'

'Tonight,' she presses, not backing down. 'It will be morning in Florida by the end of business here today. I am sure the prime minister doesn't miss his dawn prayers.'

As they leave, Fakhri holds his right hand to his left breast. 'Thank you, Madam. Thank you.'

Tai Gu holds out her hand instead, challenging. 'Goodbye, Tuan Fakhri.' The man extends his reluctantly, only bold enough to grip the ends of her fingers for a quick moment.

They stand again at the council office entrance, waiting for their driver to arrive. 'The country went to hell the minute men started being afraid of shaking women's hands,' Tai Gu mutters under her breath.

A reedy young man is smoking a cigarette across from them, leaning on one of the broad columns of the building's porte cochère. He is dressed in office attire. Jasmine catches him looking at her, his eyes scanning the length of her body. A crooked smile emerges on his lips as he raises his eyebrows, tilting his chin in an almost imperceptible nod. His sneering stare makes Jasmine want to take off her shoes and hurl them at him. She raises her chin and looks into the distance. Tai Gu turns to glare at the man, her eyes bulging with disgust.

In the car, Jasmine yearns for a drink. There should be cause to celebrate tonight, and a groundbreaking with a prime minister to plan. But her mind is instead on Kuan Yew, the blaze in his eyes, and the unsettling feeling that things between them may have shifted.

She slouches deeper into the car seat, her head tilting back, turned towards the window. The familiar sights of her home town glide by. Soon even all this will disappear for her, replaced by a city whose streets will be a new mystery.

*

A week can change a life. Burhanuddin's takes a turn for the worse. The public humiliation from the scandal with Zizi Abdullah escalates, with more photos from unknown sources being uploaded online daily. The starlet cannot go anywhere without being mobbed, shielding her face with her handbag in almost every photograph.

The media camp out in Port Dickson, in the hopes of catching a comment from Salmah. Burhanuddin delegates his ribbon-cutting and beach-cleaning public appearances to his political secretary. Besieged, he turns to the internet, drumming up support on social media from more angry youth. Jasmine is still the target, now joined by a handful of other people

Burhanuddin and gang have set their sights on – undercover apostates who have fallen out of Islam's teachings, exposed while attending Sunday mass.

Iskandar rings her that evening. 'Jaz, Burhanuddin's really going sideways. I hear your mother is divorcing him.' Iskandar's voice is strained with worry.

'So much for it being between him and God,' snaps Jasmine.

She is deciding on colour palettes for the baby's nursery in Hong Kong. The move has become very real, with the details of her new home requiring her attention. She is cautiously excited as the curtains are picked and furniture selected. The scope of her motherly ambition is forming between cots and miniature bed linens, baby mittens, socks and feeding bottle sterilizers.

In the evening, she lays out large boards bearing the new bak kwa brand design on her living room floor. Kuan Yew has been distracted the last few days, coming back later than usual. His father was found wandering their neighbourhood streets last week. They might need to put him in a home.

Not wanting to get in Kuan Yew's way, Jasmine has tiptoed around him, saying little about her own work and duties, except to flag the obvious things that need deciding. Her workspace in his Hong Kong office; he has said she can use his. Their decision to launch the bak kwa business regionally as soon as she moves there, hopefully before the baby arrives.

There is little talk of them, beyond the cursory goodnight kiss or occasional half-hour before bedtime when she leans her head on his arm as he flips channels on the TV. She steals glances at him in the bathroom mirror while they brush their teeth in the morning. He still curls his torso round her body when they go to sleep.

But the sex has dwindled since their argument, the expanding chasm between them too wide to breach, as if they have either grown used to each other or are silently pulling apart.

He walks in a little past ten, the beep of his key card announcing his hushed return. He finds her sitting on the couch, staring at the logo illustrations laid out on the floor.

She follows him with her gaze as he tosses his car keys on the side table by the front door. He looks tired, his tie already askew. Removing it, he walks to the couch and sits down, planting a brief peck on her cheek.

'Hey, sorry I couldn't make it back for dinner.'

'Is everything okay with your father?'

'We're sorting it out. Found him a home, a nice place in Shah Alam, an extended-stay hospital for the elderly.'

'You're moving him from Ipoh?'

'Most of my siblings in Malaysia are here. My sister lives in Shah Alam, so she can see him all the time. I should be able to make it there too, on weekends.'

Weekends when he was meant to be in Hong Kong, with her and baby. The prospect of having to raise the infant alone looms larger on Jasmine's horizon.

'Babe, I'm sorry. We'll make it work, okay? Somehow.' There is frustration etched in the corners of his mouth.

She is trapped on a wheel of unending somedays. Just like she was with Iskandar. 'What if I don't leave, Kuan Yew? What if I stay?'

He looks away, blinking, his eyes troubled.

'Or maybe you'd rather I didn't,' she says. 'Maybe this is all just too much. For you. I get it.'

He clutches his hair with both hands, elbows jutting out on

275

either side of his head. 'I don't know how to be there for you right now, Jasmine, not in the way that I want to. I can't. Not with my dad getting worse.'

'I could stay.'

'No, you shouldn't. Not after everything. Not with the baby, or they'll win. Your kid will be Malay and Muslim. Just like you are now, at least as far as the law here is concerned. Neither you nor Iskandar want that for her. You told me yourself.'

'But I love you.' It is the first time she has said it, and it slips out without her thinking, a secret lodged in her throat these last few days, too afraid to reveal itself. Now it has found air, tumbling out of her mouth, despite her fear. Her heart is racing, palms damp with nervousness at how he will react.

His eyes soften at her words. He pulls her towards him, kissing her, his tongue searching, his hand buried in her hair. They make love on the couch, on the living room carpet. She recognizes a yearning from her past, from a time when love was lived trapped in the confines of an hourglass. Yet there is relief, her body stretching like a spring uncoiled from its hold. She basks in the weightlessness that has accompanied her confession. She loves him and she is safe in the knowledge that he wants to be with her, despite her shortcomings.

Afterwards, she lies on the couch in the crook of his arm, shivering a little from the chill of the air conditioning.

'You're cold,' he whispers, nuzzling her neck. He fetches a blanket from the bedroom, wrapping them both in its folds.

'I'm used to being second place, Kuan Yew. We can survive this.'

A look of sadness runs over his eyes. 'I don't want to hold

you back. And you don't deserve second place. I just need a little more time to sort things out.'

'Take all the time you need. It's not like the baby and I are in a hurry. She has a whole life ahead of her. And I'd like it to be with you in it.'

'Well, the doctor did think I was the father.' He is laughing a little now, a smile returning to his lips.

'Speaking of babies, we need a new name for our company. What do you think of Kinta?'

The valley in Ipoh where everything began for her family. The place that was once the world's richest tin ore deposit, pulling her ancestors to its doorstep. A name that will root their new endeavour to its past, their past, the parts of her she still wants to keep. Unlike the new-old history, the one with her parents that she would rather forget.

She retrieves the design boards scattered all over the living room floor, straightening out cardboard edges that were crushed in their lovemaking.

He lets out a deep belly laugh. 'That's what these are? Well, this was one hell of a way to christen our new venture.'

21

The prime minister is predictably late. Jasmine sits at one end of the front row, fanning herself with a copy of the afternoon's programme. The large air-cooling unit, one of four installed under the massive canopy, blows a chilly breeze right in her face. She has to keep her sunglasses on, the rush of blown air smarting her eyes. Despite this, the heat beneath the canvas roof is stifling. She feels a little faint.

Already the requisite hangers-on have assembled at the edges of the seated crowd. Phoenix's board members are at the tent's entrance, awaiting their VIP guest's arrival alongside the councillor Fakhri Abdullah.

Finally, he arrives, a man of slight build in a tailored grey suit, looking every bit the weary but sated politician. It is rumoured he has cancer, the incurable kind, but today there is no trace of its ravages in his demeanour. Like others who have come before him, the man seems too beleaguered for the burden of his office. No wonder the country is spinning out of control.

The speeches begin, first Kevin's as Phoenix CEO, then the town councillor in his interminable drawl. The prime minister is last, rising from his seat slowly, shuffling his papers for a moment before straightening his body and raising his gaze towards the crowd.

278

Jasmine is preoccupied by the sight of Kuan Yew onstage, seated at the very edge of the row of VIPs. He is so striking with his broad shoulders, and if he is feeling the oppressive heat he shows no sign of it. His mouth wears a permanent hint of a smile, which from time to time widens minutely when he glances sideways at her. She wants to reach up and kiss him, open-mouthed. Her ankle slides against the other in a slow, long line.

He recognizes the gesture and grins briefly, before stiffening as his gaze shifts to the tent's entrance. There is a scuffle; shouts can be heard. The prime minister halts his speech. Batik-clad bodyguards spring to attention from among the audience.

A group of young men, dressed in red T-shirts, bandanas on their heads emblazoned with the party logo, try to push through the security detail at the tent's opening. They chant 'Hidup Melayu! Hidup Islam!' repeatedly, each round getting more frantic.

There is pushing and shoving at the tent's entrance, the crowd twisting back in surprise and shock. A collective gasp arises from the din. The faces of the intruders are distorted in ugly grimaces. Elbows and hands claw through the human barricade that is pushed to the point of breaking. Shouts of 'Calm down!' mingle with the rabble's chanting, rising to a crescendo.

Despite the security guards' best attempts, their numbers are too small to hold back the intruders. The red-shirted men push through, the crowd now scattering, screaming, pressing themselves against the tent's flapping walls. Kuan Yew leaps off the stage, rushing towards Jasmine, but not before she feels a rough arm pull her to her feet and put her neck in a chokehold.

She kicks and yells, one hand shielding her belly, but she is no match for the man who is yelling in her ear. 'You traitor! Jahiliyyah! Melayu tak sedar diri!' A Malay who has forgotten herself. An insult of the worst order, except she has never felt Malay, not even now.

She feels the burn of the man's moustache on her cheek as he presses her face closer to his, tightening his grip round her neck. 'Pukimak hang,' he hisses in her ear. Your mother's cunt.

She strains to catch a glimpse of his face. It is Burhanuddin.

Suddenly she is yanked backwards as someone grabs Burhanuddin by the hair. Surprised, he releases his hold on Jasmine to face his assailant.

She stumbles, crashing forward into a chair, her arm breaking her fall. A steely tang rises in her saliva and she feels the first burn of a cut inside her lip.

Turning, she sees Kuan Yew holding Burhanuddin by the scruff, his fist raised then delivering a blow to her assailant's face. Burhanuddin falls backward with a heavy thud, hitting the asphalt. The batik-clad bodyguards swiftly surround him.

Kuan Yew staggers for a moment, shaking his fist, his eyes blind with rage. Seeing Jasmine, he rushes to her side, gathering her in his arms. She feels herself being lifted and she stares at the roof of the tent as it trawls past her vision, until they reach the searing light outside.

Kuan Yew is yelling in his loud, booming voice. A group of men approach, trying to ease his burden, but he doesn't let go of her.

They lead him into the Buddhist temple. It is the heart of what will be Phoenix Village. The cool, dark interior is a drastic change from the blinding sun. She hears the hurried flap of slippered feet. They are led down a long, dim corridor behind the main altar into a room, then behind one more curtain, where Kuan Yew lays her on a small, spartan cot in the gloom.

A man, a monk, clad in saffron robes, speaks with a quiet voice: 'She will be safe here, I will make sure of it. I will not leave her.'

Jasmine hears the fierce, hushed tones of conversation between Kuan Yew and the monk. She cannot make out what is being said. Kuan Yew kisses her briefly on the forehead and sweeps aside her fringe. 'Stay here, I'll be back.'

'Be careful, Kuan Yew. Please.' She is crying now, her hot tears wetting the rough pillow, afraid she might never see him again.

*

She must have fallen asleep, because when she wakes she is still in the dark room. A square patch of light filters through a rough cheesecloth curtain. The monk is sitting next to her, watching intently.

He holds up a clean, damp face towel. 'For your lip. You are bleeding a little.'

She raises herself on her elbows, feeling dizzy. She takes the cloth from the man, dabbing her swollen lip.

'It doesn't look too bad. You won't need stitches. I think you will be okay.'

He is an old man, with permanent creases in his forehead, and small eyes that are wrinkled at the corners. His calming, wide smile lights up his face.

He pulls his robe closer, its saffron folds rustling. 'Are you with child?' he asks gently.

She nods.

'May the Buddha bless you both. When will the baby be born?'

'Sometime in December. It's a girl.'

He squints, as if doing mental sums in his head. 'A firebird, like the phoenix. She will be a survivor. Strong, fierce, passionate,' he says. 'And hot-headed,' he adds with a slow laugh.

'Sounds just like her mother,' Kuan Yew says. He is standing in the frame of the doorway, his shirt collar open, tie missing, his jacket slung behind his back.

A sob rises in Jasmine's throat, but she stops herself. She is taking shallow breaths, as if afraid to believe what she is seeing. Kuan Yew is safe. He is still here. She feels her lower lip tremble and stifles a small cry.

The monk rises from his seat, gesturing for Kuan Yew to take his place.

Kuan Yew politely declines, looking at Jasmine. 'I think we should get you to a doctor, just in case.' Turning to the monk, he says, 'Thank you, sir. Thank you for everything.'

The monk smiles, bending slightly from the waist. 'Blessings on you both, and your baby.'

Kuan Yew insists on carrying her to the car.

'I can walk, Kuan Yew, this is ridiculous,' she protests.

'Shut up, for once. Can't you just be a proper damsel in distress?'

This makes her laugh in short gasps, her mirth turning into small sobs as she buries her head in his shirt.

He stops walking. 'Hey, babe, it's okay. Shhh . . .' He kisses her softly, gazing at her face. 'You're safe. I'm here. Always.'

She looks up at him, suddenly seeing. A slow burn grows in

her belly, making her scalp tingle. Her future flashes before her eyes. Settling into her new home in Hong Kong. Finally holding her baby in her arms. The rows upon rows of Kinta pork jerky on a store shelf next Lunar New Year. And in every frame, the image of Kuan Yew next to her, his face beaming with joy. He is the home she has always searched for, the one to whom she wants to belong.

The words slip out. 'Marry me, Kuan Yew.'

His mouth drops open, eyes blinking in disbelief. 'Are you proposing to me? Right now?'

But before he can finish, Kevin runs up to them, waving his arms. 'Che Che! Are you okay? Oh my God, you didn't tell me this CEO business was going to be so dangerous!'

They laugh, just a little, at the absurdity and terror of what has transpired. Even the prime minister was upstaged for some minutes. The rebellious men were subdued quickly, thanks to the prime minister's bodyguards. They were taken away in hand-cuffs, in plain sight of the media who were there in full force, cameras clicking, reporters shoving microphones in their faces.

'Burhanuddin?' Jasmine asks.

'He's done. At least for now,' Kuan Yew says. 'Although you know what it's like with Malaysian politics. You're not really finished till you're six feet under. But I doubt he'll be able to stand for election this round.' They reach Kuan Yew's car and Kevin opens the back door. Kuan Yew bends, gently sliding Jasmine in, as she pulls herself to sit up. He swings round to the front, switching on the engine. The cool blast of air conditioning fills the car's interior.

'Kevin, stay here for a minute with her, will you? I'll just say my goodbyes to your mum.'

Kevin takes a seat next to Jasmine, his forehead wrinkled in concern. 'You sure you're okay, Che?' He eyes her belly.

'I think so. I hope so. I hope everything's okay. Now that we've come this far.'

Relieved, Kevin rolls his eyes. 'Lord, that man of yours turned you into a regular Disney princess with all that sweeping you off your feet.'

She swats his arm, a flush rising to her cheeks. 'It's embarrassing, really.'

'Oh, shut up, learn to sit back and enjoy it.' They laugh, leaning deeper into the plush leather seats. Kevin strokes the smooth cream surface. 'Shit, this is nice. Think Ma will let me get one? Now that I am CEO and all?'

Jasmine lets out a snide laugh. 'You might die trying, Kev. Your mother's more fearsome than a bunch of angry men.'

Kevin groans. 'I know. It's just . . . that old Mercedes, did you know the damn thing takes ten minutes to warm up in the morning before it will start? The driver told me on the way here. Ma just scowled.'

'The trick is, Wonder Woman, to do it when she's not looking. Talk to Mr Chew. He's your Moneypenny,' Jasmine says with a grin.

*

The waiting room is empty when they arrive at the clinic. Jasmine slumps against Kuan Yew's shoulder, a slow tiredness crawling up her spine.

The door to the consultation room opens. Jasmine sits up, Kuan Yew holding her hand.

It is April Kamila, the former Queen Bee. She is older now,

as they all are, her face a little rounder and shining. Much care has been taken with her make-up, as if to compensate for the absence of a hairdo, her hair now concealed beneath her hijab.

'Jasmine Leong, long time no see.' April Kamila extends a slim, bony hand as she eyes Jasmine with a knowing stare. Turning to Kuan Yew, she smiles. 'Always a pleasure to see you again, Olivier.'

Jasmine didn't want to come here. But most of the other town clinics are shut at lunchtime, their medical staff not returning till after 2 p.m., and Jasmine is growing weary. They are staying in Ipoh tonight. Both Kuan Yew and Dr Menezes insisted that Jasmine see a doctor as soon as possible.

Without asking, Kuan Yew follows them into the consultation room. He helps Jasmine onto the examination table.

'Take a seat, Olivier.' April points to a chair against the wall, drawing a curtain around herself and Jasmine, obscuring Kuan Yew from view.

'It's been a long time,' the doctor coos. 'I didn't realize you were pregnant.'

Jasmine manages a brittle smile, hoping to appear more in pain than reticent.

April spreads the gel onto Jasmine's stomach, scanning the surface of her belly. All the while, she asks questions about the pregnancy. Any bleeding, discharge, pain or discomfort? After the examination is complete, April whisks open the curtain. Kuan Yew jumps to his feet, helping Jasmine as she eases off the table. He doesn't let go his grip on her hand.

'The baby appears to be fine,' April says with a tight smile. 'You shouldn't have any problems carrying it to term.'

Kuan Yew gives Jasmine's hand a gentle squeeze.

'Thank you, April,' Jasmine says.

'It's Dr Kamila, actually. So, you're Muslim now, I hear? Welcome to the family.'

Jasmine is speechless for a moment. The woman still hasn't changed. She feels a gentle tug of her hand. A warning from Kuan Yew to steer clear of danger. But after this morning's incident, Jasmine feels a little reckless.

'It takes more, I think, than a piece of paper and a pair of people making babies to be Muslim, April. I am sure you know that. After all, if tomorrow you discovered you were actually Chinese, it wouldn't exactly make you give up your faith. Or would it?'

'Well.' April is unfazed. 'There is no choice, at least as far as you are concerned. Not here. You are Muslim, whether you like it or not.'

'I don't. And I am not. I daresay I never will be.'

A tiny sneer rises in the corners of April's lips. 'We're not that bad, you know.'

'I never said you were. I just don't think being like you makes things better for me.' Jasmine loops her arm through Kuan Yew's. She turns as she leaves and glances at the doctor. 'Good luck, April, with everything. I am sorry we couldn't have been friends.'

*

In the car, she tastes a tincture of blood in her mouth. She has been chewing the inside of her lip.

'I know what you're going to say, and no, I couldn't help it. I don't know why, but she's never liked me.'

Kuan Yew is silent as he starts the car's engine. He reverses, glancing in the rear-view mirror, manoeuvring out of the parking space. Once clear, he presses the accelerator, heading for Jasmine's childhood home.

As they reach the house, he pauses before exiting the car to open the front gate. 'Sweetheart, she's always envied you, that's all. It's not that difficult to figure out. To some people, your life seems better than perfect.'

'If only she knew,' Jasmine mumbles. She unlocks the front door and checks her phone; there are missed calls from Iskandar.

Kuan Yew sees the screen. 'Call him, for God's sake. The man's probably worried. You are carrying his child after all.'

Iskandar picks up on the first ring.

'I'm okay. We're all okay.'

'Shit, I saw the news. I told you that Burhanuddin's off his rocker. Jaz, I need to see you, both of you, before you leave Malaysia. Promise me.'

She is taken aback by his request, but doesn't want to discuss it right now, not with Kuan Yew by her side.

Later, she sits at the head of the formal dining table, eating a steaming bowl of sar hor fun. The slippery white noodles remind her of the time she first left for England when she was only twelve. Its sweet and salty broth tastes like a mixture of joy and tears. Kuan Yew is sitting perpendicular to her, slurping his own bowl of noodles. He glances at her from time to time. She has been quiet since the phone call to Iskandar.

'What did he want?' His voice is gentle.

'To see me. Us, actually.'

Kuan Yew looks up from his meal in mild surprise. 'Us? As in me too?'

She nods in silence, putting down her chopsticks.

287

'I guess it's finally time I met him again,' Kuan Yew says. 'I am, after all, in love with his daughter's mother.'

Later, lying in her old bed, Jasmine is unable to sleep, the mattress now too firm for her. She tosses and turns, finally settling on her side, a pillow lodged beneath her belly. She pulls Kuan Yew closer, leaning back on his weight.

'You okay, babe?' he murmurs, half asleep.

'I'm going to miss this,' she says into the night. 'When I'm in Hong Kong and you're still back here.'

'Not for too long, I hope, love. Not if I can help it.'

Jasmine recalls her unanswered proposal earlier in the day. Maybe there is a sliver of hope that he will accept.

Yet a small puncture has formed in her chest, making it hard to breathe when she thinks of Hong Kong. When she will be without him, waiting for him to arrive. Those periods in between his visits, which now might be even further apart than she first anticipated. But she knows she cannot ask for much more. Already, this man has met her more than halfway. She was unable even to do that with Iskandar.

'Kuan Yew?' There is a question she suddenly remembers. 'How on earth did you get a name like Olivier?'

He is silent for a moment before a small laugh escapes his lips. 'I'm amazed it's taken you this long to ask.'

'Did you pick it out of a book? A movie?' She turns around to face him.

'It was that old bugger who owned the pizza place. After I started deliveries, a couple of the old ladies, regulars, used to call and demand that I send over their orders.'

Jasmine tries to stifle a laugh, but fails. 'Regular Romeo, you were.'

'He used to yell out "Oi, Laurence Olivier, your girlfriends are asking for you again." It was embarrassing. The other guys in the joint used to take the piss out of me. The name stuck.'

'So you officially changed it?'

'Nah, it's just a name I use. Not that I really had a choice in the matter. I got my first job in a fund management house through my old pizza boss. There was an opening at the firm where his brother worked. He introduced me to his brother one evening, after we'd finished our shift. Said to him, "This is Olivier Lau." Told me no gwai loh would ever be able to pronounce my name.'

'Did you tell him who you were named after?'

Kuan Yew laughs. 'Yeah, I tried. Didn't wanna hear about it. Said that when I'm as rich as the Singaporean prime minister, maybe then people will bother to learn my name.'

22

The next day, the Ipoh groundbreaking is all over the papers. Photos of the prime minister and Tai Gu smiling next to a model of the new township are splashed alongside those of the protestors being led away in handcuffs. Reading the news, Jasmine imagines Poh Poh looking down with raised eyebrows, slightly appalled at the spectacle. But at least Phoenix Village will be a reality someday, just as the matriarch intended. Burhanuddin has been silenced, along with his protestors. The prime minister, very nearly a victim of the scuffle, was suitably shaken and responds swiftly, issuing a stern warning to douse insurgent ambitions. Those continuing to make trouble will be ejected from the party. The rabble retreats back into the crowd, and is lost again among its teeming masses. At least for now, there is a reprieve, until something else stirs the mud up again to the surface.

A fortnight later, Zizi Abdullah is pictured in gossip columns alongside a rising young star. Iskandar tells Jasmine that her mother has decided against divorcing Burhanuddin after all. 'Looks like it's all clear from here for you, Jaz.'

She has put aside some things for him while packing for Hong Kong. A Thelonious Monk album from their student days in London. The missing halves of pairs of socks. A stray handkerchief found under her couch. Copies of photographs they took on their trip to the Cotswolds.

His face has regained some of its boyish colour, reminding her of the first time she met him in London. They are sitting by the pool's edge, dangling their legs in the water as the evening sun slips below the horizon.

'I miss this view,' he says.

'It can't be that bad where you are now.'

'Mont Kiara is condo hell. I can't sit on my balcony without peering into my neighbour's living room. At least here the monkeys don't stare back.'

They laugh.

'I still miss you,' he says softly. 'I miss being able to talk to you. You're the only one I don't have to explain things to.'

They always somehow communicated more in their silences than words. As if there existed between them a porous membrane through which their thoughts and senses flowed unimpeded. Like two halves of a whole. Perhaps it was all those years, all those times spent apart, that cultivated it.

She is quiet, swishing her legs in the water. 'I'm sorry things didn't work out with us, Iska.'

'Please tell me at least we can still be friends?'

'We'll always be more than that. You're the father of my child.'

The door beeps. It is Kuan Yew. Seeing him, Iskandar and Jasmine tense, drawing their legs out of the pool. She had told him Iskandar was coming over and wonders now if it was a bad idea. But it is too late. They are all here together, triangulated in their entwined history, present and uncharted future.

'Don't get up, you two. Stay.' Kuan Yew walks over, planting a quick kiss on Jasmine's lips. He sits next to her, pulling the socks off his feet and loosening his tie.

Iskandar stands anyway, offering his hand to Kuan Yew. 'I owe you a proper apology. I'm really sorry, man, for what happened. Really. I shouldn't have done what I did.'

'Water under the bridge, mate,' Kuan Yew replies, rising to his feet. 'I know you weren't in a good place. We've all been there.'

'I've stopped drinking. Well, almost. One drink a day, tops. And I want to make it up to you both if I can.' Kuan Yew and Jasmine exchange looks.

'Listen, you're having this baby, Jaz. And you two are together. Well, at least I assume you're staying together, but even if you don't, I mean, I hope you do. I don't want you to have to bring this baby up by yourself, Jasmine.'

A look of alarm crosses Jasmine's face.

'Let me set up a trust fund. For the baby. So you don't have to worry about her education. It's the least I can do. I'm not going to be much of a father to her since you're moving away. I just thought I could play a small part. I know you can well afford it yourself, but . . . I just thought . . .'

Jasmine looks at Kuan Yew. His gaze is fixed on Iskandar. She wonders what is going through Kuan Yew's mind. And if he will ever be able to forget that he is not the father of her child. Perhaps her only child, given her age.

Kuan Yew claps Iskandar on the back. 'Good show, mate. I think that's a great idea. Jasmine?'

She is gobsmacked and can only nod in response. The idea of both men being in her life is not something she had really thought about before this. She assumed that, once in Hong

Kong, Iskandar would be a distant part of her past. Someone from her memories, only to be recalled once in a while when she reminisced. But now he is asking to be part of her future. She supposes it would have happened anyway, since he is the father of her child. What is the baby's birth certificate going to say? Will she name him as the father? Would Kuan Yew agree?

But the men have moved on, Iskandar telling Kuan Yew about his plans to tour with his band. She swallows hard, knowing her next words may send them both scuttling away into their corners, perhaps leaving her alone again.

'I'm not sure I want to name you as her father on the birth certificate, Iskandar. The risk, if anything like this ever happens again . . . I'm not sure I want to even entertain the thought.'

The men stare at her in silence.

'Jasmine, are you sure?' Kuan Yew starts, but she answers with a firm nod, tucking her hair behind her right ear.

'The baby will not carry his name. She will be a Leong. It's the only way. But she'll always know who you are, Iska. I'll make sure of that. And you can be part of her life too, I've said that before. I just want to make things clear.' Jasmine holds her breath.

Iskandar holds his hands open wide, palms turned up to the ceiling. 'That's more than enough for me. I don't want my family getting involved. Not after what's happened. I don't want my child growing up with that kind of mess hanging over her head. It stops here.'

Kuan Yew's face breaks into a small smile. 'Stay for dinner,' he says to Iskandar as he walks away to the bedroom. 'Just gimme a minute to change. Someone needs to help me finish a bottle of wine.'

She helps Kuan Yew cook. 'Thank you,' she whispers, their bodies brushing against one another while she reaches across him for a plate.

He puts a roast in the oven. Dinner won't be for a while. 'No worries.'

'No, thank you. For being so gracious.' She twists her body to face him, tugging on his sleeve to make him pause.

He runs his forefinger along her jaw, leans down to give her a long, slow kiss. 'We're all grown-ups. And you're raising his child. I'd hope that I'll have to see him again sometime. Because it can only mean I'll still be in your life.'

She searches for a shadow of doubt in his eyes but finds nothing except light.

'And besides,' he adds, letting out a small laugh, 'the man needs to work on his right hook.'

*

At five months into her pregnancy, Jasmine is starting to feel the strain of carrying the extra load. Her back is often sore now, wrapped in heat plasters that leave sticky tracks every time she changes them.

Tai Gu has given even stricter instructions on what Jasmine can and cannot consume: no chillies, no seafood, and a whole list of other things. Too cold, too much yin, not good for the baby. In their place are thin broths, double-boiled and strained, served in large dinner bowls. Stir-fried vegetables with not too much garlic. At one point, Tai Gu even contemplates rearing black chickens on Seh Gu's condo balcony, intending to slaughter them for soups. Thankfully, Kevin puts a stop to the notion; he has found a supplier of the charcoal-coloured fowl instead.

Jasmine's tongue feels thick and chalky from all the insipid meals. She longs for a cold sip of champagne, missing the prick of bubbles on her tongue. She hasn't had a cigarette in months now.

She is turning into a regular matron, her ankles having disappeared from sight. Her belly, like a strange, ballooning mountain attached to her middle, obscures her feet from view when she stands. Occasionally, she feels the baby kick against the wall of her womb, making her catch her breath. Kuan Yew laughs every time he feels the baby's small thump on his palm when he presses it to Jasmine's tummy. Once, she felt something push up against her sternum, causing her to gasp. The doctor said it was the baby again, maybe an elbow or knee. She wonders how she is going to endure four more months of this, especially when it will apparently get worse.

Yet there is something comforting about its heft at night, as she lies on her side to sleep. By now, Kuan Yew knows to curl up to her, his body slanted to ballast her, one arm wrapped under her breastbone. He holds her until her breath evens out, and he is certain she is in deep slumber.

Her six weeks are finally up. She travels back to Ipoh to say goodbye, at least for a while. Until after she has had the baby and settled in Hong Kong. Tonight she is throwing a dinner party. She fusses with the table – the long, formal dining one they seldom use. The champagne is chilling in the fridge, even though she cannot have any. Poh Poh's best china, with the gilt-rimmed edges, has been polished, along with the silver cutlery. Napkins ironed, starched and folded. Small bouquets of frangipani blooms adorn the table.

She pops her head into the kitchen. Ah Tin is busy

commanding her three nieces at the stove. Of course she is cooking this last dinner. She would have been insulted if Jasmine hadn't asked.

Jasmine breathes in the scents of food bubbling on the range. Salt, sugar and myriad other flavours meld into the complex dishes of her childhood. Nothing is simple when cooking for those who matter, the preparation requiring hours of labour over a hot fire. Hand-rolled yam abacus, because tonight is a reunion of sorts. The delicate, minty hints of lei cha. Pork, braised over a low, slow fire, with salted vegetables. Clouds rise from the steamer as Ah Tin raises its lid to check the fish. The kitchen is noisy with the clanging of spatulas against heavy black woks. Jasmine sniffs the sharp tang rising from the drunken chicken as it hits the roof of her palate. Maybe she can sneak a small sip of the sauce when Ah Tin is not looking.

As the sun slips beneath the horizon and the sky turns a deep, dark blue, her family arrives. Matthias pulls up in a shiny new Maserati, Kevin grinning in the front passenger seat. Tai Gu is sitting in the back, accompanied by Tunku Mahmud.

Kuan Yew is the last to get there, with his second brother, who now runs the family goldsmith shop in town. Kuan Soon and his wife, Mei – a petite, fierce woman – tumble out of the car with their three kids in tow. The rambunctious clutch of boys tears through the house the minute polite greetings are dispensed with. Their footsteps clatter as they run up the curved wooden stairs. Their mother is embarrassed, but Jasmine only laughs, relishing the chaos.

She calls to the children from the bottom of the stairs, enticing them with the promise of a gift. When they reach her, she asks them to close their eyes then slips a slim envelope into each of their hands. The boys tear the seals without hesitation, pulling out the contents with glee.

'Tickets to Hong Kong Disneyland ah?'

'Wah! Tai Pak, look! Will you take us?' Their eyes are on Kuan Yew, knowing he is the only chance of their parents acquiescing. Kuan Soon holds up his hands, resisting. His wife says it is too much. But Jasmine insists, offering to house them in her new Kowloon abode, promising to book their flight tickets as soon as they can confirm dates.

'Babe, you didn't have to do this,' Kuan Yew says.

'I thought it'd be nice to have them over for the holidays. It'll give you an excuse to come too.'

He bends down to kiss her briefly on the lips. 'I love you,' he says. 'And I don't need an excuse.'

At dinner, Tunku Mahmud proposes a toast. 'May this not be the last time we all gather here.' He beams at Jasmine, who is seated at the head of the table.

Tai Gu counters with her own proposal. 'We should celebrate every Lunar New Year here. Like we always have.'

'Perhaps the year after next,' says Jasmine. 'The baby will be too young to travel this coming February. Maybe this time, you could all come to Hong Kong.'

The baby's full-moon ceremony will fall during the festivities. She hopes they can all come visit, although Tai Gu will likely already be there. The eldest Leong is threatening to be present for the birth, confinement lady in tow.

Later, Jasmine stands at the door, dispensing hugs and promises to call as soon as she lands in Hong Kong. Kuan Yew drives his brother and family back to their home. Ah Tin embraces her, tears welling in her eyes. Jasmine makes a mental note to send her a plane ticket next year. It's high time Ah Tin had a real vacation.

Jasmine walks through every room in the house, turning off light switches and checking the windows. She leaves the chandelier above the staircase on.

Upstairs, in Poh Poh's bedroom, she spies the old trunk, on the floor where it has rested all these years. Its contents are still intact, except for her parents' marriage certificate, which she has tucked in a folder among her things to be sent to Hong Kong. She opens the photo album, flipping to the last pages, tracing her fingers over the photographs. Her mother's laughing face. Her father with his funny expression, the day he found out about Jasmine.

Her life would have been so different if he had survived. But he didn't, as fate would have it. Out of his death, she emerged, whole and complete, only to be almost torn apart by the things that brought him and her mother together. The secrets that emerged from his unexpected demise. The love that never turned to hate.

Without them, all this wouldn't have happened. Without them, there would be no her. Nor this baby that is growing each day, slowly making its presence more felt.

She shuts the album, placing it back in the trunk. These are things from her past she will leave behind. They belong here, to Poh Poh, and not to her new life.

She hears Kuan Yew coming up the stairs, his footsteps firm, sure and slow. There is no indecision, no rush to his stride. She turns to see him in the doorway, leaning with one hand on its frame.

'Yes,' he says, a tender, clear light in his eyes. She is puzzled for a moment. 'Yes, I will marry you, Jasmine Leong Lin Li.'

She tries to leap up but instead tips backwards, landing on her behind. He drops down next to her, concern in his eyes, steadying her back with his large, strong hand.

'Well, it's about bloody time,' she replies, fanning herself with the neck of her dress. 'The things a woman has to do these days to get a husband.'

He throws his head back, letting out a big laugh before he bends down to kiss her, long and deep.

When they come up for air, she looks him in the eyes. 'I thought you should be the first to know. I've decided. The baby, I am calling her Alexandra.'

'After her father,' he says.

'Yes, but that's not all. Her full name will be Alexandra Leong Kuan Yin.' After him, the Singaporean giant, and the bodhisattva of compassion.

His face breaks into a wide grin, eyes shining with pride. 'With a name like that, she and I, we should be able to keep you out of trouble. One hot little mess is more than I can handle.'

Kuan Yin, The One Who Hears the Sounds of the World. The Goddess of Mercy and Compassion. The firebird that will rise from the ashes of all their pasts, on a flight path of her own.

In her heart, Jasmine knows that she has finally done enough. At least, for the time being.

Acknowledgements

It is not often a novel gets a second breath of life.

I owe this one first to Jerome Bouchaud, whose belief in the book made this second iteration of *The Accidental Malay* possible.

To Roshani Moorjani, for being the first to champion this edition, and Orla King, who has made the edit process such a joy, thank you. The book is now so much richer because of your insights and generosity.

And thank you to the rest of the Picador team who have contributed to the delivery of this edition: Marta Catalano, Laila Rumbold-Kazzuz, Helen Hughes, Kieran Sangha and Moesha Parirenyatwa.

To the original team at Epigram and the cavalry of people in my life who were the first to stand behind *The Accidental Malay*, it is only because of all of you that my little story even first found air.

Ribuan terima kasih.